Ramya's Treasure

Essential Prose Series 158

**Canada Council Conseil des Arts
for the Arts du Canada**

**ONTARIO ARTS COUNCIL
CONSEIL DES ARTS DE L'ONTARIO**

an Ontario government agency
un organisme du gouvernement de l'Ontario

Canadä

Guernica Editions Inc. acknowledges the support of the Canada Council
for the Arts and the Ontario Arts Council. The Ontario Arts Council
is an agency of the Government of Ontario.

We acknowledge the financial support of the Government of Canada.

Ramya's Treasure

Pratap Reddy

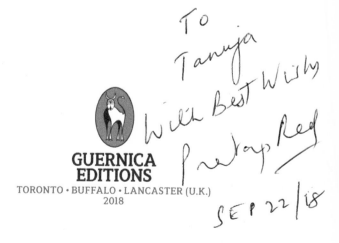

To
Tanuja
With Best Wishes
Pratap Reddy

SEP 22/18

GUERNICA
EDITIONS
TORONTO • BUFFALO • LANCASTER (U.K.)
2018

Michael Mirolla, general editor
Julie Roorda, editor
Errol F. Richardson, cover design
David Moratto, interior design
Guernica Editions Inc.
1569 Heritage Way, Oakville, (ON), Canada L6M 2Z7
2250 Military Road, Tonawanda, N.Y. 14150-6000 U.S.A.
www.guernicaeditions.com

Distributors:
University of Toronto Press Distribution,
5201 Dufferin Street, Toronto (ON), Canada M3H 5T8
Gazelle Book Services, White Cross Mills
High Town, Lancaster LA1 4XS U.K.

First edition.
Printed in Canada.

Legal Deposit—Third Quarter
Library of Congress Catalog Card Number: 2018930400
Library and Archives Canada Cataloguing in Publication
Reddy, Pratap, author
Ramya's treasure / Pratap Reddy. -- First edition.

(Essential prose series ; 158)
Issued in print and electronic formats.
ISBN 978-1-77183-328-8 (softcover).--ISBN 978-1-77183-329-5 (EPUB).
--ISBN 978-1-77183-330-1 (Kindle)

I. Title. II. Series: Essential prose series ; 158

PS8635.E337R36 2018   C813'.6   C2018-900251-4   C2018-900252-2

For the loved ones who have passed on.
In memoriam.

Contents

*"Nothing can match the treasure of common memories,
of trials endured together, of quarrels,
and reconciliations, and generous emotions."*
—ANTOINE DE SAINT-EXUPERY, *Wind, Sand, and Stars*

1

The Sandalwood Box

Ramya awakes thinking of the small sandalwood chest that has been lying undisturbed for many years on the topmost shelf of the closet in her spare bedroom. She turns on her side and squints at the clock. 7:25 A.M. Ever since being laid off from work, she's been waking up at half past eight or nine, a far cry from the days when she had to set her alarm to 5:30 in the morning. If the alarm failed to sound (or she was too deep in sleep to hear it go), there would be hell to pay.

She lolls in the bed, luxuriating in the indolence of the jobless, wondering what it was that made her think of the box. Was it the fragrance, so sweet and cloying, of the wood the casket was made of? Though the scent of sandalwood could be overpowering it would have dissipated over the years—the 8" × 12" intricately carved box must be nearly a hundred years old. Whimsically, Ramya wrinkles her pert nose and sniffs the air. She catches a hint of the Hawaiian Breeze which the automatic dispenser in her bathroom religiously farts at thirty-minute intervals.

Outside, a shy sun is mustering confidence to shine upon the world. It is the middle of January; she lost her job just before Christmas. A nice Christmas gift that was. But why should she care? She is not even a Christian. She is a Hindu, a childless, single woman (separated from her husband a few years ago), who will turn fifty soon, and is living in a characterless, cookie-cutter townhouse in a suburb of Toronto.

The overheated air, quivering like a beast, hangs over her. Maybe it's time she got up and shut off the heat. Even after living in Canada for over fifteen years, she hasn't got used to the cold. She always has to put the heater on high despite the big hydro bill she receives in the colder months — which is the better part of the year. Besides, if the room is too cold, she wakes up in the middle of the night with an urge to go to the bathroom, and then always finds it hard to get back to sleep.

But right now, she's not going to get out of bed for any reason. She lies supine on her side of the bed, the side she occupied when her spouse still lived with her. Prakash had upped and left. No, that's not exactly true, but his share of their king remains cool and empty, with the pillows in place, the sheet only a tiny bit dishevelled.

It has been so many years since she's given a thought to the sandalwood chest, and today, god knows why, it was dredged up from the unfrequented depths of her memory. As a rule, Ramya is not given to reminiscing. Crying over spilt milk isn't her cup of tea (as she proudly tells people). If she could, she'd lock up her memories in a closet in the basement, and throw away the key.

The box is exquisite, made from a scented tropical

wood that grows mostly in Karnataka, a province in the
south of India. Until recently, sandalwood trees, a pro-
tected species, belonged solely to the provincial government, even if they grew on private land. Her grandmother
gave her the box when she was a child. The old lady had
been using it to store her rosary and a pocket-sized version of the holy book, the *Bhagavad Gita*, along with other
small knickknacks.

The nine-year-old Ramya had begun to add the little
treasures of life which came her way: the good conduct
medal she had won in Grade 7; the gold locket that was
a hand-me-down from her mother; the cheap pale purple
lipstick her best friend Maunika had given her; the green
and gold Hero pen, an inducement from her college-mate
Prahalad ... Over the years, a number of small memorabilia
— some pleasant, some unpleasant — had found their way
into the box. Some of the souvenirs, which had such
cheerful connotations once, were now steeped in so much
sadness.

Ramya tries to go back to sleep, but as usual it eludes
her. Many a night has she tossed and turned, churning
up the edges of the bedsheet from where it is tucked
under the mattress. Instead of counting sheep, she should
tot up all the troubles in her life. Having had Prakash for
a partner, she doesn't have to look hard.

She'd often told herself that, on the next visit to her
family doctor, she'd ask him to prescribe her a sleeping pill.
However, when the time came, she always changed her
mind and stuck to the current ailment — most often a
stubborn cough or a cold — that brought her to the clinic.

But what could have awakened her? Unlike back

home in India, the windows here keep the sounds of birds and traffic out. How many birds trill in winter in these northern latitudes anyway? And there's so very little traffic on the street where she lives — Maple Grove Court. A dead end.

Ramya finally rises from bed to make herself a cup of coffee. On the way to the kitchen, she notices a sign on her phone's display screen, indicating a new voicemail message. Ramya ignores it. Right now, she has neither time nor inclination for voicemails. In all probability, it's the same dodgy company that calls every few days promising a free vacation for two in the Caribbean.

What if I did take up that offer? Ramya wonders, following the whimsical train of thought to its illogical conclusion. Who would I go with? She wishes she had a male friend, a thirty-five-year-old bronze hunk — like the half-dressed men you see in ads for *manly* products, holding a surfboard, with a fine dusting of white sand (like salt which may have been added for taste) on their bodies.

The only man in her life at the moment is Gerry, whose name might well be a diminutive for geriatric. Well into his sixties, he is the maintenance superintendent who can be seen doddering about the condominium property, with a tool box or a step ladder in his hand. But she has nothing more than a nodding acquaintance with him.

In the kitchen, Ramya makes herself a strong cup of Bru, a brand of south Indian coffee that she buys at the local Indian grocery. With mug in hand, she goes to the front of the house, and, opening the door just enough to let her arm slip through, she picks up her *Toronto Star*. The newspaper has come in a blue plastic bag because of the predicted bad weather. On the wrapper there are remnants of pre-dawn snow flurries, like tear drops. She goes through the paper, stopping now and then to take a bracing sip of coffee, for the news — an earthquake here, a suicide bombing there — is as gloomy as the weather that has been forecast. Snow, even rain maybe, accompanied by winds.

Ramya has made plans to go to a hairdresser in a nearby mall, to have her hair dyed and cut, and her face massaged — to knead some glow into her lifeless features. Then she'll do some window shopping — clothes, jewellery and shoes — which may turn into actual shopping if she finds a good bargain. Have a bite in the food court — there's a new takeout called Thai Express which she'd like to try. She has charted out all these activities in a mental to-do list with a view to bring some purpose back into her life. Of late, the days have begun to unfold with a boring regularity. And a terrifying sameness. She can't even remember what day it is, not even whether it is a weekday or the weekend.

She decides to test herself: What day of the week is it today? Wednesday? It's not a Tuesday, she's sure, because she wouldn't have planned to visit a hairdresser on a Tuesday. Old habits die hard — it's considered unlucky in south India to have your hair cut on that day, and most barbershops remained closed on Tuesdays. It couldn't be the weekend either — her newspaper would have announced it, changing its handle to *Saturday Star* or *Sunday Star*.

She has to look at the newspaper's masthead to verify the day of the week: It's a Thursday. How eventless her life has become!

An hour later, despite the invigorating cup of coffee, her determination to go out has all but evaporated. A kind of inertia has stolen over her. The very thought of bundling herself into voluminous winter garments dispirits her. She feels overcome with lethargy, though it's only a couple of hours since she woke up. All her energy, it appears, has been drained out of her, and no amount of self-will or second cup of the slightly acrid coffee will be able to rejuvenate her.

She potters about the house, righting the cushions on the sofa, removing old newspapers from the end tables, wiping clean coffee-mug rings from the centre table, doing any odd thing, but the one job that's crying out to be done.

There's an urgent need to complete the Employment Insurance form. It's long overdue, but Ramya's been irresponsibly putting it off. Really, there's no excuse at all for the procrastination — but it's not going to happen today, that's for certain. Unreasonable though it is, the very thought of taking on all those demanding forms online fills her with an emotion which is almost revulsion.

On an impulse, she goes into the spare bedroom to retrieve her old sandalwood casket. She has to stand on her toes to reach it. There's a layer of ceiling-dust, as if someone had sprinkled Pond's talcum powder — the old-fashioned cosmetic she still buys from an Indian shop — on the wooden box. A faint halo of fragrance clings to the chest even after all these decades. She brought the box from India, wrapping it in a turkey towel before jamming it down into her already overflowing suitcase.

Blowing the dust off, Ramya carries the box into the dining room. She settles down at the far end of the dining table, an area that doubles as her study table — though in her basement there is an office-like set-up with an executive table and a plush swivel chair. The table and chair in the basement room are placed next to an unwieldy bar — a feature that made a delighted Prakash decide on the place at once when they were hunting for a house ten years ago. The bar still harbours Prakash's old beer mugs and wine glasses, turning misty with abandonment. Nowadays, she never goes down into the basement except to vacuum the place once in a blue moon. While it's surprising how much dust an untenanted and unfrequented part of the house can collect, even that chore has become infrequent of late.

Ramya opens the casket ...

There's a jumble of objects in it, curios and souvenirs of her life, mere bagatelles — random milestones on a road going nowhere. Unlike the mythical box of Pandora, there's nothing in her box which even remotely resembles Hope.

2

Plans for Departure

ANOTHER DAY, a clone of the previous one: grey, with the promise of more snow. The sun is playing truant again —it must have gone south to an island destination to bask on a beach lapped by an aquamarine sea. Only loons stay in Canada in winter.

In the low adrenaline period of a wintry day, an hour or so before lunchtime, having nothing better to do, she once again returns to her sandalwood box and rummages in it ... She fishes out a small transparent plastic canister from the job lot of memories. The canister rattles like a coin box. It contains brownish-black seeds, blurry through the plastic. Ramya knows that they are only kidney beans. A hundred and eight of them, if she has not mislaid any. She has been misplacing things a lot lately. Her husband, for instance.

Ramya unscrews the container, and pours a few of the dried-up beans on to the palm of her hand ...

9

It all started a little over fifteen years ago. Prakash and Ramya were in the kitchen rustling up an elaborate Sunday morning brunch. On such occasions Prakash would always want Ramya to make traditional Hyderabadi cuisine, for no other reason than she hailed from Hyderabad. In Hyderabad, if her family wanted to savour typically Hyderabadi food they would go to a restaurant. At home they, especially Amma, prepared only a humdrum variety of food. This meant Ramya had to consult a cookbook or download recipes from the internet if she had to make bagara baingan or mirchi ka saalan.

The phone rang. Prakash gleefully abandoned the task of chopping onions, which he had manfully volunteered to do, and skipped out of the kitchen to take the call.

Ramya could hear the intermittent mumbling of the telephone conversation in the living room. Then suddenly: "Hey, Ramya!"

Prakash had a deep, carrying voice.

"What's it? I'm busy," Ramya said, teary-eyed from the onions.

"I want to see today's *Deccan Herald*."

Prakash could have got it himself. The folded paper lay sedately on the centre table, less than a few feet from where he stood. Not half an hour ago, Ramya had patiently reassembled the newspaper after Prakash had a go at it and left the pages scattered all over the living room furniture.

Ramya had to rush out of the kitchen, leaving a simmering pan unattended to hand the newspaper to

Prakash, and returned to the kitchen to finish the dishes by herself.

When Ramya re-entered the living room, sweaty and tired, Prakash said: "Have a look at this." Ramya glanced absently at the newspaper, folded into a quarter, which Prakash was holding.

"Read the ad," Prakash said, tapping the paper with this forefinger.

It was a good-sized advertisement on the cover page of the paper. It was about a seminar on immigration to Canada being held that evening in a five-star hotel.

"What about it?" Ramya asked. For some reason a chill crept into her heart. What wildcat scheme was Prakash thinking of now? Ramya knew, once Prakash mounted on a new hobbyhorse, which might have had the name From Westward Ho By Canada, nothing could unsaddle him.

"Shall we check it out? There's no harm in seeing what it's all about. Ramesh and Suri and their families are also going."

It was Ramya's considered opinion that there *was* harm in whatever Prakash chose to do, but she refrained from saying so to his face. She also knew full well the futility of arguing with him. So, she decided to accompany him to the event—just to keep any eye on him, if not anything else.

She combed her shiny hair, smelling of Dabur's herbal hair oil, and let it fall loosely on her shoulders. She wore a pretty pink-and-blue patterned Poachampalli silk sari and ran an Angel Face powder-pad over her face. Prakash, wearing Ray Ban sunglasses and leather gloves as if he were going to a drag race, drove his silver Ford Ikon, which had all the bells and whistles, to the hotel. Cursing fluently, he jackrabbited through the traffic, surprisingly heavy for a weekend afternoon.

The meeting was held in a large conference room, with thick pile floor covering underfoot. Hanging ponderously from the ceiling were giant chandeliers, which looked like bursts of fireworks frozen in time. The temperature was cold as a freezer and the room smelled of recently shampooed carpet. They listened to a hyper-lively talk from a moustachioed speaker who smiled and smiled as he revealed all the hidden glories of Canada — its universal healthcare, its educational system, and its high living standards. Anyone would think that Canada was the best-kept secret in the world. The speaker did not mention that most of the year Canada was cold, and in winters the temperatures could dip to minus thirty degrees Celsius even in a southern city like Toronto — after all they were competing with other aggressive immigrant-seeking countries like Australia and New Zealand, which had weather on their side.

Even Ramya, in spite of her innate scepticism, was impressed. The cost, however, seemed a bit prohibitive — there were so many components, like landing fees, visa charges, consultant's commission and proof of funds. The consultant promised to make it easy by taking his money in instalments, a ruse which never failed to succeed in baiting the undecided. Prakash and all his friends resolved to take the plunge in unison. There was a sense of security, however false, when one did things collectively — Canada's atrocious weather and its chronic unemployment be damned.

Ramya was not sure if it was a good decision—Prakash
had only recently come out of his alcohol addiction problem. But going to Canada certainly had it attractions. It
was not just a matter of individual ambition to do something for themselves. There was a strong societal movement
in India which encouraged the young to emigrate to the
West, or failing which, to at least move to the Middle
East where pots of black gold could be had for the asking.
There was not a home where at least one child had not
emigrated. In fact, there were many homes where the
entire younger generation had left the Indian shores, leaving the older family members to fend for themselves in a
world which was turning increasingly inconvenient, expensive and unsafe. Could she convince Daddy to immigrate with them? She thought not.

Prakash and his friends filled out their applications
in duplicate—or was it in triplicate?—and sent the moun-
tainous piles to the consultant. While Ramya went about
her life in normal fashion, Prakash waited in a state of
expectation similar to what a teenage boy would experience on his first date, excited and anxious at the same
time. But as months passed, there being no news from
the consultant, Prakash went almost crazy. He was that
kind of a person, impetuous and impatient. He lacked
the ballast of stability which mature men appeared to
have.

Prakash kept following up with the consultant's office
in New Delhi every couple of months, and eventually
stopped, when the only reply he got was the refrain: "Your
application is under process, sir. The High Commission
will let you know of their decision in due course."

Almost two years went by, and all the applicants had come to believe that their hope to immigrate was a lost cause when, all of a sudden, there was a letter from the High Commission of Canada asking Prakash and Ramya to undergo medical exams. But for reasons unknown Prakash's friends did not receive such a letter—thanks to the vagaries of the points system. One never quite knew which applicant would win and which applicant would lose. Having to immigrate all by themselves added another layer of anxiety for Prakash and Ramya.

From the recommended panel of doctors, they chose one who had a reputation for being a little lenient. They were just being cautious. With Prakash coming out of his severe drinking habit only recently, they did not want to meet any speed bumps. Prakash had not kicked the habit completely either, though he had reduced his consumption drastically. Earlier, he would drink almost every day either at parties to which they were being constantly invited, or all by himself if he was at home, listening to rock music or watching *Baywatch*. Even after his so-called cure (a word Prakash would use proudly), he'd have a small one once in a while, calling himself a social drinker, leaving Ramya to imagine what unsocial drinkers would be like—going berserk in the streets, smashing shop windows or knifing each other?

They need not have feared at all. The medical exams were a breeze—the doctor only pointed out that they both should watch their weight and monitor their blood pressure which was a bit on the higher side. When they came out of the clinic both sighed with relief—Ramya because she always expected the worst, and Prakash because he once again escaped the consequences by the skin of his teeth. Ramya was not too enthusiastic about immigrating, but having parted with a small fortune, she did not want their application rejected. To celebrate, Prakash bought a bottle of Bacardi on the way home.

Now that their medical exams were behind them, Ramya knew it was only a matter of time. Three months later they received the visa, and the landing paper printed on a mucous-green parchment-like paper. When Ramya unfolded the document, uncovering the prominent seal, reality struck her. Until then the entire idea of applying for migration to Canada had a will-o'-the-wisp quality, something in the realm of fantasy, like Parsifal seeking the Holy Grail, or Christopher Columbus looking for another sea-route to India.

Within the next few weeks, they would be lifting anchor and setting sail to a new land on the opposite side of the globe. They knew not what lay ahead, and would be starting their life from scratch. They would be leaving behind a world of relatives and friends — especially her father, who was nearing seventy. Over the years, they had built relationships of varying degrees of intimacy. Soon these myriad bonds which moored them to India would be severed in one fell swoop. Of course, they could always keep in touch by mail and email, but Ramya knew it would be an entirely different ball game. Once they went away for good, a great many of these bonds, seemingly strong now, would wither and die spontaneously, ceasing to have any relevance in the distant future.

They booked their passage on a date just one week before their visa was due to expire. There were innumerable farewell parties, some of which were hosted by those who wanted to find out about immigration. India was a me-too country, where people rushed to do what their neighbours or colleagues did. Many of their friends discovered, between mouthfuls of nan and butter chicken, that Canada's extreme cold was not for them, and decided to try their luck with Australia.

Ramya and Prakash vacated their flat in Bengaluru, selling most of their expensive handpicked furniture at rock-bottom prices. How Prakash hated parting with his car, unmoved by the fact they were going to North America, the happiest of happy hunting grounds for automobiles!

"I'm sure you'll be able get a better car in Canada. They must be having countless models to choose from." In India, everything seemed to be limited, except population and corruption.

"That's true," Prakash said. "But that's not the point."

His feelings were akin to the heart-wrenching a mother would have if she were separated from her child. He took pains to ensure that his car would be in good hands, and, rather than hawking it to the highest bidder, he sold it to someone he thought would treasure it.

Having disposed of all their worldly belongings, they moved to Hyderabad and stayed with Ramya's father until it was time to leave.

"Daddy, once we reach Canada we'll see that you can join us as soon as possible," Ramya said.

"Ramya darling, I hope you don't mind my saying so, I prefer to remain in India. I certainly wish you the very best, and hope Prakash finds life in Canada even more congenial than it was for him in India. As for myself, I wouldn't want to move out of my own house if I can help it."

"You'll say that now, Daddy. But in a few years, you will find it very lonely here."

"Ramya dear, let's cross the bridge when we come to it."

The last important thing they did just before leaving for Canada was to visit a small temple at a village called Chilukuru in the outskirts of Hyderabad. Prakash had a vow to fulfill. They started at the crack of dawn, when the sky was salmon pink in the east, and the air was deliciously cool. Prakash did not put on the air conditioning, and kept the windows rolled down. The road, one of the old highways, was lovely with ancient trees standing guard on both sides. The landscape was peppered with incredible rock formations. They were the trademark of Hyderabad, even more so than the redoubtable Golconda fort, which one could discern in the distant hills, making a bulwark against the lightening sky. Golconda was once a fabled city, and so known for its riches that it had become a byword in the English language for fabulous wealth — as was mentioned in the Chambers dictionary which Ramya always kept on her study table.

The shrine had a bucolic setting, snuggling amidst farms and orchards, a spitting distance from the shore of a lake. A trickle of a road led to the centuries-old temple. Once lost in obscurity, the place began to acquire an awesome reputation for granting the wishes of its devotees, and since many of them, at least the younger ones, were aspiring to get a visa to the United States of America, the deity got the nickname of Visa Venkateshwara. Prakash had sought a Canadian visa from God, and it was comforting to know that He had not discriminated against America's northerly neighbour.

There was a fair sprinkling of people in the courtyard of the temple, making rounds of the temple. It was a tradition at the temple that those who had their wishes fulfilled would walk around the temple one hundred and eight times. To keep count Ramya had taken hundred and eight kidney beans in a plastic box. But Prakash fished out with a flourish a handy little electronic gadget with which he intended to keep count. Even then, Ramya emptied all the beans into the palm of her hand and placed the empty box in a corner of the temple courtyard. At the end of every round, called a pradakshina, Ramya dropped a bean into the plastic box. Ten minutes into their penance, Prakash said: "Hell!"— and returned the counter to his trouser pocket. Ramya didn't have to ask if he had forgotten to press the button at the end of some rounds.

Every now and then Prakash would ask: "How many rounds to go?"

"How would I know?" Ramya would say, opening her palm to reveal the collection of remaining beans. "Care to count?"

It was almost an hour and a half since they had started their circumambulations, when Ramya, feeling slightly dizzy and her calf muscles aching, tossed the last bean into the plastic box. They then entered the sanctum sanctorum, joining the tail end of a queue. Many of the devotees in the line had completed the requisite rounds, and not all of them looked as if they were the type to seek visas to the U.S.A. or any other country for that matter. They must have come because they were cured of a deadly disease, or found a job, or passed exams, or found a marriage alliance for their daughter. The queue moved sluggishly as the priests there allowed the devotees to have darshan of the Lord to their hearts' content, a rarity since in most temples security guards were employed to prod the dawdling devotees to move on, hardly giving them time to stand before His idol and commune with Him.

After coming out of the temple they spent some time loitering in the cool shade cast by the tall trees surrounding the temple. They rambled along the edge of the lake, drinking in the beauty of the place. They could hear the sweet warbling of birds nestling among the foliage, and the guttural grumblings of frogs splashing about in the water. The April sun was up and beating down on the silky stillness of the lake, and when a light breeze ruffled over the treetops, Ramya's heart filled with an indescribable exhilaration. How lovely the day was! It seemed as if the world itself was a temple, with divinity imbued in everything—every wildflower, every blade of grass, every pebble, and every boulder.

The next day, they would be taking the flight to faraway Toronto, via Mumbai and London. Ramya's eyes filled with tears.

There are no two ways about it. The EI forms must be completed. Ramya should have done it within two weeks of the date she was laid off, but she keeps deferring it.

Now she must come up with a credible excuse for her tardiness. What pretext could she use? PLSD — post lay-off stress disorder? Would the employment insurance guys buy that? Or maybe good old chronic depression would be easier to sell.

Neither of the excuses is far off the mark, and she has to do something about the bouts of depression she gets into every now and then. Though laid-off, her workplace insurance for health and dental benefits will continue for some time. Like a hangover after the party.

So, she calls the Employment Assistance Program provider of the insurance company, taking the telephone number from the magnetic sticker on her fridge, and arranges for an appointment with a psychologist. The sticker has been affixed there for many years, and until now she had no reason to take recourse to it. Not even when Prakash and she parted ways.

3

Arrival

ONE OF THE few things that Ramya put into her box after coming to Canada is her citizenship card. It's oblong and laminated, slightly bigger than a credit card. A prize, almost. Like a good conduct medal, which an immigrant receives for his or her three-year penance.

The penance of living in the country for one thousand and one hundred days. Or nights, if you prefer, as in the Arabian tales. After all, there's a fairy tale quality to the idea of successful immigration. Poverty to prosperity in one short hop, as some people would like to believe. Besides, immigrants smuggle in so many of their stories and histories. Like contraband, which no one cares to frisk for at the border. Guards can only pat down bodies.

How many tales must have entered the country in this manner! Yet they remain largely untold, unheard, unrecognized, unchronicled, lost in the remote vastness of a large, cold, sparsely tenanted country, which often turns a deaf ear to newcomers.

The citizenship card has nestled there in the sweet-smelling box from India undisturbed all these years. It was rarely needed; her driver's licence sufficed in most situations. During elections, while waiting for her turn to cast her ballot, she saw prospective voters who brought only their citizenship cards as proof of identity being turned away by the officers. Those who drove suffered no such fate. Proof positive that life in North America centres on the automobile.

What catches Ramya's eye is not so much the card itself, but the photograph affixed to it. It might as well belong to a stranger — a stranger with a youthful, even vivacious, face, a face in no need of a facelift ...

It was a cold, wet evening when the Air Canada plane touched down in Toronto. The journey had been long and tiring — with two boring and tiresome layovers; one in Sahaar, Mumbai, and the other in Heathrow, London. No merry hop, skip and jump was immigration. It was an expedition of over twenty thousand miles to a destination halfway across the globe. It was undertaken not on a magic carpet from the East, but on the wings of the combined effort of three airlines — Indian Airlines, British Airways and Air Canada. All these capers only to start an uncertain life.

The plane had landed with an unsettling thud, and rapidly decelerated, screeching all the while. A cheery co-pilot gave them a welcome speech including details of weather conditions in Toronto which seemed laughably mild (such was the dread immigrants usually had of Canada's climate). No sooner had the plane ground to a stop than most of the passengers popped out of their seats, as if they were required to give a standing ovation to a successful flight. While Ramya remained seated, waiting for the line-up to start moving, Prakash slid into the seat closest to the aisle, as if he couldn't contain his eagerness to step on to Canadian soil. One of the passengers, trying to pull out his cabin luggage, dislodged a few pieces from the overhead locker. One of the bags fell smack on Prakash's head.

"Welcome to Canada," Ramya said. Prakash gave her one of his looks, a kind of glare he fetched up when he felt silly and angry at the same time.

Dragging their hand-luggage after them, Ramya and Prakash followed the retreating backs of passengers. They shuffled through the aerobridge, and trudged along what seemed like an endless corridor to the immigration office, eschewing a long travellator, because Ramya had never ridden on one before and her legs felt wobbly after the long journey. This was an early reminder that immigration meant getting used to things in so many surprising ways.

They waited in a cheerless hall, full of artificial light and without a single window, if her memory served her right. All the prospective immigrants were herded like felons into a holding cell. Ramya looked around. Most of immigrants seemed to be from India, especially Sikhs from Punjab. Not surprising since their flight had connected to other flights originating in different parts of India. There were a few people of other nationalities too, like Filipinos and possibly Eastern Europeans. At a table a black couple whose landing papers were not in order were loudly remonstrating with a border security officer. This made Ramya all the more nervous.

Ramya had grown up in a country where law was an instrument to strike terror in the hearts of the innocent. The unscrupulous always had the ways and means to keep the enforcement authorities at bay, often colluding with them. Ramya half-expected the immigration officers to find some pretext to bar their entry into the country. As one after another passenger was called to meet with an officer, Ramya felt the butterflies in her stomach grow larger and flap their wings faster.

"Do you want to use the toilet?" Prakash asked.

"No!" Ramya said, almost screaming. "Don't keep asking me that silly question."

Prakash had been plying her with that query from the moment they boarded the flight. Once ensconced, Ramya did not feel like getting up from her seat. Every hour or so, Prakash would struggle to his feet, and lope away on mysterious errands. Her father, who was a retired doctor, had warned Ramya about DVT — Deep Vein Thrombosis, a condition which was increasingly found to cause death of passengers on long-haul flights. So Ramya had staggered up and down the aircraft's semi-dark aisles a couple of times, hoping to ginger up her blood circulation.

"I'll be back in a minute," Prakash said for the umpteenth time and wandered away. Hardly five minutes had passed, but Ramya grew frantic. Anytime now their number could be called. Where was Prakash? It was just like him to leave her in the lurch! But he returned a few min-

utes later with a smile on his face which was almost a
smirk. Though he said nothing, the smirk translated itself
as: "Why do you always get so panicky?"

Soon afterwards, it was their turn. They entered the
immigration officer's cubicle and took their seats. The
official collected their passports and landing papers, and
solemnly checked each item. He consulted a computer,
turned his head and peered at their faces, and then compared them with the mugshots in their passports. He
double-checked to make sure that they had brought sufficient funds into the country. Satisfied with the booty,
he smiled, returned the passports, and extended his hand,
uttering the words: "Welcome to Canada!"

Prakash's hand involuntarily went to the bump on his
forehead. Ramya had to lean across the table and take the
border officer's proffered hand.

They went to the carousel to collect their luggage. A
paroxysm of panic seized Ramya when they couldn't locate one of their suitcases. Prakash shambled away, and
returned ten minutes later with the bag, like a hunter
dragging a carcass. They looked around for a baggage
trolley. Trolleys weren't available for the asking; they
needed Canadian small change to unlock them from the
mechanized stack. Resourceful in ways Ramya could
never fathom, Prakash materialized a two-dollar Canadian coin — which they came to know later was called
a toonie — from his pocket. They loaded their suitcases
on to the trolley, and proceeded to the taxi stand, following the overhead signs.

It was a spring evening with a shy sun taking cover
behind a veil of clouds. The ground was wet as it had

rained earlier in the afternoon. There was a nip in the air, sharp as a stiletto — that's how it felt to her tropical skin.

They stayed for a fortnight at a guesthouse run by a family from Delhi. They had heard of the guesthouse from one of Prakash's colleagues in Bengaluru. It was far cheaper than a hotel or a motel. Not surprisingly, the quality of service was slipshod and left much to be desired.

Since they were a couple they got a room to themselves. The room was small, more like a broom cupboard, with just enough space for two beds. The bed linen looked as if it hadn't been changed since the time of Samuel de Champlain. (Ramya had read up on Canada before coming over.) There was no other furniture; they had to shoehorn their humongous suitcases into the room. There was a common bathroom adjacent, smelling of overuse and a nauseating room freshener likely procured from a dollar store.

The guesthouse provided a barely edible breakfast and dinner. Mostly bread with butter, jam, and boatloads of tomato ketchup for some incomprehensible reason, since they never served eggs or sausages or any such thing. For lunch you had to fend for yourself, the rationale being you would be out during the day, trying to figure out the system and making the first moves to settle down — like opening a bank account, applying for a Social Insurance card, and looking for the most elusive of quarries in Canada: a job.

The other inmates in the guesthouse were friendly and companionable in their own way. After all, they were in the same boat. Many of them were from small towns in India, and not fluent in English. They were mostly bachelors in their twenties. They were looking for, or already working at, jobs in warehouses and factories, and, to Ramya's astonishment, seemed content with it. While Prakash socialized with the other residents in his hearty nonjudgmental manner, Ramya thought them to be a shifty lot, not averse to cutting corners or exploiting Canada's welfare system.

Without even waiting for the jetlag to subside, they began to look in earnest for a place to live. A free local newspaper you could pick up at grocery stores listed rental properties. When they converted the rent into Indian Rupees for a place, comparable to the one they had back home, it seemed astronomical.

Eventually they decided on a basement apartment. When they managed to find an affordable one — a dingy place with an entrance located in the owner's garage, like a trap door in a horror movie, they snapped it up.

They had to cough up two months' rent in advance (called first and last), but didn't mind, such a relief it was to get out of the guesthouse. The couple running the joint were friendly, helpful souls, but the place could be depressing. Some of the residents had to stay for months because they couldn't break free from the low-paying survival jobs they were sentenced to. They may as well have been breaking stones or picking oakum.

It was only when Ramya and Prakash started looking for employment themselves that they realized all their education and the years of experience they had accrued in their line of work were of no account in Canada. It seemed new immigrants were debarred from white-collar jobs; the only job openings were in warehouses and factories, mostly labour-intensive work. Even these were not easy to come by.

Prakash enrolled at an employment agency whose owner was of Indian stock, though he hailed from the West Indies. A sympathetic soul, he provided Prakash with a series of short stints in all kinds of places — factories, warehouses, condos, and offices. Prakash went without protest to wherever his services were required and at whatever time of day. The jobs were all menial, and were not regular, full time work. There was no guarantee how much he would make in a week. The fortnightly paycheque he received had an element of either a pleasant surprise or a nasty shock attached to it.

Ramya, appalled by the requirement to be able to lift sixty pounds or so, avoided applying to warehouses and tried her luck with fast food places and garment stores. While all the establishments accepted her résumé (some of them even had a 'Now Hiring' sign stuck to the store front), not one of them called her for an interview or even bothered to respond in any way.

Though it made a huge dent in their savings, Prakash bought a second-hand car — pre-owned, they called it here — as soon as he could. Nothing fancy, no bells, no whistles, just a serviceable Chevy. Prakash had realized early that if you had a car in this country you improved your chances of landing a job. But for many immigrants you needed to have a job to be able to buy a car. It was the chicken-or-the-egg conundrum with a Canuck flavour.

Driving for over twenty years on Indian roads mattered little here; Prakash had to take the drive test three times before he was rewarded with a driver's licence. It was like being awarded the Victoria Cross or the Purple Heart — not pinned to your chest but carried in a wallet on your hip.

Though the process was humbling, especially for one who had driven with so much self-assurance (to say nothing of his goggles and leather gloves), Prakash said: "Ramya, it's good if you too got yourself a licence. It's the most important ID card in North America." Ramya could never understand how casually men picked up such odd little nuggets of information in whichever corner of the world they were in. Not only did such gen have a lot of practical value, it also made the men seem so worldly wise. Even if undeservedly.

Ramya never drove when she was in India, though as a matter of routine she had got herself a licence in her late teens.

"I think I'll wait until I find a full-time job," Ramya said. "The car insurance rates are much too high."

"It's true that the rates are unbelievably high here, but it doesn't cost so much to add an additional driver," Prakash said, street-smart, as always.

But Ramya did not want to rush. It stressed her to even to think about the elaborate system of licensing: a written test followed by two levels of road testing. In India it was different. In theory the driving test back home required the applicant to perform a formidable array of feats (making a figure eight in reverse gear with stones set on the ground as the only markers, or making a sharp right angle turn between two narrow posts or some such crap), but in practice it was child's play because the driving instructor "took care of everything".

But how right Prakash was about the driving licence. Proof of identity and residence was demanded at examination halls, banks, post offices, anywhere and everywhere. Her PR (Permanent Residence) card was inadequate because it did not display her address; in addition, she was required to show an envelope which had been mailed to their address as corroborative evidence.

Four and a half years later, when they stood in the hall of the local citizenship office to take their oath, raising an open palm shoulder high, one could say with some conviction that they had managed to settle down in Canada. Prakash had a job in a factory; though his job title was that of a lead hand, the pay was relatively good. Ramya, by sheer dint of persistence, had managed to steer herself into an office job. To reach her goal, she had attended night school and worked at a series of short-term contract jobs during the day. They bought their townhouse taking a mortgage from the Royal Bank of Canada. Most importantly, each had a car: They had arrived.

At the citizenship function they joined others in singing "O Canada," with Ramya having to refer frequently to the words on the pamphlet provided to the newly converted. Prakash sang with the passion of a proselyte, and didn't cast so much as a glance at the text. The anthem had a chest-thumping feel to it. Its Indian counterpart, which Ramya had sung—or stood at attention to—several hundred times, was little more than a short and incomplete geographical tour of India, even though penned by a winner of a Nobel Prize for literature. At the end of the performance, Ramya felt a bit of a quisling.

The magistrate made an uplifting speech, and then distributed the letter-sized rust-brown certificates of citizenship. Outside, there was a Canadian flag—a tomato-red maple leaf adrift on an empty field of snow—hanging from a pole, kept at readiness as a prop. The place had a touristy air, as many new citizens posed for pictures standing in front of the flag. Prakash made Ramya take his picture with his cellphone. He stood in front of the flag with his fingers raised in a V salute. With his dark glasses and winter coat, he almost looked like a mountaineer who had ascended a formidable peak. Prakash had conquered Canada.

It's only five in the evening, but it's already dark, and Ramya can see the wintry orange glow of the night through her living-room window. She has shelved her plans to go to a nearby Canadian Tire for some antifreeze. If she runs out of the fluid, she and Ms. Peggy—Ramya's pet name for her car—could wait. Neither Ramya nor Ms. Peggy has any pressing jobs waiting to be accomplished (if one discounts the filling of EI forms, but Ms. Peggy is of little help there). Both are at loose ends with plenty of time on their hands.

Ramya remembers about the voicemail and reaches out for the phone. She has walked past the phone many times, but never felt the urge to pick up the receiver and access her message. Surely, it couldn't be her ex-boss Randy McLaughlin inviting her back to work? Ramya gives a bitter chuckle at the improbability of the thought.

When the message comes on, the voice is not very familiar, but the man introduces himself as Mrs. Rao's son-in-law.

"Subbalakshmi Rao suffered a severe stroke and has been admitted to William Osler hospital ..."

Ramya catches her breath. Sudden tears sting her eyes.

Mr. and Mrs. Rao were some of the first friends they made when they landed in Canada. The Raos too are from Hyderabad and are related to one of Daddy's patients. They immigrated way back in the sixties when things were not so difficult. Mr. Rao got a well-paid job in the provincial government, and Subbalakshmi, or Subbu-Auntie as Ramya called her, as a teller in a bank. They own a huge house, with an extensive backyard, and a large garage packed with a slew of shiny cars, with a couple more sitting on the broad tree-lined driveway.

She has a vague recollection of meeting Sudhakar, Mrs. Rao's son-in-law, a few years ago. He's a pleasant and deferential person, a bit wishy-washy perhaps. He has the tendency to be formal in the presence of his elders. Like most people who grew up in India, he would never address anyone older than him by their first name, and often added 'sir' or the Telugu honorific 'garu' at the end of the name.

Was it this phone call that had awakened her early in the morning that day? It must have started crowing insistently at dawn and then slyly crept into the voicemail. Was there something premonitory about its ringing? Something telepathic which reminded her of the sandalwood box? Her box which is chock-full of memories ... memories of people who grow old, of people who fall seriously ill, of people who die and pass over to another world — the final emigration.

She has not seen the Raos in recent years. As a single woman — a fate she brought upon herself, people said, Ramya has kept herself to herself. Subbu-Auntie is neither a blood relation nor a person in her age group—yet she was a source of support and strength when they were new to Canada. Ramya wondered if Subbu-Auntie ever cast a thought in her direction, surrounded as she was by her children and grandchildren. She couldn't be faulted if she completely forgot about Ramya's unenviable existence. Now she is grievously ill and close to dying. A person of Mrs. Rao's age could hardly be expected to survive a massive stroke.

Ramya dials Mrs. Rao's residence. The call goes into the accursed voicemail. Ramya always feels inept when it comes to leaving a message. Though disturbed, Ramya overcomes the temptation to hang up, and plants her message hoping it doesn't sound too disjointed. "Rao-garu, this is Ramya. I'm sorry to hear about Subbu-Auntie. I will call later and talk to you."

Still feeling unsettled, but having nothing better to do, Ramya walks over to the glass-topped dining table at the end of which the sandalwood casket lies. There's a small mirror, now dull and spotty, stuck to the underside of the lid. It could well be the looking glass through which you can see into the past.

But now she only sees parts of a tired, lifeless face. An eye with a bag under it, a nose with a sprinkling of blackheads, a ringlet of black hair entwined with grey …

Ramya sits down at the table and rummages in the box. Pulling out one memento after another, she lays them down on the table. A gold chain with a pendant, a filigreed dog-collar, a paperback signed by its author, and a small vial with Tik 20 written on its label … and many more.

4

Witch & Doctor

THE OUTSIDE WORLD is suffused with golden light. It's another matter that the temperature is minus twenty-one Celsius. A bar of refracted light, entering through the glass window of the dining room, falls upon the heart-shaped gold pendant Ramya holds in the palm of her hand. Inside the locket, which opens like a miniature book, there is a picture of a young, wispy, good-looking woman on the left-hand side, and on the right, that of a young man, almost dandy in appearance.

Ramya has to throw her head back a little, and crinkle her eyes to peer at the small black and white photos. She cannot see so well nowadays, and her reading glasses, which she picked up at a dollar store on a whim, are on the bedside table upstairs. Even though her company-provided insurance paid for proper reading glasses — which otherwise cost a packet if one factors in the op-tometrist's fee, she has neglected to buy them all these months. (Why the resistance? Are reading glasses, like grey hair and wrinkles, an unhappy harbinger old age?)

But there's time yet. Her insurance will last a few more weeks ... There! One more item in her to-do list.

There's no doubt that the pictures are of her mother and father, in the dew-fresh bloom of youth. In the images she carries of them in her mind, they look much older: heads daubed with grey, faces etched with lines. These are the people she called Mummy and Daddy — a little shamefacedly, if her friends were around. Her childhood friends called their parents mamma, papa, amma, nana, ma, pa or some such non-English appellation. There's something ridiculous about calling your parents Mummy and Daddy in India, a country which boasts of hundreds of indigenous languages. What's worse, it's almost elitist. It's something about having the privilege of getting educated in English, in a country where millions have never stepped into a school.

In that small photograph — surprise! surprise! — Mummy has a faint smile that almost approaches a suppressed laugh. It couldn't be true; Ramya doesn't remember ever seeing her mother smile, let alone laugh. Perhaps, at the photographer's behest, she'd loosened the thin lips of an otherwise tightly set mouth to utter the word 'cheese!' Louder than required apparently, going by the generous size of the smile. Her habitual expression had been a cross between a frown and a pout. Frout — if Ramya could be allowed to invent a portmanteau word.

Though Mummy's delicate beauty is never in question, there's a certain datedness to it — as is often the case with people in old photographs. Mummy has sharply chiselled features, which Ramya recognizes even without the aid of reading glasses. If an artist were to make a portrait of her mother in her youth, he'd choose a pointy pencil, and be tempted to use the services of a ruler.

On the other hand, her father's foppish good looks — she can make out the collar of a lounge suit and the knot of a tie — hides a soft, kind-hearted man, but much lacking in will and determination. In his profession, his almost Buddha-like gentleness was much admired by the sick and the dying.

Ramya remembers seeing a row of dry-cleaned suits, in hopelessly sombre tones, hanging in an olive-green Godrej steel almirah. Hardly ever used, they might have been raiment for the skeletons in the family cupboard. (Mummy's cupboard was the colour of hot-chocolate, and with an additional lockable compartment to stow her gold jewellery and silver puja utensils. On the shelves, the stacks and stacks of pressed and folded silk saris could well provide enough clothing for a national conference of distaff skeletons.)

Daddy dressed up in a suit only on special occasions, like attending medical conferences or wedding receptions. For everyday work, he preferred to wear, under his baggy doctor's coat, a loose comfortable white shirt and a pair of dark-coloured trousers. Every morning, before picking up his car keys and the doctor's bag, he would lift little Ramya into the air to give her a goodbye peck on each cheek. He had the very smell of freshness, a mingling of fragrances of Cinthol bath soap, and Brylcreem, the stuff he applied to his hair.

When Ramya was growing up, if she needed something, she wouldn't approach her mother. She would ask the cook or one of the maidservants who was in their employ then—maids never stuck around for long. (Over the years they had an ever-changing procession of servants, coming and going as if their intricately carved teak front door were a revolving one.)

Most of the time, Ramya's mother was as good as incommunicado. She would barricade herself in the puja room, indulging in elaborate worship of God. Though her mother's eyes glowed with uncommon intensity, they had a distant gaze to them.

If Ramya ever blundered into the puja room and found Mummy there, seated with her legs folded in a yogic pose in front of the altar, she'd withdraw. Otherwise, she'd linger for a few minutes out of curiosity, basking in the sanctity of the place. Every morning before leaving for school, she was required to stand before the assemblage of gods, wearing her full uniform (minus the shoes), join her palms, and whisper a short prayer. It was considered a time-tested recipe for success, whatever the nature of the endeavour. (She should have prayed more ardently and perhaps recited longer prayers to save her marriage.) But to give the gods their due, the prayers had worked as far as her school exams were concerned.

Mummy's puja room was drenched in the smell of red kumkum and turmeric powder, wilting flowers, and the groundnut oil used for lighting wick-lamps. The heady combination of smells, even if a jot unpleasant, had an unquestionably holy edge to it.

The altar, which was an alcove cut into the wall, had a multitude of silver statuettes: Rama, Lakshmana and Sita; Krishna and Radha; Shiva and Parvati; the roly-poly elephant-headed Ganesa, and his solemn-faced brother Muruga with his invincible spear. The wall around the alcove was plastered with framed pictures in earthy colours of even more Hindu gods. On every figurine and picture was a daub of kumkum, and flowers, a tiny portion clipped from a garland of white jasmines.

In the evenings, her mother would wander into their small garden in front of the house, plucking white jasmine buds from shrubs to weave them into a trailer. There were never enough for all the deities who had foregathered in her puja room, so an itinerant flower-seller came every day to their house with a supply of fresh jasmine, already strung into a garland. Arifuddin, the flower vendor, would stand outside their wrought-iron gate and yelling in Urdu: "*Fool*! *Amma, Fool*!" Flowers! Mother, Flowers!

A maidservant would then rush out, taking a couple of pink two-rupee notes kept in readiness on the console table. The maid would engage in harmless flirtation with the flower-seller, giggling at his funnily-accented Telugu. Arifuddin was no Casanova, though he claimed to have four wives. He was short and portly and bald. His small build was the secret of his success in the flower trade. Traditionally, flower sellers sold garlands not by weight or number, but by length, the standard being the distance between the vendor's forefinger and his elbow. Had Arifuddin been a tall, strong man he would have lost a lot of money.

The maid would return with a humongous mound of flowers in a shallow wickerwork basket—Mummy bought *fool* by the mile.

The phone rings. Ramya hastens to answer it, thinking it must be a mental health counsellor. But it's Sandeep.

"Hello, Mom," he says. "I hope I'm not disturbing you?"

Sandeep is her stepson. She didn't know about his existence when she married Prakash. He was Prakash's secret progeny, and she came to know about him only years later. Sandeep lived in Detroit, south of the border, with his wife. He worked for an Indian software company which did contract work in the U.S.A.

"No, Sandeep, not at all. How are you? How's Vidya?"

"We are fine. But ..."

"Yes?"

"I've some bad news. Our company's contract was suddenly terminated. Which means we have to go back to India soon."

"That's really bad news! What happened? Why was the contract terminated?"

"A local newspaper published an article about outsourcing and loss of jobs in the community. There was a lot of brouhaha with many politicians jumping in. Our American partner got nervous and pulled the plug,"

"Such things happening here too. When do you leave?"

Sandeep and Vidya got married about a year and a half ago; it's only been a few months since Vidya moved to the U.S.A. from India. Having no appropriate visa (H something or the other) that allowed her to work, she was forced to be a homemaker. This new development must have come as a rude shock to her.

"By the end of the month most likely," Sandeep says.

Ramya is swamped by an inexplicable feeling of desolation. Why does she feel this sudden bout of loneliness?

Sandeep is not even her biological son. He was nine years old when she first saw him, a quiet, gentle, affectionate boy who addressed her as Ramya-auntie. Prakash made Sandeep call them Mom and Dad—to Prakash it sounded hip, not being called Nana or Papa or some such word from the local language. Prakash cultivated hipness with fervour—he was that kind of guy.

Sandeep hadn't lived with them. He grew up in his grandparents' house, leading the life of an orphan even though both his natural parents were alive. His mother lived by herself in an ashram, a religious commune. Occasionally, he'd come over for a short vacation when Prakash and Ramya were living in Bengaluru. A sweet-natured boy, he went about his life in his own quiet way, rarely bothering adults. Though he's in his twenties now, he retains his pleasing childhood qualities, unaffected by his father's caprices.

"Mom, are you there?" Sandeep asks.

"Yes, very much. I feel a little disappointed, Sandeep."

"I knew you'd be. I'm sorry."

"Why don't you plan a quick trip to Canada? A weekend getaway, you know. You could show Vidya Toronto before she goes back to India."

"That would be a good idea, but I'm not sure. We'd like to see the Niagara too … and of course look you up before we return to India."

"That will be nice. And I believe the falls are more spectacular from the Canadian side."

Ramya replaces the receiver with a feeling that is quite indescribable. Really, how lonely can one get? She hopes Sandeep and Vidya will find time to visit Canada. Sandeep had mentioned her and the most famous waterfall in the world in the same breath. Two see-worthy attractions. That's some consolation no doubt, though both are falling —one in a headlong rush down a gully, the other helplessly coming down in life, piteously complaining.

To distract herself, Ramya picks up the novel she's halfway through. The book was borrowed from the local library more than a month ago, and is long overdue. Despite her idleness, Ramya hasn't found the time to either finish or return it. There are at least half a dozen books she has stopped reading midway. She doesn't know if the fault lies with her, or the writers who are unable to make their books gripping enough.

Ramya soldiers through a couple of pages, then shuts the book with a slap. It's like a war of attrition: Sometimes the book's readability wins the day, and sometimes her own ennui has the last word. The story is not uninteresting—about a character who escapes the confines of the novel, and later returns to murder the author. The way books are written nowadays, she thinks, this ought to be the fate of many a writer.

She wonders if the story of her chequered life would evoke a reader's interest. If not exactly an autobiography (for she is neither famous nor notorious, so of no interest to any publisher), she could always try her hand at creative nonfiction, the new and lucrative genre. Her misadventures with Prakash certainly had potential, and if she could wring out a bestseller from her failed marriage, it would be the saving grace.

Even as a toddler Ramya knew that she had what people called a peculiar person for a mother. Such knowledge would've been an uncomfortable cross to bear for anyone, let alone a sensitive child like Ramya.

She was eight when she got the first hint of a reasonable explanation for her mother's eccentric behaviour from Atom Auntie, her father's younger sister. To Ramya, Atom Auntie was the most fascinating person on the earth. She was always recounting stories — from the books she'd read, the films she'd seen, the gossip from her work place, the things that happened to neighbours, or simply bits of family history.

Ramya sat on a moda — a cotton-fibre cushion crowning a wickerwork stool — while Atom Auntie made her a sweet called sheera. It was made with semolina and sugar fried in ghee, and garnished with cashew and raisins. As was her wont, Atom Auntie brooded over her gas stove, stirring and chatting incessantly to her little niece.

"This stove cooks so much faster than my old kerosene one," Atom Auntie said. The stove was a dull grey rectangle with two sooty burners. It was connected to a cherry-red cylinder of butane with a lime green hosepipe. "The stove was a gift from your Daddy, by the way."

"Yes, I know."

"For a little girl you know a lot. Your Daddy is a good, kind brother. Did you know that you too had a brother?"

"No," Ramya said. "What happened to him?"

"How silly of me! I shouldn't have opened my mouth. You're much too young to understand."

"How come I never saw him?"

"You were just two years old when it happened."

"What happened?"

"Dear me. How persistent you are! I won't say another word. Forget that I told you anything about him. I'll get into trouble if your Mummy hears about it. I've enough troubles in my life as it is."

"Please tell me the secret, Atom Auntie. I promise! I won't tell anyone."

"No," Atom said, putting her ivory-like forefinger over her lips. "Mum's the word."

Though Ramya never asked her mother about the dead brother, she never forgot him either. Years later, she would learn about the incident from another source.

As the years passed Mummy's behaviour became more and more bizarre. Though she hardly socialized, and except for pottering about the garden, never ever ventured out, news had a way of getting around. By the time Ramya was in Grade 3, many of the children at the local convent school had got to know of Mummy's reputation. One day Sister Bernadette, who taught them moral science, put a question to one of Ramya's classmates: "Prabha, do you know who the Holy Mother is?"

Without a moment's hesitation, the small chubby girl answered: "Ramya's mummy."

As Mummy grew older, the children in their neighbourhood began to call Mummy a witch. Her sharp features, including the slightly hooked nose, didn't help. Though still in her forties, she looked gaunt and haggard. Mummy didn't wear a floppy hat, but she began to resemble, even to Ramya, the witches in the illustrations accompanying the fairy tales she read.

Ramya's car is a brown weather-beaten Mazda. She thinks of it as a sorrel mare. At first blush, the Ms. Peggy moniker sounds a bit whimsical, but it's actually a diminutive for Missus Pegasus. The choice of the name can be attributed to Atom Auntie's lasting influence, though she's herself long dead. Atom Auntie was a schoolteacher and she fed young Ramya's mind with fascinating tidbits from history, mythology and literature.

Ramya prefers to keep Ms. Peggy in the garage, her stable so to speak, not leave her in the driveway as some people, Prakash included, would do—as if their car is some kind of totem pole.

Perhaps it is.

Life in North America is inescapably regulated by the automobile. Buses, streetcars, bicyclists and pedestrians are treated like interlopers on the roads. An automobile is a symbol of personal freedom, a substitute for the Arabian of the Wild West—like Lone Ranger's Silver or Red Ryder's Thunder. SUVs that could accommodate seven often tear down the streets with only one rider.

Prakash was always after Ramya to get a licence and drive a car. She initially rebuffed his advice, but a few years later, when she had a stable job and they were relatively well off, she took driving lessons with a Desi instructor. Though she had learned to drive in India, her father, no expert driver himself, had felt too nervous to let his young daughter take the car out on her own in the chaotic, unruly traffic of Hyderabad's roads.

Ramya's driving instructor in Canada was resourceful enough to make her take her road tests in out-of-the-way places, rather than in centres in and around Toronto where the failure rate was high. Much to Prakash's chagrin, Ramya passed in her second attempt. Unlike the surly inspector in Burlington during her debut road test, his good-humoured colleague in St. Catharines found her nemesis, parallel parking, up to the mark, and gave her a clean chit. Even today, almost a decade later, she finds parallel parking a perpetual challenge, and tries to avoid it. Also, with roundabouts scarce in North America, she finds making a left turn, in the split-second interval between the green light going out and the red coming on, a real nightmare. She's terrified that an oncoming car will T-bone her. She has heard of so many people who'd met that fate, and wouldn't have survived to tell the tale, but for airbags.

Ramya believes automobiles, much like pets, begin to resemble their masters over time. Or vice-versa. Her Mazda is middle-aged, stodgy, grungy, and in urgent need of a bath. It certainly looks a trifle undesirable. But Ramya doesn't intend to get the car washed in winter. What a waste it would be to get the car cleaned and detailed, she has convinced herself, then have a small winter storm come along and ruin the shining exterior. She'd rather do nothing until spring, the life-breathing season, when the yellow warblers start to serenade, and the denuded trees begin to wear a modest cover.

Nowadays for Ramya, any reason is good enough for procrastinating, moreover she doesn't like sitting alone in the car with a billowing cloud of foam enveloping her. It makes her spine tingle, reminding her unaccountably of Hitchcock movies. But procrastination is not new for Ramya; She's been prone to it as far back as she can remember. When she was preparing for school exams, she made a small placard with the words *Procrastination is a Thief of Time*, and stuck it on the wall above her study table. But the procrastination she's indulging in now has a feeling of hopelessness attached to it. It wasn't the same when she was young, when things got postponed because there were more engaging diversions. Now, it comes from the feeling that no chore on earth is worth the while.

In India when Ramya was young, owning a car was a mark of social status. Only a few could afford one. Being a doctor and a gentleman of property, her father had the resources to buy a sedate, sage green made-in-England Standard Companion. Though comfortable and utilitarian, the ungainly model found few takers when first introduced in Great Britain in the sixties. Tastes had changed, and there were flashier models in the fray. Standard Motors, the crafty manufacturer, shipped the unsold stock to India where it found a ready market. For all Ramya knew, the story might be apocryphal. Indians have a huge chip on the shoulder—they always think companies in the West dump substandard goods on them.

Daddy's car was a convenient pocketsize station wagon, meaning it had extra cabin space instead of a boot at the back. Ramya often demanded to sit there, where she could kneel, and look at the drivers of cars following theirs. She'd get a great kick out of pulling funny faces at them. Some of them would raise their fists or glare at her in pretend anger, which only made her laugh.

Daddy wasn't a very confident driver and that made him overly cautious. He lacked the necessary spunk to drive in the disorderly traffic typical of Indian roads. One day, when Ramya missed the school bus, he volunteered to drop her off. On the way to her school, he got trapped at a roundabout, and went around and around numerous times, not having enough pluck to peel away from the island in the heavy, unceasing traffic. They were so late that her father had to accompany her to the classroom to apologize to the teacher in person.

A small icon on the telephone indicates there's a voice-mail message secreted in its innards. The message is from a psychologist named Renata Schrink, who introduces herself in a chirpy voice and leaves a number for Ramya to call back. "Hope to talk to you soon," she ends bright-ly. There's so much sunshine in her voice that it can hardly be real. Is it meant to be an antidote for her pro-spective patients' chronic depression? A marathon game of tag has begun, thinks Ramya, each leaving a meaning-less message for the other. She's no longer keen to talk to Schrink, though her mood-swings themselves may need the attention of a psychologist. By the way, could Schrink be her real name or just a professional handle, a *nom de gloom*, so to speak?

But right now, she must do something about her bod-
ily needs: in this instance, her totally depleted larder. If
she procrastinates, she won't even be able to cook herself
a decent meal. Reluctantly, Ramya picks up a writing pad
and a ballpoint pen. With the concentration of a poet,
something she always wanted to be, she writes:

Bread
Bagels
Priya Avakkai pickle
Bru Coffee powder
Taj Mahal loose-leaf tea
Rice (Sona Masoori)
Rice (Basmati)
Toor Dal
Channa Dal
Tamarind
Turmeric powder
Red chillies
Karela
Brinjals (round)
Cabbage
Potatoes
Roma tomatoes

Then she adds:

Homo Milk

When they first came to Canada and found little to cheer
them, Prakash thought it was a hoot. This must be the

only time she's thought of Prakash without feeling a negative emotion.

Ramya pauses and tries to remember what other groceries and produce she may need for the next two weeks. Unable to think of anything in particular, she adds:

Samosas

Then scores it out. Ramya can't believe how popular samosas have become in Canada—they have come to represent the best of Indian cuisine. In India, samosas, no one's favourite, are considered a crude, greasy snack. She herself would disdain them. But in Canada she finds herself eating them with some relish, and buys them regularly from the Indian store. Perhaps samosas are more suited to a cold country like Canada—they're spicy, filling, and even tasty if eaten hot. And they are, as they say in India, cheap and best.

Ramya puts the paper and pen down abruptly, like a poet suffering from a pang of writer's block. She's lost all interest in shopping. There's nothing in the house, not even a half a loaf of bread. But she's in no mood to put on those voluminous winter garments and drive down to the store. Besides, Ms. Peggy is a such a disgrace, with swathes of white road dust on her body. Not fit to be seen in public. Like her mistress.

She'll have to order a pizza over the phone.

❦

There were times when Daddy drove down to the big local market. In ordinary circumstances, one of the servants would fetch vegetables and provisions from shops in the immediate neighbourhood. But if there was a big party in the offing, Daddy liked to do the shopping himself.

Typically, it would be a somnolent Sunday morning, and after a heavy breakfast of idli, sambar and chutney, her father would set out. If Ramya asked to go with him, Daddy would happily take her along—he was that kind of a father. Ramya would accompany him, even though it would take a long time, and the market was an incredibly smelly place. There was something entertaining, even thrilling, about a trip to the bazaar.

Daddy would also take a young, able-bodied servant —someone like Sailoo. The servant boy was needed to carry the provisions so that you could avoid hiring coolies, the scantily clad, muscular men who carried your purchases in big round baskets placed on their heads. They smelled of stale sweat, and were notorious for their recalcitrance and aggressive bargaining skills. It was best to avoid them.

The bazaar was spread over many hundreds of acres, or so it seemed to Ramya. It had a large section devoted to fresh vegetables. There were separate areas earmarked for fruits, flowers, dry vegetables, spices, meat and fish. In the periphery of the market there were jewellers, sweets vendors, stationers, clothiers and what have you.

It was a riotous world where bicycles, cycle-rickshaws, auto-rickshaws, pushcarts, bullock carts, scooters, motorcycles, cars, minivans, and lorries, to say nothing of jaywalking cattle and devil-may-care pi-dogs, jockeyed for road space. Thousands of people jostled each other, and the vehicular traffic on the narrow roads often ground to a halt. There was a constant din—a kind of gigantic susurration which, if one paid attention, would separate itself into the component noises of internal combustion engines, newfangled electric horns and old-fashioned bellow horns, radios blaring in cafes, bells ringing in temples, cows mooing with hunger, dogs barking at one another, people shouting, people talking, people laughing.

Taking the hand of either Daddy or Sailoo in hers, lest she get separated from her elders in the maelstrom of people, little Ramya would scurry after them, her rubber slippers squelching in the slush. There was always slush on the ground, great streams of it, like black, wet soil. With her free hand, she would cover her oversensitive nose to ward off the smell of rotting fruit and blocked drains.

The vegetable vendors sat on low stools, surrounded by scores of baskets which were steeped with vegetables: tomatoes, brinjal, cauliflower, carrots, cabbage, a variety of gourds, a selection of legumes, and an assortment of leafy vegetables. Every transaction was an exercise in good-natured banter, yet it sounded as if it was on the threshold of a no-holds-barred brawl. The air was thick with accusations and insinuations of sellers and buyers, hurled like hand-grenades at each other.

"You can't pick and choose," the vegetable-seller yelled to a customer who was stuffing vegetables into a small dirty wickerwork tray. The tray with vegetables would be handed back to the vegetable-seller to be weighed.

"Do you expect me to pay for rotten vegetables?" the customer shot back.

"Am I supposed to take back home all the vegetables that are not good?" the seller countered.

"Weigh properly, weigh properly," another customer

would remonstrate. "Hold the scales the correct way, or else I'll report you to the authorities."

"You can complain to the Prime Minister for all I care!"

"Eight annas for a kilo? Look at these beans, they're all dried up!"

"Take them for six annas. Special price, just for you."

"I'll give four annas, not a paisa more."

Such momentous bargains were being struck all the while. That was the norm: Negotiation was part of the buying process, and even more so, a social skill. But Daddy was too shy a person to haggle with small vendors. In the early days, it was said, he made valiant if uncertain-sounding counter offers. The sellers, prescient in such matters, simply stood their ground. Daddy always buckled under and ended up paying what was demanded. So he stopped making even a token attempt to beat down the price. Anyway, the cost of food was so small in comparison to his earnings that it didn't matter much. That's how Daddy comforted himself.

Each time, Daddy followed the same routine, buying the same vegetables, the same meats, from the same shopkeepers because for every party they would have the same menu (as though it was something ordained by the scriptures): peas palao, fried mutton, chicken curry, vegetable korma, and raita. And of course, there would be poppadum or garelu (a doughnut shaped savoury) or some such fried stuff for a side. On occasion, fried fish would be thrown in as an afterthought, or a couple of vegetable dishes, if there were any uncompromising vegetarians in the guestlist.

After buying fresh vegetables, the threesome would

move on to the section that sold dry merchandise like spices. As soon as Ramya stepped into the lane, her justly famous nose would start to twitch. Hanging over the entire area was a nuclear cloud of aroma caused by the warring smells of various spices.

From there, to proceed to the butcher's shop one needed a very strong stomach — simply covering your nose wasn't enough. Dangling from hooks were skinned, blood-smeared carcasses of goats, as if they were so many wet clothes hung out to dry. When Ramya was very little, the sight had disturbed her so much that she stayed off meat for many months. The butcher wielding an enormous cleaver would chop up hunks of meat with astonishing speed and dexterity. To little Ramya it was a wonder that he didn't slice off the ends of his fingers. When one asked for minced meat, it was fascinating to watch him dice meat at a demoniac speed, the butcher's knife sounding as if it were transmitting a message in Morse — *Tchak! Tchak! tchak! I'll have you for lunch! Tchak! Tchak! Tchak! I'll have you for dinner! Tchak! Tchak! Tchak! I'll even have you for evening snack!*

The next stop, the poultry. In those days, one often bought chickens live. The birds were housed in crowded, noisy enclosures, reeking of fear and death. The shopkeeper would grab a hen by its legs, singing the praises of its gastronomic qualities. The bird, squawking in terror, would be held aloft for inspection. If approved, he would kill the bird by snapping its neck. He'd pluck out the feathers, skin the fowl, dice it into bite-size pieces, and wrap them in a large leaf of a wild plant before handing it over to the customer.

Of all sections in the market, the Nobel Prize for sheer stink would go to the fish stall. The fish from the sea, having come by overnight trains from the distant coast, would lie with their eyes open, staring unwaveringly at Ramya, reminding her of her stern science teacher. The lake or river fish would sometimes be alive, swimming sluggishly within the confines of a dark, malodourous tank.

Once Daddy checked the shopping list he brought with him, and ascertained that he had bought all the items, they returned to the car — Sailoo weighed down by a large round wickerwork tub balanced over his head, and Dad carrying a jute bag or two. Ramya would get into the cabin space at the back of the car, where she'd have the advantage of views offered by three windows — a kind of wide screen experience of the vivid drama that was the Indian bazaar. Daddy would steer the car through the traffic, nudging a cow here, bumping into a rickshaw there, honking all the while, to make the sea of apparently deaf people part for them.

On the evening of the party, when they began to prepare the food, the whole house would smell of the delicious spices that went into the cooking. The appetizing aroma would waft through the rooms, like a special guest who'd been given free run of the entire house. Ramya always associated a party or a festival with the smell of spices, heady and cloying, rather than anything else. Not the rearrangement of furniture in the living room to accommodate the large number of guests; not the decorations, when mandatory bunches of multi-coloured balloons blossomed on the walls and ceilings on birthdays; not the shimmering daisy-chains of tiny clay lamps that snaked along the parapet-walls during the festival of Deepavali; not the sudden appearance of a large metal tub with iceberg-sized blocks of ice submerging bottles of soda and beer. Nothing, nothing—but the all-pervading smell of cooking, as palpable as a three-dimensional object.

The guests would begin to trickle in much after the stated time, as if it was bad manners to arrive at a party on schedule. The menfolk would stay back in the living room where an impromptu bar had been set up, but the women, dressed in party finery of silk saris and heavy jewellery, would coast on, carrying with them a halo of the scent they'd doused their armpits with. They proceeded to the bedrooms where they'd settle down on beds or sundry chairs.

The ladies, having transformed a part of the house into a fortified seraglio, would sip Kissan's orange or pineapple squash from tumblers hardly bigger than shot glasses. In their cozy seclusion, they'd talk about films, new recipes, and illnesses, like measles and whooping cough, which befell their respective families. Sitting amidst her guests, with a preoccupied look, Mummy would participate little, if at all, in the desultory conversation. She behaved more like a reluctant invitee rather than the hostess. Her only concession to the occasion was to wear a Kanchi silk sari (with an ill-fitting and mismatched blouse), and stick random pieces of jewellery on her ears, neck and hands—like someone indifferently hanging Christmas ornaments.

Only for get-togethers of the extended family would

children be invited. Ramya rejoiced if there were no children present — she hated having to play "house-house" with other girls, pulling out her collection of dolls and toy cooking utensils. If there were boys among the guests, they'd have to play "I spy" in the front yard, which was even worse.

If Ramya was all by herself, she'd do what she liked doing most — man the makeshift bar. Bottles of liquor stood shoulder to shoulder on the counter, like stalwart generals on parade. Most of the bottles were of whiskies made in India with names drummed up to evoke the Scottish Highlands — like Bagpiper or Peter Scot. But the pride of place was given to the one or two bottles of Scotch with illustrious names like Chivas Regal or Vat 69 — presents for Daddy from grateful patients who'd bought them at duty-free shops in airports on their way back from a foreign jaunt.

Ramya would clamber on to the barstool, replacing the versatile Sailoo, who'd until then assumed the avatar of a bartender. Though displaced, he'd stand by Ramya's side, like an avuncular ghost, as she dished out large pegs of whisky. Daddy's misty-eyed friends coming up for refills would chat her up, pretending she was a barmaid.

"So Ramya darling, how's business today?"

"Not good. Krishna Rao uncle is not drinking anything today."

"He has a bad liver. Your Daddy must have ordered him to stay away from liquor ... So Ramya what do you want to become when you grow up? A doctor like your father or remain a barmaid?"

Sliding soda water carefully from a bottle into the

tumbler with the peg of scotch (Sailoo having prised opened the rusty bottle-cap, as Ramya did not have the required strength in her small, thin wrists), she said: "I want to become a teacher like Atom Auntie."

She was a little girl then, around six years. But somewhere down the road, she dropped her overvaulting ambition to become a schoolmarm. She couldn't pinpoint exactly when the momentous realisation occurred. Was it when her poem was published for the first time in the school magazine? Or when she'd finished reading Daphne Du Maurier's *Rebecca* in her preteen years? The book's enchantment was so powerful that she'd felt there was nothing more wonderful than being a writer. In a society which encouraged boys to become engineers and girls doctors, Ramya had kept her counsel, biding her time.

Daddy's parties would drag on late into the night, propelled by the men's reluctance to call it a day. The famished wives had to make brave sorties into the men's stronghold repeatedly to persuade their husbands to have dinner. It was a custom in those days for men to have dinner first, and only then would their wives follow suit.

At the end of a sumptuous meal, as always, paan was distributed. These were small green trapezoid tidbits made of betel leaves folded over areca nuts, coconut shavings and rose jelly. It was the perfect antidote to the lingering masala flavour in your mouth or the stubborn nicotine smell in your breath. The moment the guests partook of the paan, the party ended for all intents and purposes. The guests would slip away, in incredibly quick succession, to their waiting cars, calling out their thank yous and goodnights.

After the precipitate evacuation of the guests, a sudden hush would descend on the house. The drawing room would have a bereft aspect, like the lounge of a sinking ship abandoned in a hurry. Later the servants would turn up to collect the glasses and empty the ashtrays. By then Ramya who wasn't used to late nights would begin to doze, her eyes stinging with sleep. Curled up on a sofa in the drawing room, she would sleep contentedly until Daddy or a maid carried her to her bedroom upstairs.

⎯⎯⎯⎯⎯⎯

Ramya telephones Mrs. Rao's home. An overdue call, which cannot be put off for any reason. Mrs. Rao's daughter picks up the phone.

"Jayanti, I'm sorry to hear about your mother. How is she?"

Ramya remembers Jayanti as a teenager. Outwardly she looked very much Indian, but when she spoke she sounded like a native-born Canadian. Though not impolite, she had a confident and direct way of speaking, even to her elders, which had sounded curt to Ramya's unaccustomed ears when she first came to Canada.

"I meant to call you today, Ramya. Mother passed away late in the night yesterday."

"My god! I'm really sorry ... How is your father keeping? May I speak to him?"

"He's resting right now. He's taken mother's loss very badly."

"I'm not surprised. They were close. I'd like to come and see him."

"That will be nice. But please call before coming."

Ramya puts down the receiver, overwhelmed with intense sadness.

⌒———⌒

When Ramya was in Grade 8 her own mother died after a prolonged illness, ending a tug-o-war between a puzzled but indefatigable team of doctors and the relentless and determined hosts of the Lord of Death. A few weeks before, Ramya's parents had been to the port city of Chennai (called Madras then) for a couple of days to attend the wedding of a close family friend's daughter. On their return to Hyderabad, Mummy fell ill — she felt too queasy to eat and had a slight fever. When the symptoms persisted, her condition was diagnosed as jaundice and she was put on appropriate medication. Weeks passed but there was no improvement. Test after test was done, and Daddy consulted his specialist friends, but the deterioration was unstoppable. She was not responding to drugs; the entire regimen of treatment had no effect on her. Thin as a rail at the best of times, the illness reduced her to a two-dimensional object spread out on the mattress. Like a large inflatable doll from which all air had escaped, leaving a limp, wrinkled plastic sheath.

In desperation, Daddy admitted her into a hospital. When Ramya visited her mother there, she found her lying inert on a metal cot, in a dead faint, with tubes sticking in and out of her — as if she were a processing machine designed to improve the quality of running water in the hospital. All the gallons of intravenous glucose were of no avail. For Daddy it was a terrible blow, twice over. Besides the personal loss, the fact that he was a doctor, and yet could not help her, weighed heavily on him.

Ramya felt sad, but not in an immediate, soul-wrenching kind of way. She acknowledged the loss but didn't feel it. It was the suddenness, more than the loss itself that was the gravamen of her sorrow. When they brought Mummy's body home, slow, silent tears trickled down her cheeks, but there was no outpouring of grief. Daddy looked more bewildered than he did at normal times, and fortunately for him, his relatives and friends stepped forward unhesitatingly to help with the funeral arrangements. The kind of support he received was not surprising at all since Daddy had always provided medical consultation, and often medicines, free of charge to his friends and relatives.

Mummy was laid out in the living room on a bed of ice-blocks, which shed copious tears for her. Quantities and quantities of flowers were arranged over the body: Arifuddin the flower vendor went out of his way to deliver a huge number of garlands for Mummy, his biggest customer. Of course, Daddy insisted on paying for the flowers, and Arifuddin reluctantly accepted it. However large-hearted and magnanimous, Arifuddin was, when all was said and done, only a petty businessman.

Incense sticks and lighted lamps were placed on the floor at the foot of the bed of ice. The incense was of the same fragrance Mummy had used for daily worship. In death she smelled just like her puja room, the place she'd spent most of her time.

There was a steady stream of visitors. Even out-of-town

relatives came, and not all of them could be accommodated in the house. They had to take rooms in nearby hotels, or they went back the same night. The house was full of strangers, many of them clad in white, who'd come to pay their last respects. There was so much hustle and bustle, with servants running hither and thither, that it grated on Ramya's nerves. One maid's exclusive task was to mop up the water from the melting ice-blocks.

Her mother was cremated in a faraway burial ground, and only the male relatives went to witness it. Daddy returned home carrying, in the crook of his arm as if it were a child, a large earthenware urn which contained Mummy's ashes. He couldn't bear to dispose of Mummy's remains right away in the traditional way. He must have thought it too callous to jettison Mummy out of their lives in one heave.

All the guests and visitors had left, and an unnatural silence, an emptiness like curfew, descended on the house. It felt as if the house was filled with an invisible fog, and the inmates maundered about, not knowing what to do next.

Daddy sent word for one of his patients who was a jeweller to have a decorative silver container made to store the ashes. Until the silver casket arrived, the earthenware pot was placed on the sideboard like an ethnic artefact bought from a Cottage Industries showroom. A horrified Amma, Ramya's grandmother, had it moved to a corner of the front yard. It was considered inauspicious to bring the remains of a dead person into the house.

Then Daddy got the brainwave to bury the ashes in the bed of Mummy's beloved jasmine bushes. Amma would have none of it—she instructed Daddy to disperse her daughter's ashes in a holy river so that her soul would have eternal peace.

So, Daddy pored over a map of the district and decided to empty the urn into the Krishna River. In the meanwhile, the earthenware got broken by a careless maid sweeping the compound. Amma transferred the ashes to an empty biscuit tin that had been washed and wiped dry. The tin had the word Britannia printed on in bold, gothic letters, lending a kind of grandeur and solemnity no decorative silver container or ethnic artefact could match.

Daddy and Ramya hit the road in their new made-in-India Ambassador, a model which grew out of the old British Morris Oxford. A symbol of India's self-reliance, the Ambassador was one of the most popular cars ever made in India, and remained on the roads, almost unchanged in appearance, for nearly half a century. Daddy had to go in for a new car after their venerable Standard refused to budge one fine morning. Cars too die.

They travelled for miles and miles, Daddy faithfully following the map. It was beginning to get dark, and they were nowhere near the temple town where they intended to scatter Mummy's ashes. It slowly dawned on them that they were lost. Daddy tried to read the map in the dim ceiling-light of the car, but it was useless. He recalled crossing a small bridge about twenty miles behind them, so they made a U-turn and headed back. He stopped the car on the middle of the narrow bridge. There weren't many vehicles on the road at that time of the day. They'd seen only a lumbering state transport bus and a couple of straw-laden bullock carts in the last half hour.

They stepped out of the car and went over to the railing—a set of pipes running through a few uprights. Some of the pipes were askew; some were missing. When Ramya leaned over them and looked down, she was relieved to make out a grumbling but steadily flowing ribbon of water in the light of the moon.

"Do you think it's the River Krishna?" Ramya asked, in a voice fraught with doubt.

"Who knows," Daddy said. "Anyway, all streams and rivers eventually flow into the mighty ocean."

Daddy uttered the words in a matter-of-fact manner, but in the dark still night, with only the distant but tireless cicadas strumming a dirge for Mummy, it sounded deep and philosophical. Daddy prised open the lid with his thumbnail, and stretching his arms out, inverted the box. Just then, a gust of wind came up the stream, flinging back some of Mummy's ashes on them. Startled, Daddy let go of the box. They heard a soft splash and a thud as the biscuit tin fell into shallow water.

They stamped their feet and ruffled their hair, trying to shake off the ashes. They got back into the car and drove away. But some of the ashes must have remained, clinging to their clothes and body. In a way, a small part of Mummy came back home with them.

5

Atom Auntie

R AMYA CANNOT BELIEVE her eyes …

From the odds and ends in her box she has unearthed a lemon-flavoured lollipop. It's wrapped in translucent paper which is twisted into a tuft at the top. She can make out the dull yellow candy behind the veil of limp, greying paper that was once crackling crisp and snow white. With the passing years the candy has lost its delectable appeal, a sign that even nonliving things are not immune to aging.

But what about its taste? Does it remain the same? Candies are nothing but boiled sugar with artificial colour and flavour. Is it palatable after all these years?

Rather sketchily she remembers reading in a newspaper about a jar of honey (or was it wine?) discovered in an ancient Egyptian (or was it a Greek?) tomb. The report said it was still unspoilt and edible. Though not of similar vintage, the lollipop was nearly four decades old. It may also be safe to eat after all these years, but Ramya is no frame of mind to try.

As to who gave her that lollipop she doesn't have to
speculate: It was none other than her aunt—her beloved
Atom Auntie, her father's younger sister. Ramya remembers Atom Auntie always giving her candies, cookies and
sundry gifts. She was the only person in the world who
never uttered an unkind word to Ramya, nor ever spoke
to her in a sharp tone. Despite the obvious difference in
their ages, Atom Auntie always treated her as if she was
her equal. She would regale her with stories—sometimes
so comical and improbable, that Ramya, even as a child,
suspected her aunt of making them up.

Atom Auntie's real name was Sunanda, and she got her
nickname in a peculiar way. Daddy expected Ramya to
call his sister Auntie, having a decided preference for
English nomenclature. After all, he'd been educated in a
school run by the Jesuits. He thought it reflected a modern outlook. But Mummy used to employ the Telugu
word *Attamma*, which meant an aunt, while referring to
Sunanda, like: "I can't tell you stories the way to your
Attamma does." Or: "Your Attamma has all the patience
in the world." It was no wonder then that little Ramya
started calling her aunt Attamma Auntie, a frightful tau-
tology. But mercifully it was shortened to Atom Auntie,
coming as it did straight from a babe's mouth.

Atom Auntie was unmarried, and remained single all
her not-so-long life. When speaking to Ramya, some people
referred to her as "your spinster aunt," piercing Ramya's
heart. It sounded so demeaning, though they didn't mean

to be unkind. They were merely stating an incontestable fact in an age when political correctness was practically nonexistent. Atom Auntie was good-looking, light of skin, and 5 feet 6 — tallish for an Indian woman. One would have expected her to be besieged by suitors, even in a tradition-bound society where marriages were made, not in heaven, but in comfortable living rooms abuzz with busybody relatives. Young men always had an eye for attractive women, and traditions be damned. Yet Atom Auntie, for seemingly inexplicable reasons, remained in a state of bachelorette-hood.

The answer to this mystery lay in her horoscope. According to the pundits, she was born at a time when Saturn was in ascendance, and there was also the matter of a wayward Mars. Or some such rigmarole, but, in a word, it meant Atom Auntie's horoscope was not auspicious for the groom's mother. Any man marrying her ran the risk of his mother meeting a sudden and untimely death. Despite the dire astrological prediction, Ramya's father tried to broker a match. He was Atom Auntie's elder brother, so it was his responsibility as much as their parents' (who lived in their ancestral village in the back of beyond) to see she was duly married — in effect, to hand her over to the care of an upright and dependable male member of society. It turned out to be more of an uphill task than he could imagine.

Daddy did his best. He first enquired among his relatives; then, with rising desperation, among educated young men within the community; and later, in a last-ditch effort, among his friends and acquaintances of any caste or creed. But all his attempts came to naught. Maybe because he was upfront about what the horoscope said. He couldn't find a single rational and courageous young man who would disregard the horoscope. Even dangling the carrot of a nice, fat dowry — Daddy didn't mind selling his lands in their village if the need arose — was of no avail. The horrendous future which the stars foretold was enough to dissuade the bravest of young men.

But, surprising as it may seem, Atom Auntie did have a suitor, and was even formally engaged to be married for a brief while. And it happened, not because of her brother's perseverance, but as a matter of pure chance.

Daddy had just completed building their two-storey house, using his savings and an immense loan from a bank. The house, the same one in which Ramya grew up, was in a nice clean neighbourhood where the roads were lined with shady gulmohar trees, and pretty roundabouts graced every intersection. The upper floor of the building was rented out to meet the loan repayments. The family which moved in had a daughter of marriageable age. It so happened that a young man, with his family in attendance, dropped by to determine the suitability of a match. The boy didn't take to the girl, but on his way out he spotted Atom Auntie in the garden — she was watering the lawn with a hosepipe. She was laughing and chatting with the maids who were lounging on the front steps. The maids were content to allow Atom Auntie to do their work while they leisurely folded betel leaves into paans and popped them into their mouths.

In the crystalline evening sunshine, Atom Auntie, who always cut such a pleasing figure, must have looked like a vision to the young man's eyes, jaded from viewing so many prospective brides in quick succession.

The very next day, their tenant, who was distantly related to the young man, came down, and with a sour face, conveyed the young man's wish to Daddy. Daddy at once cautioned their tenant about the minefield in Atom Auntie's horoscope.

"I've already told him about it," the tenant said, his face turning a shade more sour, "but you know how young men are. He's most insistent."

"Well, if he doesn't mind, then we'll invite him over. Let's see what will come out of it."

Soon Atom Auntie and the young man were engaged. His name was Satyavan and he worked in a bank as a loans officer.

A few weeks before the wedding day, Satyavan and his mother were returning from Moazzamjahi Market where they'd been to buy small green mangoes and red chillies to make avakkai pickle. His mother, who was slightly on the heavier side, was perched precariously on the back saddle of his Lambretta. She was clutching a jute bag which contained their purchases. An elderly Bedford lorry roared out of nowhere, and with scant regard to traffic rules, made a beeline towards them. At its helm was a man in an infernal hurry. It was later discovered that he was completely intoxicated with vast quantities of toddy, a potent country liquor. Terrified, Satyavan's mother jumped off the scooter, startling poor Satyavan into losing his balance. The Lambretta took a tumble, but the accident, mercifully, wasn't fatal: Satyavan escaped with a few bruises, but his mother, who fell on the road like a dhobi's bundle of unwashed clothes, had her leg — tibia, as Daddy pointed out with a physician's exactitude — broken.

Every man, woman, and dog recalled the oracular warning of the pundits. It wasn't a nice situation for Atom Auntie to be in. Very awkward for Daddy too. He and Atom Auntie visited the hospital, taking half a dozen expensive but mournful looking apples (the best they could buy in the local market) along with a packet of rusk, the standard offerings for a patient in a hospital. Satyavan and his mother were engaged in earnest conversation, which Satyavan broke off when he saw Atom Auntie and her brother. Seated on an easy chair provided for family attendants, he looked sullen. He had masses of plaster and wads of iodine-soaked cotton stuck on various parts of his body.

His mother, a plump lady of fifty years, lay trussed up on a metal cot whose ancient white paint was bruised with rust. The light brown bed sheets, which had once been lily-white, sported beige floral patterns — ghosts of bloodstains of past patients which repeated washing couldn't completely exorcise. She too had her fair share of bandages and one of her legs was in a cast. When she spotted Atom Auntie, a wave of terror swept over her face.

"Hello, Hello, Hello," Daddy said, making a brave attempt at cheeriness. "How are you all feeling?"

Daddy engaged Satyavan in light breezy conversation hoping to improve his mood, while the two ladies remained silent — Atom Auntie out of respect, Satyavan's mother with a lack of graciousness. Daddy glanced at the hospital reports and said: "Nothing to worry, Satyavan, we'll have your mother out of the hospital in no time." Daddy had a number of friends in the hospital though he himself didn't work there, and as a consequence Satyavan and his mother got special treatment.

When Satyavan's mother was released a week later, Daddy left early from work to drive her in his elderly but handy Standard Companion to her house. In the days that followed, Daddy visited Satyavan and his mother regularly.

"They are coming along nicely," he told Atom Auntie. "Satyavan can return to work coming Monday."

When they didn't hear from Satyavan in the next few days, they weren't unduly perturbed. Satyavan's family didn't have a phone in their house, and he would have a lot of catching up to do at work. But one day their tenant turned up at their front door unannounced. He didn't sport a sour look this time round, rather a shadow of a smile lurked at the corners of his mouth. Still, he started off in a grave tone: "Satyavan has sent word ..."

"Yes?" Daddy asked.

"His family is very upset. He'll speak to you in person when he gets better. In the meantime, he has sent this letter for you."

Even before Daddy could unfold the single sheet of paper, Atom Auntie guessed what it would contain. Her brief flirtation with matrimony was over. Daddy read through the letter, and said, with an air of distraction: "I can understand how Satyavan feels. But he shouldn't decide in haste ... Anyway, thank you for bringing the letter."

It was said that Atom Auntie, given short shrift in such an undeserving manner, neither wept nor expressed any resentment. She accepted her fate with a stoicism which comes from long experience of living in a world that was fickle and heartless.

All this happened when Ramya was a toddler. She heard the story in bits and pieces from Amma and the maids. Though a gifted storyteller herself, Atom Auntie had neglected to recount her own story, which was the very stuff Bollywood cinema was made of, except that in Indian films there's always a happy ending.

In the aftermath of the broken engagement, Daddy searched, not for a groom, but for a job for Atom Auntie. He correctly reckoned that having something to do would keep her mind from brooding. She got a job as a teacher in a small primary school. It was only meant to be a stop gap arrangement as the school was far away in the suburbs. Atom Auntie was good with children because she could empathize with them so well, and her students adored her in return. She made a proficient teacher too; being a natural raconteur, she could even make dreary subjects like civics or grammar sound fascinating. So Atom Auntie stuck to her job, though it wasn't well-paying and required her to take a bus and a local train to get to her place of work.

Ramya sits in front of the TV idly watching a shopping channel airing a pitch for cosmetics for aging women. The rapturous anchors mention the word décolleté repeatedly like it is some kind of mantra, pricking Ramya conscience. Her own décolleté is fine and does not need attention for the next few years, but it reminds her of the inexorable passage of time, and the long list of things she needs to get done (even if improving her décolleté is not at the top of her list).

Ramya doesn't know why she's put the TV on, or why

she's stopped by at this particular channel while surfing, except that TV, God bless the idiot box, does have the power to keep loneliness at bay, a feature not even its inventor could have foreseen in his most optimistic moment. A TV can be a substitute for live human company, even if a poor one.

Ramya's mind drifts from the show, reflecting whether she would have been better off if she had made different choices in the past. When she immigrated to Canada she presumed that jobs were plentiful, and you could indulge in cherry picking. Things didn't turn out so rosy, but as she could afford to pay for education — they'd brought a substantial sum of money from India, she surveyed all the learning avenues available.

One of the first things she learned was that getting another management degree in Canada was a waste of time and money, as she wouldn't have Canadian experience to go with it.

She seriously contemplated enrolling in a teacher's training college, but then she learned that newly qualified teachers often languished as supply teachers. Unattached to any specific school, they had to wait to be called as a stand-in for a teacher who hadn't showed up. Such a teaching stint could last for a day, a week, a month or even a year, depending on the type of leave the regular teachers took. Ramya heard horror stories of supply teachers who got no more than a few days of work in a year.

Somebody suggested Ramya train as a nurse. Unlike in India, a nurse's pay was nothing to be sneezed at, but being a doctor's daughter, and a pampered one at that, she couldn't countenance working as a nurse. It also needed a kind of empathetic disposition Ramya knew she didn't possess, to say nothing of the time and study required to become a Registered Professional Nurse.

Eventually realizing you couldn't be too picky if you're a new immigrant, Ramya took the first job that came her way. She started at a Tim Hortons coffee shop as a cashier, then cut and chopped her way, via The Bay and Walmart, to — at last! — an office job in a car parts factory, where she got health and dental benefits on top of a reasonable fortnightly paycheque.

Wherever Ramya worked, whether in India or Canada, she was liked by her supervisors and employers. It was gratifying to learn that she was perceived as diligent, reliable and hardworking — a sure-fire cocktail of attributes any recruiter would fall for. Totally engaged, Ramya always gave her best to her job. She never worked with her face turned to the clock, never minded working late if there was an urgent task to be finished.

Yet, when it came to the crunch, her employer cast her out in a heartbeat. Just like that, without even an iota of compunction. Ramya suspected that it wasn't such a simple matter — there may have been racism and nepotism at play.

She had never felt so worthless in her life as when she was laid off, not even when Prakash went out of her life. Their separation was a matter of mutual incompatibility years in the making, having stopped liking each other as far back as she could remember. But losing her job had cut her to the quick, undermining her self-esteem. Not many of her cashiered colleagues appeared to take it so badly. Was it because she was an immigrant, and had found looking for a job a herculean task? Besides, it wasn't that the company had closed its shutters, leaving the entire workforce in the lurch. The layoff had affected only a few employees, and the company was running and making profits for its share- and stockholders.

Ramya remembers the fateful Friday in the third week of December as if it's yesterday. Just before the close of day, nearly fifty employees were told not to turn up for work the following Monday. (The home office in Michigan had asked the Canadian operations to reduce the workforce by ten percent to improve their financial outlook. There were 485 employees, so they cashiered 49 hands, rounding off the number.) Veronica, her colleague who worked in the accounts payable department, was a petite woman who was five feet nothing in her stilettoes. She said: "I must be that half employee who's getting the sack."

It's a good thing that Ramya's finances are in order. Even without fortnightly cheques getting deposited in her bank account, she isn't in any pecuniary distress. Besides having a variety of investments, she has already paid off the mortgage with the help of the money she had realized from selling her father's house in India—and there was enough left over for a nest egg, too. And if she could motivate herself to fill in and submit the unemployment insurance forms, her fortnightly paycheques could be re-kindled for another eight months at least, if what she heard was right.

It isn't such a bleak scenario after all, yet a sort of lassitude has crept into her being in the last few weeks. She feels no enthusiasm, no sense of expectation, just a desire to let things be.

How can she crawl out of her cocoon of lethargy and aimlessness?

Maybe, this was the right time to reassess her priorities. It was an opportunity to have re-look at her life. She should focus on finding things to do, things which would give her real joy, things which are meaningful, things she always wanted to do but had neglected, all these years, to act on because of distractions of family and career.

Deep down in her heart there's a dream, however incipient and insubstantial, waiting to be realized. A youthful dream that should have been pursued. A pipe dream, ambitious and asinine at once.

The dream to be an author.

A cynic would have opined that it was unrealistic; and elders in India would have declared it irresponsible. After all, how many writers could live on proceeds derived solely from writing?

Even then, this was the opportune time to breathe some life into that half-forgotten ambition. She may not have the talent to make it, but at least now she has the time to try.

⁓

Atom Auntie had to commute quite a distance to get to her school. In those days, it was uncommon for people to travel far to work. Usually, they found a job in their neighbourhood. But Atom Auntie always got a raw deal. She would leave the house at the crack of dawn and return just before dusk. She had to walk to the bus stand, take a bus to the railway station, ride a local train, and then walk again to reach her school. Despite this, she always had time for Ramya. And little Ramya would wait at the front of the house with growing impatience to catch the first glimpse of her beloved Atom Auntie turning into the street. Ramya would push the side gate open, and start running towards her, shouting: *"Atom Auntie! Atom Auntie!"*

On the other hand, as a teacher, she got long spells of holidays: summer holidays, Christmas holidays and term breaks. She spent all her leisure hours with Ramya.

Atom Auntie read a lot of books and as such was privy to an enormous fund of stories. Often at dinnertime she would sit on the parapet wall of the roof, and feed Ramya from a silver bowl. Though the utensil was tarnished and smelled peculiar, how heavenly it was to dine in the open air! Under a canopy crowded with twinkling stars — it was an era when lights on the earth were too modest to outshine their celestial counterparts, Atom Auntie would tell Ramya tales which would hold her captive with enchantment. And how delicious the food tasted, even if it was just plain dal and rice, when served with sides of chivalry and chicanery! When Atom Auntie wasn't around, Ramya would refuse to eat, clamping her jaws shut with a strength that was surprising in a child. No pleas or threats could make her open her mouth again. Unless, of course, a story was told. But for Ramya's mother, or any of the maids, it was quite a challenge to fetch up a tale to conform to Ramya's exacting standards. If the story didn't grab her attention or was one she'd heard before (which often was the case, considering how limited her Mummy's or the maids' repertoire was), Ramya would say: "The food doesn't taste good today." That was that—she'd stop eating, and turn her determined mouth, ringed with crumbs of food, away.

When it came to storytelling Atom Auntie was in a different class altogether. She would point out star-clusters, calling them Orion and Pegasus or Cassiopeia, and narrate their background stories. It would be years before poor Ramya could connect the random sprinkling of stars to form the picture of a hunter or a winged horse. The only exception was the Big Dipper, which fortunately looked its name.

Atom Auntie's choice of stories was eclectic, often taken from Greek or Norse mythology, rather than from Indian sources. In those days, just over a decade after India's independence from Britain, English books with Indian content were hard to come by. So, Atom Auntie would rather recount the exploits of King Arthur and Robin Hood than the adventures of Rama and Krishna. She was more at ease with Mother Goose tales than she was with Jataka stories.

It was left for Amma, her grandmother, to correct this asymmetry, albeit unintentionally, when she read out stories years later from an eagerly awaited Telugu periodical called *Chandamama*. It was printed in lurid tones of green, blue and pink, and served up Indian folklore and mythology by the ladleful. That was how Ramya became acquainted with stories of King Vikramaditya and his ghostly burden Vetala, and Emperor Krishna Devaraya and his witty minister Tenali Ramakrishna.

Amma had her own take on astronomy. In summer, when it got too warm, Amma and Ramya would go onto the roof to sleep. The flat roof, often called a terrace in

India, had a parapet wall on all sides. As they unrolled
the beds to sleep in the cool night breeze, Amma would
explain the mysteries of the night sky with a mytho-
logical slant. The very same Big Dipper, also known as
the Great Bear, would be called by its Indian name of
Saptarishi Mandala, the abode of the seven great sages,
and Arundati, the perfect wife — hardly visible — dimly
simpering next to her hermit husband.

"If you look hard, you will find her," Amma said, as
though a perfect wife wasn't someone easy to come by.

She would tell Ramya about Surya the Sun God and
his wife Chaaya, the Shadow; about Soma the Moon
God and how he was afflicted with consumption which
made him wax and wane; about black, sinister serpents
that would try to swallow up the Sun and Moon, causing
eclipses.

The most gruesome story Ramya ever heard was re-
counted by Atom Auntie. It wasn't a story at all in the real
sense of the word, but a tragic incident that happened at
a school. One of Atom Auntie's friends who taught in
an exclusive girls' school had invited her to attend their
annual day event which was touted to be spectacular.
The school had deep pockets, so they had an excellent
music and dance department which was staffed with
talented teachers. In consequence, the school children
put on a show every year which was of a very high order,
almost professional in its execution.

The event was held in an attractive open-air theatre.
A rich navy curtain hung in scalloped gathers, and pinned
to it were letters made from satiny pink ribbons, which
read: "Welcome to Our Annual Day Celebrations." The

bright strobe lights focused on the message heightened the sense of expectation.

It was an evening in late November; the sun had just set, leaving splashes of gold and orange along the western horizon. Overhead, the sky was a throw of inky velvet with sequins. Shy wintry stars, peering down through a veil of haze, had turned up to watch the show, as if they knew that something unexpected was about to happen. It was a chilly night, giving the audience the perfect excuse to dig out their moth-balled winter wear — men wore suits and cardigans, young men jackets and jerseys, and women and girls stoles and sweaters. Atom Auntie wore her usual chocolate brown pashmina shawl, with a tiny paisley pattern in light ochre (a gift from your mother, she told Ramya), to go with her crisply starched cream-coloured Venkatagiri sari with a thin gold border.

In front of the stage, hundreds of metal folding chairs were arranged in neat, serried phalanxes. A red carpet was laid out in the aisle, and there were potted plants everywhere, adding to the décor. The audience section was fast filling up with guests.

A male teacher selected for his voice — a kind of syrupy baritone — was the invisible master of ceremonies. As he began to welcome the guests in his deep voice, the outer strobes dimmed, and the curtain rose to reveal a stage flooded with light. On the stage was a long table with half a dozen high, ornate chairs placed on the farther side. Glasses of water covered with coasters were placed on the table, as if arranged for a phantom feast. The disembodied voice of the compere invited, one by one, the principal, the members of the school board, and the chief guest — a local cricket hero—on to the stage. The principal handed over large bouquets of blood-red roses to the guests. The chief guest in particular had an enormous and uncomfortably heavy garland made of white lilies and red roses put around his neck. Then began a series of unbelievably dull speeches; starting with the principal, everyone seated on the stage had a go at the mic. Taking gulps of water —for preaching parches the throat, the many speakers showered clichés on the bored, restive children who made up the bulk of the audience.

Almost an hour later the last of the speakers fell silent. Then all the guests on the stage rose *en masse* and filed out, taking a narrow flight of steps on one side of the proscenium. When they returned to their seats in the front row, the curtains came down, and from behind it issued sounds of hurrying feet, and furniture being dragged away. The curtains went up again to reveal a large statue of Nataraja, the dancing god. Two students were seated on a mat on the floor, and in front of them were their musical instruments, a veena and a pair of tablas. Tentatively they began to play, and the show started at last.

A dancer sashayed in, deliberately stomping on the floor of the stage to make her ankle-bells ring out. After bowing to the figure on the stage, she began to dance to the accompaniment of the music provided by her two fellow students. Though Atom Auntie had seen similar classical dances performed in schools before, they paled in comparison to what unfolded before her eyes. Most of the acts which followed—whether one-act plays, mime or folk dances—had a finesse not common in school performances, certainly not at the school where Atom Auntie taught. All the children were either extremely talented or had put in hours of practice. All the acts had that aura of professionalism which came when no expense was spared.

Grade after grade put on enjoyable acts, much to delight of the parents who'd come to see their children perform. One of the items was a dance number by the Grade 8 students which promised to be not the usual Indian classical or folk dance, but a modernistic one choreographed by a new dance teacher. It was an ensemble of ten dancers dressed exotically, if inaccurately, as birds of paradise. Each dancer wore an elaborate costume made with brightly coloured plumes. The dance was exquisite to behold as the dancers flapped their arms, and wove around the stage with fluid movements, grouping themselves into patterns, then moving away, dissolving the formations, and then re-grouping to form another.

The background score was a medley of movements from western classical music—Mozart, Beethoven and Wagner. In the final round, burning sparklers were handed out to the dancers. The dancers twirled the sparklers around, as the music picked up pace, rising in a crescendo towards a grand finale. The audience watched spellbound.

One of children accidentally dropped a sparkler on her costume. The flimsy synthetic feathers burst into flames. Some of the other dancers, sparklers in hand, ran to help their classmate, and before anyone realized what was happening, the costumes of three or four children were on fire.

Screaming, the girls ran hither and thither like celestial firebirds, while the taped music played on relentlessly with a manic verve.

Some foolhardy members of the audience rushed to

the narrow staircase the led to the stage, with no clear plan of rescue, unwittingly blocking the way to others bearing fire extinguishers, having torn them down from the walls of the main school building, to douse the flames.

"Roll! Roll!" their dance teacher shouted, tears welling in her eyes because there was no way she could clamber on to the stage which came up to her chest. "Roll on the floor!"

To many in the audience, judging from their reaction, she may have been merely giving stage directions. Were they transfixed with horror or did they presume, in their confusion, that it was all part of the spectacular dance routine? But luckily, some young men who had come to watch their younger siblings perform vaulted themselves on to the stage and, taking off their outer garments, swiped at the burning costumes with them. Wrapping the burning girls in their coats, they succeeded in snuffing out the flames.

There was confusion all around, the audience dispersing helter-skelter. Never before in her life had Atom Auntie witnessed such a horrific scene. There was so much wailing and weeping, Auntie Atom herself had begun to sob without even realising it. What the parents were undergoing, especially those who saw their children go up in flames before their eyes, was difficult to imagine.

The affected children were moved to a nearby hospital in school vans. Much later, a solitary fire engine turned up, with a fireman standing in the rumble, ringing a brass bell lustily. There was nothing for the firefighters to do. The stage was deserted but for residue of foam from the extinguishers and burnt pieces of cloth fluttering in the breeze. Many of the chairs were strewn about, lying on their sides. Some of the potted plants had toppled, the red earth spilling out like bloodstains.

Three or four children received first-degree burns on their hands and back. It could've been a lot worse but luckily the plumes were away from their body, and the costumes themselves were made of thick cotton. Nonetheless, the children would carry the scars for life, some on their bodies, and some in their minds.

Atom Auntie wept again, as she ended the story.

"Why are you crying, Atom Auntie?" Ramya asked. "They were not your children."

"It doesn't matter whose children they were," Atom Auntie said, taking Ramya in her arms and hugging her.

A little later, Atom Auntie narrated another story — a funny one, she said — as an antidote.

Atom Auntie had a friend and colleague named Thilakam. She was a short lady in her late fifties, with bold brushstrokes of grey in her hair. She wore diamond ear- and nose-studs whose lustre had dimmed long ago for want of proper cleaning. She was a good-natured, friendly person but a wee bit eccentric, so her colleagues referred to her as thikka-Thilakam. The prefix thikka meant crazy in Telugu.

One evening, after school, the two of them went shopping. Thilakam was an inveterate bargain-hunter, and she wanted to buy a pair of slippers. As usual they went to the fancy Bata showroom on the main street, inevitably called Mahatma Gandhi Road. After walking around the store, gazing at the footwear on display with prices as fancy as the shop, Thilakam declared: "They don't have a wide variety."

So, they left the showroom and sought out a small competitor nearby who styled himself Baba Footwear. Despite the shop being small and ill lit, its walls were crammed with racks that reached up to the ceiling. The shelves were stuffed, without a sliver of empty space, with long white cardboard boxes containing a dizzying variety of footwear: men's shoes, ladies' shoes, children's shoes, leather shoes, PVC shoes, rubber boots, factory safety shoes, dancing shoes. Though the display cabinet was dusty and flyblown, sporting a very limited range, all you had to do was to ask for the type of footwear you had in mind, like "PVC sandals in mithai pink," something cheap and waterproof that went with your shalwar kameez when you were taking the school children out for a picnic on a cloudy day. The salesman would nod his head, go inside the storeroom at the back of the shop, and re-emerge with just the pair you were looking for.

Thilakam and Atom Auntie made themselves comfortable on the lime-green faux leather and chromium chairs. The salesman switched on a ceiling fan, which groaned as it began to rotate, but soon enough sent down a hurricane force of draft at them. He then placed a shoe-sizing stool in front of Atom Auntie. Thilakam quickly dragged the stool towards herself and plonked her dry, dusty foot on it. The blood-red polish on her toenails was chipped, making her toes look as if they were bleeding.

The salesman read her foot-size with a studied deadpan expression and made his way to one of the racks. He pulled out a dozen boxes and brought them over. Slapping the soles of the slippers together to produce an explosive sound, he offered them one by one for Thilakam to try on. She would wear each one, examine it from every

angle, even take a few tentative steps to test the comfort of
the soles. Then she would remove her foot, and shaking
her head, turn the slipper over to read the price-sticker
on the instep.

When she had tried on all the slippers, she told the
salesman in a commanding voice: "*Andar se dikhao*! Show
me from the stock kept inside!"

The salesman went to the back of the shop through
a narrow, curtained doorway and re-emerged with another armful of boxes. Thilakam slowly and steadily went
through the motions of trying on the pairs, before shaking her head with fastidious disapproval. When she had
tried out all the slippers, she barked: "*Andar se dikhao!*"

The salesman, with a harried look, returned to the back
of the shop and came back with some more boxes.
Thilakam made short work of them, finding nothing to
her taste.

"*Andar se dikhao! Andar se dikhao!*"

The salesman sallied forth once again to the storeroom. He returned and, unloading the boxes on to the
floor, said: "These are all the slippers we have in the
shop." He looked tired and altogether omitted slapping
the slippers against each other as he gravely handed pair
after pair to Thilakam who sat amongst a sea of open
boxes and rejected slippers.

But Thilakam was insatiable. Again, she said in a
rasping tone: "*Andar se dikhao*! Show me from the stock
inside!"

With a weary look, he shambled away and returned
with a few more boxes which had a red and gold design
on them, instead of the standard white.

"These pairs are for brides," the salesman said, sounding like a pent-up volcano. "They are very expensive."

"So what?" Thilakam said, stuffing her unlovely foot into the slipper. She traipsed up and down the limited space in the shop. She even raised the hem of her sari to examine her feet with close attention.

When she had tried all the footwear in the bridal collection, she said insistently: *Andar se dikhao! Andar se dikhao!*

"Do you really want to see what I have inside?" the salesman asked with an edge to his voice. Without further ado, he unzipped his fly and thrust out his pelvis.

Thilakam gave a shriek shot up like pheasant from a bush. Saying, "How dare you! How dare you!" she ran out of the shop. Atom Auntie followed her, not quite knowing whether to be amused or outraged.

"That wicked man!" Thilakam said, when Atom Auntie joined her on the street. "How could he do that? I should have him arrested for lewd behaviour! Cheap fellow—cheap like the quality of his footwear!"

"But you must accept," Atom Auntie said, "that he had variety."

When she finished the story, Atom Auntie laughed so much that tears streamed once again out of her eyes. As she couldn't continue to stir the sheera, she reduced the heat to simmer on her gas stove, to give her time to recover from the merry recollection.

"Did he show his puppy shame?" Ramya asked breathlessly.

"Not quite," Atom Auntie said laughing. "He had his underwear on. Green and blue striped."

When Ramya turned nine, Atom Auntie moved out of their house. She rented a small apartment near the school where she taught. The commute was getting to be more and more exhausting. The city was growing, the population exploding by leaps and bounds because of the migration of people from the rural areas seeking jobs and facilities. All this exerted pressure on an already overburdened infrastructure.

There was also the matter of mild tension between Mummy and Atom Auntie for no apparent reason. While each was polite to the other, there was a coolness between them. Ramya, uncannily perceptive as children are, felt she was the cause of the friction between her mother and aunt. Mummy must have resented Atom Auntie monopolizing Ramya's affections, but what else could one expect? If Mummy had taken care of Ramya properly by herself, she would surely have been the object of her daughter's adoration, with no other contenders.

The world of grownups was too complicated for little Ramya.

Whenever Daddy went to Atom Auntie's house to look her up, he never failed to take Ramya with him. For Ramya these trips were the most precious of her life. No pilgrimage or sightseeing tour could ever hold a candle to a visit to Atom Auntie's home.

Her new home was on the outskirts of the city. It took nearly an hour to get there. The neighbourhood had a rustic look, which isn't to say that there were glens, brooks and haystacks about. It was rustic in the sense that the streets were made of dirt and were potholed, and not lined with sidewalks. Dogs, cows, goats, pigs and hens moved about freely, dotting the street with their excreta. The unpaved road became so narrow that Daddy couldn't drive the car right up to the building in which Atom Auntie lived. He parked it a few hundred yards away at a convenient spot, and the two of them walked the rest of the way.

She lived in a small portion of the second floor of the building. The view from her tiny living room was pretty: They could see a small temple surrounded by trees. It was a shrine dedicated to Hanuman, the monkey god. They could see devotees going to or coming out from the temple. Now and then they could hear the temple bells ring.

Atom Auntie as usual had made sweets and salty snacks for Ramya. The entire house carried the aroma of the food. While Ramya had kheer or some such sweet, Daddy would drink foaming south Indian coffee from a small stainless-steel tumbler. Once he finished his coffee he'd go back to his clinic, leaving Ramya behind. He'd return late in the evening to take her home.

There was nothing Ramya liked more than being in Atom Auntie's house. It was no patch on their palatial home, manned by many servants, in the heart of the city, yet Ramya felt far happier here than anywhere else in the world. Atom Auntie kept her small house spotlessly clean. Every nook and corner had the sweet smell of the incense sticks Atom Auntie burned for the morning prayer. There were many dolls and toys for Ramya to play with, but more importantly Atom Auntie always joined in as if she were a playmate of Ramya's.

But the thing Ramya enjoyed most was having her palm read. Atom Auntie had become a palmist of sorts.

There was a book by Cheiro or some such person in the small niche in the wall which Atom Auntie used as a bookshelf. Some of the other books occupying the niche were Brewer's Dictionary of Phrase and Fable, Bullfinch's Greek Mythology, Bartlett's Familiar Quotations, and the Buddhist *Dhammapada*.

While Ramya never questioned why Atom Auntie, of all people, would take to palmistry, as she grew older she often wondered about it. Did Atom Auntie presume she could change her destiny by knowing what the future held in store for her? Or did she simply want to be forewarned about other dreadful things which were to come her way? On the other hand, Atom Auntie, well-read as she was, would often quote the lines from *Rubaiyat* of Omar Khayyam: "Moving finger writes, and, having writ moves on/ Nor all thy Piety nor Wit/ Shall lure it back to cancel half a Line/ Nor all thy Tears wash out a Word of it."

Once Ramya had finished eating her snack, a murukku or some chudva, she'd ask, wiping her hand on her skirt: "Can you read my hand, Atom Auntie?"

"First, go and wash your hands like a good girl. You shouldn't wipe your hands on your skirt," Atom Auntie said with a sigh. What could one expect of a child who was in care of a capricious team of servants?

After washing her hands in the tiny washbasin placed outside the bathroom, Ramya went up to Atom Auntie and extended her palm, which now reeked of Rexona soap.

"No, give me your left hand. A woman's future is written on her left hand."

"Isn't that the dirty hand?" Ramya said.

"Whoever said so?" Atom Auntie said, knowing full

well who might have said that. Who else but Amma?
"Ramya!" Amma would say. "Don't eat the biscuit with
your dirty hand. Use your right hand."

"Now let me see …" Atom Auntie said, shaking her
head, as she took Ramya's unmanicured hand with prominent mourning borders outlining the nails.

"How beautiful your hands look compared to mine!"
Ramya said, sitting on a stool opposite Atom Auntie's mini
living room. Atom Auntie sat on a divan converted from
a large iron trunk.

It was undeniable that Atom Auntie had beautiful,
fair hands, the colour of pale sandalwood. And she kept
them well manicured, painting her long tapering nails a
pearly pink. The gold bangles she wore always seemed to
shine with an extra lustre on her wrists.

"Whose beautiful hands are you talking about?"
Atom Auntie asked, momentarily sidetracked. Thrusting
her palm under Ramya's nose, she said: "Look at my palm.
See how many lines there are! Criss-crossing like railway
lines in Vijayawada junction. They say a person who has
so many lines would lead a very unhappy life."

There was moment of silence. Ramya looked at her
own palm; there didn't seem to be too many lines. What
a relief!

Atom Auntie went to her study table and pulled a
drawer out. After rummaging in it, she came back with a
magnifying glass and a telescopic pointer. Atom Auntie
never did anything by halves. Studying the lines on
Ramya's hand through the glass, as though for the first
time, she said: "This is your life-line." Simultaneously,
she traced the line, using the pointer for Ramya's benefit.

"Do you see how long the line is? That means you have a very long life ahead of you. And this is your line of education ... You will be a very well-qualified young woman. And this is your love line — you will marry a very rich and handsome man."

"How many children will I have?"

"Let me see ..." Atom Auntie peered at some hachures on the side of Ramya's palm, counting them aloud, "One-two-three."

"Three children! How nice! I can play with them every day! Can I take them to school with me?"

"They will be happy to go to school with you. And you can play with them all day," Atom Auntie said laughing.

Ramya never forgot the day Atom Auntie gave her the lemon-flavoured lollipop. She was in Grade 9, too old to crave a lollipop. It was given to Atom Auntie by a student celebrating her birthday. As with all the gifts that came her way, she saved it for Ramya. How thrilled Atom Auntie was to see her. She hugged Ramya and showered her with kisses. Atom Auntie looked thin and tired and there were streaks of grey in her hair. To see her beloved aunt in that condition brought a lump to Ramya's throat.

Daddy took Atom Auntie's wrist, and checked her pulse while staring at his HMT watch. Then he disinterred the BP apparatus from his bag, and opened the long rectangular machine. He wore his steth, and pumped air into the BP machine, and the column of mercury began to rise briskly. Then he released the air, letting the mercury in the machine drop in slow degrees.

"Everything's normal," Daddy declared, removing the steth from his ears. He returned the doctor's paraphernalia to his bag, and then handed over a whole hoard of physician's samples he had brought along with him.

While Atom Auntie made coffee for Daddy, Ramya ate the Mysore pak and Bombay mixture served in small stainless-steel plates. Atom Auntie had made them specially for Ramya, sparing neither effort nor expense, and Ramya could taste her aunt's affection in the snacks. No snacks in the world tasted as delicious as the ones Atom Auntie made for her.

It began to grow dark as the winter evening drew to a close. The sky was filling with darker shades, purple and Prussian blue. Atom Auntie switched on a small forty-watt bulb. The wiring in the house was so old and weak that she had to be careful of how much power she used. There was no way you could use an electric water heater in the house; so Atom Auntie took her bath with cold water every day, even in winter.

When they were about to leave, Atom Auntie came down the stairs to see them off. As Ramya and her father walked away, she stood at the gate waving to them. Every now and then Ramya stopped, her heart growing heavier by the minute, to turn around and look at her aunt. As the distance grew between them, Atom Auntie seemed to shrink in size. Just before turning the corner, Ramya looked back for the last time. In the dim light of the street lamp, she saw Atom Auntie, unsubstantial as a shadow, still standing by the gate with her hand raised in farewell.

Ramya never saw Atom Auntie alive again.

6

Amma

Ramya finds Amma's japmala, her rosary, in her box. Ramya had been so close to her grandmother, her Ammamma, that she used to call her Amma, which means mother. The rosary has 108 beads—at least there ought to be; she has never bothered to count them. 108 is an auspicious number in the Hindu tradition. The beads are pale brown, made from the wood of holy basil, known locally as tulasi, a sacred, strong-smelling medicinal shrub. Ramya remembers seeing her grandmother sitting in silence, her lips working overtime, repeatedly invoking any one of the 330 million Hindu gods, while her fingers rolled over the beads as if she were winding a watch.

In the box, Ramya also discovers a pair of peculiar objects which bring a smile to her lips. They are made of silver but have blackened with age—time is such a merciless phenomenon. One of the utensils is shaped like a small thin spoon, and the other a tiny spear. They have eyeholes at their ends, and are held together by a silver wire, like a key ring. Amma never used them but kept them as souvenirs.

"What are these funny things, Amma?" Ramya remembers asking her grandmother.

"My brother gave them to me, long, long ago," Amma had said, taking the silver tools from Ramya. "This one is for cleaning the wax from the ears and this for picking your teeth."

"Really?" Ramya had said, quickly taking back the objects. "Can I use them?"

"You'll do nothing of the sort. You'll end up getting ear or gum infection if use these things. Besides, they are just keepsakes."

Digging further into her box, Ramya is surprised *not* to find the old, well-thumbed copy of the *Bhagavad Gita*. What could have happened to it? She can't even recollect when she last saw it. All she can say with certainty is that it was very much there, in the first few months of owning the chest, when she opened and closed the lid a million times, her eyes lovingly dwelling on her newly-acquired possessions.

She seems to have mislaid the holy book, just like she has done with her faith. Irretrievably. Without realizing it, she'd let her belief fall off the radar — a casualty of the hurly-burly of modern life. It is years since she visited a temple, or genuflected before the silver figurines she has in the house. These idols, which originally belonged to her mother, are now stowed somewhere in her basement, out of sight. And out of mind.

She'd like to read a holy book now, just to see if it would provide comfort in these difficult times. Who knows, at this stage in her life, it could be just what the doctor ordered. She can't even recall in what language her grandmother's copy of the *Gita* was. The volume with its browned pages was already old then, and had been rebound by a local bookbinder, using a blue, marble-patterned cardboard for its covers, and wine-red cloth for its spine. Was the commentary on the primordial verse in Telugu? If so, she could have coped, though perhaps with some difficulty. If it was in Hindi, then too it was man-ageable, though the going would've been tougher. What if it had no commentary at all and was all in the original Sanskrit, that ancient if moribund tongue? She sincerely hoped it wasn't. She would make very little headway, though Sanskrit was possibly the forerunner of all Indo-European languages.

***

Long before Amma came to stay with them for good, she visited them in their house in Hyderabad. In those early days she was merely Ammamma, Ramya's mother's moth-er. Having taken an overnight train, she materialized on their doorstep at the crack of dawn, with her big bulging holdall, and her shining brass goglet in which she carried drinking water for the journey. She would have taken a cycle-rickshaw, after much haggling, and come on her own from the railway station. It was an age when distan-ces were short, and the world a much safer planet. Often, the price of the ride was not finalized until after rickshaw arrived at the destination. One heard Amma's imperious voice and the importunate tone of the rickshaw puller

outside the compound gate, in the final round of negotiation. If the rickshaw-puller got the better of Amma, he
blessed her and all her descendants, and chirpily ride
away, tinkling his bell. But if he was worsted, he cursed
her to damnation for all the world to hear, and furiously
pedalled away to the ratcheting noise of his rickshaw.

Unfazed, Amma entered the house with a proprietorial air and headed straight to the spare bedroom on the
ground floor. Whether she was occupying it or not, the
room always harboured the smell of the snuff tobacco she
used, staking her territorial rights.

One of the first things Amma did after settling down
was to unpack the loads of sweets and pickles she'd made
over the preceding weeks. Boxes and jars would be piled
high on the sideboard in the dining room.

"See what I've brought for you," Amma said to the
sleepy-eyed but excited Ramya. The two of them sat on
the floor beside the unrolled holdall lying supine, with
its many pouches open-mouthed as if yawning after a
long sleepless journey. Amma never failed to bring something for her granddaughter—a gaudily painted doll or
rustic-looking toy, the likes of which one could never find
in a city.

"Thank you, Ammamma," Ramya said primly in English, like a well-brought-up girl who attends a convent
school.

Then Amma added unthinkingly, hurting Ramya to
the core of her being: "How thin you've become!" To
Ramya, her much commented-upon skinniness felt like
a personal failing, a moral shortcoming. But the punish-
ment Amma had in mind for her had a delicious ring to

it: "Now that I'm here, I'll make all your favourite dishes. You can eat to your heart's content!" She added as an aside: "Hopefully, you will put on some weight!"

Amma's khaki holdall was an object of endless fascination for Ramya. There was a light mattress and a pillow inserted into a tough canvas-like outer cover, which had many pockets and compartments stitched into it. The holdall waned and waxed like the moon during the course of Amma's stay. First, Amma emptied the things she'd brought from her town, making the holdall a skinny relic, and then, in the days before her return, the holdall started growing in size like a balloon, getting stuffed with the purchases Amma made to take back with her. On the day of her departure, the holdall stood like a gigantic jam roll. The leather straps which stretched tightly around it were secured with a lock. The goglet, scrubbed with tamarind juice once more in preparation for the return journey, sparkled like burnished gold.

When it was time to leave, Amma, surrounded by a ring of servants who gathered to see her off, wept a little, and soon all the maids joined in like an enthusiastic Greek chorus, adding an operatic touch.

In addition to giving tips to the servants — the money painstakingly extracted from cloth-bag tucked away at her waist, Amma often made a present of twenty rupees or so to Ramya. Once when she was very young, mistaking the currency notes for trash, she'd taken the smelly, tightly-folded wad and waddled up to the wickerwork wastepaper basket in the drawing room. Saying, "Ghaleez!" which meant dirt in Urdu, she'd tossed the money into the wastepaper basket, much to the merriment of the maids.

Once the vails were distributed, Amma would ask one of the servants to flag down a passing cycle-rickshaw. But if Daddy was at home, he offered to drop Amma at the station. Being a GP, he was usually at his private clinic in the heart of the city, or out on house calls. One knew whether he was in the house by the presence of his doctor's bag, with his name emblazoned in gold, standing on the console table. The leather bag was a rectangular pyramid in shape. It contained medical bric-a-brac like glass syringes, needles, ampoules of distilled water, a spirit lamp, BP apparatus, and a stethoscope, the last of which Daddy fondly called his steth. It sounded like an endearment, like calling someone named Elizabeth, Beth.

Before leaving for the station with Amma, he asked Ramya: "Would you like to come along, love?"

"Yes, yes!" Ramya said, so thrilled that one would think she was being taken to the zoo or the cinema.

A major railway station in India was a throbbing, living organism. It was awake 24/7. A continuous stream of people entered its immense portals, while waves of people poured out in batches. The roads leading to the station were always busy with cars, taxis, scooters, motorcycles, bicycles, auto-rickshaws, manpowered-rickshaws and what have you rushing up and down, trying to avoid jaywalkers who were swarming the place. The incredible clamour, within and without the station premises, had a festive ring to it. Little wonder then that Ramya associated going on vacation, or merely visiting the railway station, with joyous excitement.

She entered the station with bated breath. Holding her Daddy's hand, she climbed the wide but short flight of stairs under the giant portico. But before she could savour the delights that awaited her, first Daddy had to join a queue—how slowly the line seemed to progress!—to buy a platform ticket for himself. Amma already had her sleeper-ticket which was bought much in advance. It was stashed away in her cloth-bag. Ramya was too young to need a platform ticket. At the entrance to the platform, Amma brought the fast-moving line to a complete standstill while she pulled out her bag, and burrowed into it to dig out her ticket to show it to the stationmaster. The size and colour of a biscuit, it was most likely wet and stained, having jostled for space with betel leaves, nut powder and lime paste. The station master grimaced and snipped a miniscule wedge off her ticket with a stainless-steel instrument that looked like a nail-clipper.

On the platform, there were vendors with carts and vendors with trays, selling toys, balloons, magazines, newspapers, snacks, soft drinks, tea, coffee, cigarettes, and paan. Regular shops and restaurants alternated with waiting rooms and toilets. Hanging over everything was a canopy of pungent odour, a combination of smells from toilets, antiseptic, smoke, and whatnot, unique to a railway station in India.

To Ramya, the most fascinating object in the station was the vending machine. The only one of its kind, it dispensed, for a small fee, a ticket-like card with your weight stamped on it. Ramya's visit to the station was never complete without getting herself weighed, scraggy as she was.

Then there were the trains themselves, thundering into the station, or parked at the platform, huffing and puffing with irate impatience. The steam engines of old were the real stars — black, demonic beasts belching steam from every pore. Hungry fires raged in their bellies; Ramya would gaze with utter fascination, while the engineer fed them with shovel-loads of coal. (The magic disappeared when steam locomotives were displaced first by diesel and then electric ones, locomotives with no personality, almost indistinct from the coaches they hauled behind them.)

After the stationmaster's frantic flag-waving, the whistle was blown. The train gave a lurch and, mustering its strength, heaved itself out of the station. Amma put her hand out the window and waved at Ramya as the train bore her away, slowly at first, then gaining so much speed that the carriages racing past became a blur.

During the summer holidays, Ramya took the same train with her mother or father to visit Amma. She lived in a small bungalow perched halfway up a hill. From the bedroom window, you could see a sliver of sea in the distance, grey and flecked with silver, sandwiched between unruffled blue sky and the ragged tops of coconut palms. The house was surrounded by fruit trees — mango, jackfruit and cashew — and wild undergrowth. In the forecourt was an ornamental urn built into the ground. It housed the sacred tulasi shrub. The housemaid watered the plant every day and drew geometric patterns with rice flour on the ground around the urn.

At the back of the house, there was a well with an ancient windlass. When Ramya was young she would like to peer into its smelly, mossy depths. She would drop a pebble, wait to hear the plop, then watch the silken ripples placidly spreading across the green-black surface.

Amma came out of the kitchen onto the verandah from time to time to check on Ramya. If she lingered near the well for too long, Amma yelled: "Don't play near the well. Come back, it's not safe!"

On one occasion, Amma said: "Do you know Niranjani who lives in the house beside the cycle repair shop? Her granddaughter was a year or two older than you. She used to come down for holidays from Delhi. She would do nothing but play near their well all day long, not paying heed to her grandmother's warnings. One day do you know what happened?" Amma paused, partly to catch her breath and partly for dramatic effect. When Ramya shook her head, she went on: "A crocodile crawled out and dragged her in."

"Dragged whom?" Ramya asked. "Niranjani-amma?"

"You little imp. You're the limit!" Amma said.

There were not many children in the neighbourhood—the houses were few and far between in that part of the town. There was also the matter of caste: in those days, Ramya was not allowed to play with the half-clad children she sometimes saw running about in joyous abandon.

So she spent hour after hour leaning back on the cement seats on the veranda, reading books. When she was very young they were mostly fairy tales by Hans Christian Andersen and the Grimm brothers; later, when Ramya was in middle school, she graduated to Enid Blyton. What a fantastic world Enid Blyton created for children! Secret Seven, Famous Five, The Five Find-Outers, the very names of the series evoked mystery and suspense. And then there were the school stories, set in invented institutions like

St. Claire's and Mallory Towers, humorous and exciting at the same time. No wonder Ramya devoured books, while bees serenaded the flowers in the gardens and butterflies flitted from bush to bush. Sometimes Amma would come to the verandah with a plate of juicy wedges of freshly sliced mangoes, or golden-yellow segments of jackfruit smeared with oil. The inside of a jackfruit is so waxy that if you didn't apply cooking oil to the blade you wouldn't be able to get the unbelievably sticky stuff off the knife.

Those were the blessed years when TV was restricted to large cities like Mumbai and Delhi, and neither Hyderabad nor Bengaluru, let alone rural areas, had coverage.

One day when Ramya was deep in a book, Amma said: "How much you read, Ramya! You'll spoil your eyes if you go on like this. I wish you had more things to do here. Would you like to go up the hill in the evening?"

So the two did a spot of mountain-climbing of sorts, scaling the steep hillside at the back of the house. Ramya scrabbled up the slope, lightly hopping across screes, while Amma, carrying a jute bag, made slow, grunting progress behind her. The hillside was strewn with stones and boulders, and stunted trees and wind-flattened scrub grew here and there with heroic determination. Right at the top there were the remains of an old temple — a small, flat plinth of concrete, and a few low, crumbling stone walls. Years ago, gale-force winds from the sea had hurled themselves shoreward and blotted out the temple no sooner than it was built.

While Amma sat on the leftover stonework, Ramya pranced around, pretending to be the Queen of Jhansi, scything the bushes with a switch as if she were mowing down British troops. Soon she tired of her sanguinary sport, and decided to return to where Amma sat. On the way, she spotted a discarded cigarette pack on the ground, and with the magpie instinct of children she pounced on it. She was thrilled to see the brand name 'Charminar'. The yellow sleeve had a picture of the most famous monument in Hyderabad. It gave her incredible pleasure to chance upon something that reminded her of her home many hundreds of miles away. With excited yelps, she ran to her grandmother with the crushed and weather-beaten cigarette pack in her hand.

"Look what I found!"

"Throw it away at once!" Amma said. "You'll get all sorts of diseases if you touch dirty things. You're a doctor's daughter, and you should know better."

Chastened, a disappointed Ramya threw away the empty cigarette pack, and wiping her hand on her skirt despite being a doctor's daughter, sat down on a stone not too far from Amma.

The distant sea from their new vantage point was a broad swathe of blue. Ramya saw the silhouette of a steamer, a seemingly stationary purple smudge on the horizon, but it was chugging to a port, a hundred miles up the coast.

"Don't look so glum. See what I've brought for you," Amma said, as she pulled out a thin bar of Cadbury's milk chocolate, wrapped in its unmistakeable purple and silver foil.

When Ramya extended her hand, Amma said: "Not right away. You must have your lunch first." She pulled out a newspaper-wrapped parcel from her bag.

Amma had made her special idlis — a batter of ground

rice and lentils steam cooked in small containers made from jackfruit leaves. The idlis acquired a subtle taste and aroma from the leaves. All this was lost upon the seven-year-old Ramya, who was more of an unabashed gourmand, in spite of her much-remarked thinness, than a discerning gourmet.

"Do you come first in the class?" Amma asked, as they peeled away the leafy covering from the idlis.

"Never. There's a girl called Prabha — she's so good, nobody can ever beat her."

"Maybe, but if you worked harder you could beat her?"

"She's too good. She always gets hundred out of hundred in maths and science. I get more than her only in English."

"I'm not surprised, seeing the number of books you read!"

"What about Mummy? Did she come first in the class?"

"No, she was good only at one subject."

"Which one?"

"Moral Science," Amma said with a sigh. "Come, let's pack up. It's time to go back home."

On the way back, as they carefully picked their way around stones and boulders, Ramya saw a barefoot woman coming up the hill. She wore a loose robe of dull orange, and was thrumming a slender stringed instrument which was little more than a toy. Turning to look in their direction, she flashed a beatific smile. When Amma raised both her hands in a namaste, she nodded in a manner that could only be described as beneficent.

"Ammamma, who is she? Do you know her?"

"No, she's a holy person, a wandering sadhvi. She must have been visiting the ashram."

"What's a sadhvi?"

"She's a woman who gives up everything in life to attain her ambition."

"What is her ambition?"

"To liberate her soul from mortal coils of life," Amma said easily, as if living in the holy proximity of an ashram had honed her vocabulary in such matters. "She devotes herself only to the worship of God."

"Like Mummy? Did she give up taking care of me for that reason?"

"Not exactly … Ramya you ask too many questions."

"I don't understand why the sadhvi has to give up everything."

"You must sacrifice many things to achieve your goal. Success doesn't come easily."

Later in the evening, they sat on the cement seats in the verandah, talking. As the darkness advanced upon them with stealthy steps, Amma told Ramya about her mother and her little brother.

When Mummy was pregnant with her second baby, the gynaecologist warned her that it would be a difficult pregnancy as the placenta was located at an unsafe spot. The doctor counselled Mummy and Daddy to take adequate precautions. The lady doctor presumed that Daddy, being a doctor himself, would realize the implications, and be careful—like making Mummy take sufficient bed rest and restrict unnecessary movement.

One evening, a few months into her pregnancy, Mummy evinced a keen desire to see a Hindi film that featured her favourite hero, Rajendra Kumar. The film was running in a cinema hall called Minerva, which was housed on the second floor of an old imposing colonial building in Secunderabad. Daddy, not being a *firm person* (Amma's emphasis), could never put his foot down and say no. Unwilling to displease Mummy, they went to see the film. As it was an old building with no elevators, Mummy had to climb the uncommonly long and steep flight of stairs. When she reached the top, she was slightly out of breath, but otherwise didn't feel any discomfort. But halfway through the film, her abdomen started to hurt unbearably. When she mentioned it to Daddy, he decided they should leave at once. He took her hand and stumbled out of the semi-dark cinema hall. A trail of tiny droplets of blood followed Mummy out of the theatre. She had to make a slow, agonizing descent of those infernal stairs. Though Daddy rushed her to the hospital, driving his car at a speed he'd never done before and imperilling all the three lives, the doctors in casualty couldn't save the child.

"Your Mummy blamed herself for her unborn son's death, and was just not the same *after that*," Amma said, *After That*, like *Before Christ*, or some such watershed occurrence.

"If the child wasn't yet born, how do you know it was a boy or a girl?"

"Well ... I suppose the doctors can know whether the child was a boy or a girl. Anyway, your Mummy and Daddy were very keen to have a baby boy."

"Oh," was all that little Ramya said.

Amma looked at Ramya and said in a sharp tone:

"Now don't you think for a minute that your parents didn't want you. How much your Daddy adores you! I've never seen anyone pampering their child, whether boy or girl, the way your Daddy pampers you."

"I suppose so."

"As for your Mummy, she began to withdraw into a shell. She lost interest in the world around her, and immersed herself in religion."

So that was Mummy's backstory.

In the evenings, the two of them often attended the evening prayers at the nearby ashram. The ashram was the reason why her grandfather had moved here in the first place. The ashram and its environs were spotlessly clean and profuse with greenery. It was chockablock with fruit trees, and there were proper gardens laid out with flowers and vegetables. The produce from the garden was used in the shrine and the communal kitchen.

The prayer hall of the ashram was full of natural light and air which came in from the many wide-arched windows. Adorning the altar was a life-sized photograph of the guru seated on the floor with his legs properly folded, and his right hand held up, the open palm facing outward, the traditional gesture of benediction. His left hand dropped limply and innocently on his inner thigh, but it looked as if he was scratching his crotch. The picture, draped with a garland made from fresh flowers, was placed on a large luxurious cushion encased in a saffron silk cover. Two orange bolsters were thrown in for extra comfort.

Ramya and Amma, along with other devotees, sat on the straw mats on the stone floor facing the image of the long dead guru, and sang bhajans — devotional songs.

One of the devotees played the harmonium, a musical instrument that was like a floor-top accordion. Another beat on the tablas, the Indian drums, and a few others struck the small cymbals. Sometimes, one of the musicians would humour Ramya by giving her a pair of cymbals, two brass hemispheres held together by a short length of thin rope, to clap together as they all sang with devout enthusiasm. The audience didn't mind at all when Ramya's playing refused to keep time with the hymns. As she grew up Ramya discovered that in life not everyone was so cheerfully forgiving—she had better keep time with others, or else ...

Though Ramya was born in a city and grew up in the lap of luxury, she found living with Amma in her spartan and parsimonious house very pleasant. Away from the rough and tumble of the city, she had plenty of time on her hands: time to read books and above all time to be by herself, indulging in extravagant daydreams. Very early in life she learned to enjoy being alone, with nothing but the elements for company.

The sky was so different in the village. In the daytime it was a wide blue empty dome where silence seemed to echo. The nights were dark and thick, quivering with the noise of crickets, and the sky seemed so low that you felt you could reach out and pluck the stars.

⌒─────⌒

The afternoon is deceptively bright—the temperature is minus fifteen. Ramya decides to go to a temple. She's been feeling low for many weeks now, the surest sign of depression. Unable to connect with Renata, Ramya had planned to consult her family doctor, and talk to him about her low spirits, hoping he could prescribe some convenient, sugar-coated pills, but changed her mind in the sudden whimsical way she has acquired.

A large dose of religion may have better therapeutic effect on her and maybe even uplift her spirits. More importantly, she also wants to buy a copy of the *Bhagavad Gita*, preferably with an English translation. She knows that the temple on Derry Road has a small shop attached to it where they sell, with a hefty mark-up, religious books and CDs along with utensils for worship like lamps, bells, incense, and incense-stands. And images of countless Hindu gods, though the collection was no match for what Mummy had in her puja room.

It's not strictly true that she hasn't visited a temple in a long time. She'd gone to see the new Swaminarayan temple that had cropped up north of Toronto near Finch and Highway 427. The *Toronto Star* had regularly carried features and news reports about the project. It had taken nearly two years to build the temple because traditional methods of construction, which disdained steel and concrete, were employed. Hundreds of blocks of stone were piled one on top of the other, Lego style. Each of these blocks was dressed and elaborately carved by hand before being shipped from India. The Prime Minister of Canada had inaugurated the temple, and the event was broadcast on all news channels.

So, on the occasion of "Doors Open Toronto," when many landmark buildings in the city are thrown open to the public, she drove down to see the temple for herself,

as one might go to see tourist spots like the CN Tower or
Casa Loma. Ramya had to admit that the temple was
quite a marvel of architecture, a gargantuan heap of shape-
ly marble. It was a little too ornate for her taste. Ramya
was more moved by the workmanship of the masons, a
veritable prayer in stone, than by the actual spirituality
of the place.

In the evening she and Ms. Peggy take Highway 10
to Derry. It's past the rush hour, but the road still has
considerable traffic. Progress is slow, and she wishes Missus Pegasus could fly like her male namesake in mythology. Maybe, the name wasn't the best choice. She was
never good at giving names. When she was ten she'd
come up with name of Barghest for her pet dog — thanks
to Atom Auntie's eclectic and exhaustive choice of bed-
time reading for Ramya.

Snow flurries are sweeping down from the sky, making the night look darker. There are a handful of cars
parked outside the temple. She notices with some surprise
that the temple is now sporting an elongated dome, like
a gigantic plump white radish. When she last visited the
place, there was no dome; the temple was just a rectangular block with glass sliding doors like an office building,
looking like no temple in India ever does. Yet, inside it
had, and still has, an ambience, even if faint, of a holy
place which makes its many devotees want to come back.

Ramya slips in through the automatic door that slides
back making screechy, protesting sounds. She feels like a
prodigal daughter returning; deep inside she's not sure if
she's welcome. Religion has a way of making her feel
uncomfortable. In a religious place, or in the presence of

pious people, she is sometimes overcome with a feeling of inadequacy. She feels like an interloper. No, more of a pariah.

The walkways inside the temple are made of granite. In the foyer, she removes her boots and hangs her coat on a rack. In socked feet, she goes inside. The sanctum sanctorum is carpeted — something unimaginable in India, and so spotlessly clean — more like a 5-star hotel — that it almost robs the place of its sanctity.

On a large platform on the eastern side, a series of statues of Hindu gods are arranged, some standing, some seated on lotuses, some reclining on serpents. They look familiar, like old friends. She approaches them, her head bent, her palms pressed together, and recites the short mantras Amma had taught her. Her mother, steeped though she was in religion and rituals, and able to rattle out passages and passages from scriptures, never taught Ramya a single sacred line to communicate with God.

It's arati time. The poojari lights tablets of camphor on a salver and traces circles in the air with it in front of the deities. All the devotees sing the sacred song *Om jaya Jagadisha haré*. For those who don't know the lyrics, the words in Devanagari and Roman scripts are electronically projected on a dropdown screen operated by a remote. Worship has come a long way. Many of the miracles narrated in scriptures which wowed you can now be wrought by a schoolboy with a handheld device.

Ramya takes blessings from the priest, holy water and prasad, and makes her way to the bookshop. There she buys a copy of the *Bhagavad Gita*, fat as a dictionary and with an exuberantly colourful cover showing Krishna the

charioteer raising a didactic finger at a contrite looking
Arjuna kneeling on the ground. The book has verses in
Sanskrit written in Devanagari, but it also has a trans-
literation in Roman script and a translation in English.
Triple whammy!

Amma moved to Hyderabad when Ramya's mother fell
seriously ill. Amma sold Grandpa's ancestral home, Grandpa having died years ago. The only recollection Ramya
has of her grandfather is his sitting on the floor in front
of a collection of pictures of Hindu gods, deep in prayer.
The sunlight coming in from the window fell on his bald,
oily pate which shone like silver.

Mummy's sickness made her so weak that she could
hardly take care of herself, let alone Ramya. As far back
as Ramya could recollect, her mother had had a delicate
constitution, and was always falling ill. In those days,
they used a special word for people like Mummy; it was
'valetudinarian'. Her daily communions with God must
have completely enervated her, consuming what little
energy she had. Even as her health was failing, Mummy
tried steadfastly to observe all rituals and festivals.

Unlike her daughter, Amma was a strong, robust
woman, who started putting the house in order from the
very moment she stepped in. As Amma loved to put it,
the house had going to rack and ruin. Mummy anyway
was too preoccupied with religious duties to have any
oversight of the house. Daddy was busy with his profession, and being a man, was not expected to deal with the

domestic issues the way a lady of the house would. Was it any wonder that the servants had had a field day?

It was only after Amma came to stay with them that they began to have tasty wholesome meals. There were always extras like homemade pickles, poppadums, bhajjis and sweets. The house began to acquire a clean, nice smelling aspect. Amma made one of the servant girls adorn the front of the house with rangoli, the colourful geometric patterns, every morning.

Amma always used the spare room on the ground floor. It was cool and dark, smelling of the snuff powder she tooted and the Sloan's liniment she rubbed on her aching limbs. The floor was sparkling clean and almost cold to the touch even in the height of summer. There was always a zero-watt bulb aglow even in the daytime. Amma kept the windows shuttered, the heavy curtains drawn to meet, so that there wasn't a single interstice through which the sun, insects or dust could enter. Once a day in the morning she'd have the servants open the windows and part the curtains to air the room. If Ramya was there, she'd sit on the cot, and gaze fascinatedly at the dust motes jiving in the shaft of golden sunlight let in by the open window.

When Ramya was sixteen, Amma, who was getting on in years, showed a keen desire to go on a pilgrimage. She wanted to visit any one of the innumerable holy sites in the country. After all, until she'd moved to Hyderabad, her house was a stone's throw from an ashram, which was as good as living cheek by jowl with divinity. So Daddy made arrangements for the two to go to Tirupati. When Ramya was a little girl she'd been taken to the place a couple of times by her parents, and on one occasion had her head tonsured.

Daddy bought Ramya and Amma first class train tickets, a luxury they didn't enjoy as a rule. It was considered a safer alternative as two women were travelling by themselves. Tirupati is a sacred place in the southern part of Andhra Pradesh, one of the most visited holy places in India, if not in the world.

They got off at Tirupati railway station and then took a sky-blue bus to the temple town proper, ensconced on one of the summits of a series of hills. The bus took a narrow road which clung perilously to the sides of the hills and made many treacherous hairpin bends. Sometimes the bus slowed down to a crawl, unable to ascend a steep curve, and on more than one occasion it even rolled back a little, terrifying the passengers. But the bus would pause as if to gather its strength, and then, after groaning in agony as the driver forcibly changed gears, it would crawl up the incline. Even if the drive was a frightening experience, in that early morning air, they were privy to the exhilarating views of the forest-clad hills with mist rising like smoke from the valleys.

They checked into a guesthouse, one of the thousands dotting the hills. After having a quick bath, the two of them walked to the temple. Amma looked tired after the overnight journey, and found the walk exhausting. There were buses zipping up and down the streets which were free to ride on. But Ramya couldn't make out where the bus-stops were, and she wasn't sure if her grandmother could board the bus with ease, hauling herself up the narrow, steep steps. Outside the temple, there were thousands of devotees, many of them — both men and women — with shaved heads, standing in a serpentine queue which seemed miles long.

They joined the slow-moving line and were on their feet for five hours, without food or water, before they could enter the heart of the temple. In that seething mass of people, they didn't get even twenty seconds to have a glimpse of the deity, who stood bespattered with jewels from head to toe, oblivious to the smoke from incense, oil lamps, and camphor. There was an enormous din — the continual ringing of bells and people chanting: "Govinda! Govinda!" The temple guards pushed and shoved the devotees, exhorting them to move on. There were tens of thousands of out-of-town pilgrims waiting outside, some having travelled hundreds, if not thousands of miles, to get a chance to pray before the idol.

Amma endured the calvary with uncomplaining devotion. Even as she was taking halting steps on their way back to their guest house, Amma said: "I'm so happy, we came. This may well be the last time for me."

Once they reached the guesthouse, Amma lay down on her holdall which was unrolled over a wooden cot. She didn't even have the strength to accompany Ramya to the restaurant for a bite. Ramya went out alone, in the dimly lit streets, looking for a canteen or a mess. She found a small place at a crossroads not too far away that sold tea, coffee and south Indian fast food. She bought a few idlis and vadas, which the vendor packed in a parcel made from sheets of dry leaves stitched together. Amma ate only a few morsels, preferring to drink water from her brass goglet.

Their return journey was the most arduous one Ramya had ever experienced. Thinking back, she was always to wonder how they'd managed to complete it: the slow excruciating progress on foot to the bus station; the ride to the railway station in Tirupati with the bus continually making vertiginous turns; and the overnight train seeming to take an eternity to reach its destination, stopping at every wayside station.

Luckily for them, Daddy came to the station to receive them, and seeing him standing on the platform with his usual thin, watery smile, Ramya felt so much joy and relief that it brought tears to her eyes. In India, the hardest part of a journey often begins after arrival: One has to bargain with temperamental porters called coolies, and all over again with belligerent auto rickshaw drivers outside the station, before you finally reach your home. But when Ramya got into their own car, the familiar smell of seat leather, with an undertone of motor grease, made her feel she was already home.

The trip to Tirupati proved too much for Amma. She was nearly seventy-five and it undermined her health for good. She spent most her time confined to her bed and could only stumble about with the help of a cane. Gone were the days when she tramped about the house like an Amazonian general, barking commands to her foot soldiers.

Without question, the person who took most care of Ramya was Amma. Though she'd had a sharp tongue, she was loving in her own way. She'd watched over Ramya during her adolescent years — those trying times! At the onset of puberty, how helpful Amma was with her sage advice and comforting presence. Amma had ensured

that Ramya grew up in clean, healthy, and safe surroundings, and got to enjoy the privileges that came with her
father's position in society. Sometimes Ramya wondered
what would have happened to her if Amma hadn't elect-
ed to leave her home to come and stay with them. Before
Amma came, she was growing up like a waif, receiving
random care and affection from the many servants in
their household.

When Ramya was in Grade 10, on Children's Day,
which falls on November 14th, the birthday of India's first
Prime Minister Jawaharlal Nehru, her teacher gave the
students an assignment to compose a poem about their
mother or father.

The teacher was very young and new to the school
—she had very little experience but boatloads of enthusiasm, and this alone made her a great teacher, though she
herself may not have known it. Perhaps fearing some of
her students were orphans, she quickly amended: "Or
write about your pet animal." Then, when she realised
that only a handful of her pupils could afford to keep a
pet animal, she added hastily: "Write about anything.
Anything, as long as your poem doesn't rhyme!"

Ramya pondered on her well-liked teacher's param-
eters for great verse. She decided against writing about
Barghest the pet dog she once had. As to Daddy, he simply didn't make good copy. So she wrote a poem on her
mother. Of course, she couldn't write the actual fact. She
composed the poem about a persona who was part
Mummy, part Atom Auntie but mostly Amma.

The teacher had liked the poem so much that she had
it printed in the school's annual magazine called *Excelsior*.
It was a good thing that Ramya no longer attended the

old neighbourhood school. Had her old classmates read the poem, Ramya was sure, they would've only tittered, since they'd had a ringside view of Mummy's excesses.

The poem, which unfortunately rhymed for the most part, read:

Mother

You nurtured me with love and care
All the birth pangs you did bear
When I cried for company
You were always there
In my joy or sorrow
You always had a share
Like a ministering angel beside my bed
With your soothing hands, so soft and fair
Quelling all the ills I had a dread
An aura of comfort and joy you spread
When growing up blues haunted
The elder frowned and peers taunted
You were the pillar on whom I leaned
Till from all fears I was weaned
I miss you, my dearest mother
I am a boat yawing in bad weather
A ship on the rough seas without a rudder
I wait for the day when we shall be together

Though Ramya had to exploit a creative vein in her writing skills to come up with the poem, the part about missing her mother — all her idiosyncrasies notwithstanding — was true.

7

Barghest

THERE'S A SILVER medallion that has a brown patina that Time, the merciless god who spares no thing and no one, has conferred on it. The word "Barghest" is inscribed on it in stylized letters. The medallion had come surmounting a leather dog-collar that their neighbour Saroja had gifted Barghest on his first birthday. Ramya kept the medallion, even as Barghest went out of her life for good, collar, leash and all, like an item of household junk an itinerant peddler carries. It was no merchant of used goods, but their faithful manservant Sailoo, who led away that more than willing canine.

In retrospect, Barghest was the first, perhaps, the only being other than her immediate family whom she'd loved. Never mind how fleeting that love was — evanescent as a wild flower in bloom or a shower of rain on a summer evening. But it had roused intense passion in her. It was a love that, unlike a storybook love, had a sad and tempestuous ending.

A few days before her 10th birthday, Ramya's father asked
her what she'd like for a gift. It was his annual routine
— in the week preceding her birthday, Daddy would put
that question to Ramya, prefixing it with an endearment
like "Ramya darling ..." or "Ramya sweetheart ..." even
though he'd already made up his mind on what to give
her. Ramya, weighing the question seriously, would come
up with a wish: a set of sketch pens, bewitchingly arrayed
in a clear plastic case, or a magic slate on which all your
doodling would disappear at the press of a button.

The item she wanted was invariably something she'd
recently seen in the possession of one or the other of her
classmates. In those days, when the country suffered from
socialism (it may well have been a disease like eczema or
tuberculosis), and populist slogans like *Gharibi Hatao!
Get Rid of Poverty!* were energetically spouted by politicians, the shopkeepers' shelves were stocked not with
eye-catching merchandise, but with dismal locally-made
run of the mill stuff. There was also a chronic shortage
of all goods, and poverty was widespread. There was very
little purchasing power in the hands of the people — so
much for sloganeering.

Being a moneyed GP, Daddy would not only get
Ramya whatever she had wished for (even if he had to
request his out-of-town friends to procure it from the
Burma Bazaar in Chennai, that haven for smuggled
goods), but would also surprise her with the gift he had
in mind — a rocking horse or a tricycle or a gold-plated
watch.

But this year it was different: Ramya was waiting impatiently for the 'birthday-present' question to be popped, her mind fully made up. No sooner had her father begun, "Ramya, my precious, what would ..." than she interrupted him with breathless excitement: "A puppy!"

Daddy smiled in his fatuous absent-minded way, and walking up to her, leaned forward and bussed her forehead. A touching display of paternal love no doubt but obviously not so satisfying for Ramya.

"Da-*ddy*!" Ramya said, sighing with exasperation. "I meant a small dog. A *pet dog*."

"Really?" Daddy said, taken aback. In Hindi, the word *pappi* meant a kiss. "Are you sure you want to have a pet dog?"

"Yes, of course!" Ramya said, nodding her head vigorously — she'd received enough paternal expressions of affection to last a lifetime.

"So, my little girl wants a pooch and not a smooch!" he said with a nervous laugh.

He looked puzzled, unable to understand why his daughter would want such a peculiar thing for a birthday present. He may have been expecting her to ask for a bicycle, a pair of roller skates, or some such thing. Very few of their relatives or friends kept pets; some of the patients did, but you could count them on the fingers of one hand.

One of Daddy's acquaintances kept a collection of birds — budgies, parrots, lovebirds — which transformed the man's house into a smelly, fluttery aviary. Guests balked at coming to his house parties, not just because of the icky, unattractive ambience, but because being surrounded by live specimens of birds made the thought of eating meat unappetizing.

Then there was a patient who had a passion for snakes, and kept half a dozen of them hissing and twisting in glass and chicken-mesh enclosures. In this creepy atmosphere, when Ramya's father was preparing to jab a needle into the patient's buttock, he felt a grue crawl up his back. He half-expected a cobra to slither up his trousers and bite him on his butt to avenge his master.

Ramya's father was always of the opinion that the rightful place for an animal was, if not the jungle, at least a farm or a zoo. Now, his little daughter was demanding he bring home a quadruped! Though it went against his belief, he was loath to displease Ramya. He also realized that the fault was partly his. A few months back, he'd taken Ramya to see the Hollywood film *The Incredible Journey*. Not being an animal lover, he'd found it a drag, but for Ramya's sake, soldiered through it. He would've preferred to watch westerns with their fast-paced plots and racy music. In these spaghetti westerns, the animals, were they horses or coyotes, had a specific function—they were in no way objects of adoration. Anyway, he never went to the cinema much nowadays, but when he was a medico in Chennai he'd been a great fan of John Wayne.

Surprisingly—or unsurprisingly, if one thought about it—Ramya too found the movie boring, at least in parts. She was unused to being closeted in the dark for almost two hours, staring at the gigantic images flickering in front of her, and the actors speaking English with an accent she found hard to follow.

What a welcome relief the interval was! On the rare

occasions they went to the cinema—to watch *101 Dalmatians* or *Mary Poppins*—Daddy would buy her potato chips, which came in small white grease-soaked paper bags, or popcorn in polythene bags, shaped like small pillows, with labels printed in blue for salty and red for masala. Ramya always chose masala, the spicier of the two, and for a reason. When she complained that the popcorn was too hot, not in so many words, but by making loud sucking noises, Daddy would invariably buy her Spenses' Fruitola, a locally made soft drink, from the vendors who zipped up and down the gangways, balancing a crate of sodas on one shoulder. They'd run a cast-iron bottle-opener against the bottles for musical effect—as successful a ploy as any advertising jingle.

Even if the film failed to engage Ramya wholly, the images remained etched in her memory long after she left the dark unwholesome movie hall. The next day, as she was excitedly discussing the film with her classmates, a random and reckless thought occurred to her: Wouldn't it be nice to own a pet dog? It would make Ramya look special in the eyes of her classmates as none of them seemed to have one.

Some of the houses in her neighbourhood had dogs, guard animals really, which would poke their snouts through the grille-work of the gate, revealing menacing eyeteeth, and bark vociferously at every passer-by. And there were a few strays in their neighbourhood—Ramya found them skulking around the garbage bin at the end of the street. They were skinny and mangy, so different from the sleek, silky animals in the film.

But the most remarkable of the dogs in their neighbourhood was neither entirely a street dog nor an actual

pet. It lived near their house and answered to the name
of Manikyam. In a way, it belonged to Saroja, their
neighbour who lived three houses away on the other side
of the lane. Saroja was nineteen and was doing her BSc in
a local college. She was a gentle and kind soul whose face
easily lit up with a dazzling smile—her unpainted, slightly chapped lips framing sparkling but a tad out of kilter
teeth. Saroja always seemed to be in a hurry, and was often
seen purposefully striding up and down the street, with
Manikyam bouncing behind her like a trailer van. Saroja
was a popular and well-liked young woman and was acquainted with everyone in the neighbourhood. She could
always be relied upon for any kind of assistance: free
tuition before final exams, unpaid babysitting, or accompanying a patient to a specialist's appointment. The kids
in the area addressed her as *Akka*—elder sister.

Manikyam was a wiry, leggy creature of an indeter-
minate breed, having white and brown fur and a thin firm
tail shaped like a reclining question mark. He'd been
adopted by Saroja a few years before, when he was a
mewling puppy just a few weeks old. He'd slid through
the gap under their gate, and sat on his haunches, staring
meditatively at the front door.

When Saroja opened the door to step out, she nearly
stumbled over the pup which she initially mistook for a
soft toy dropped by a child. It shocked her when the
small ball of brown fur let out a weak cry and skittered
away. From a safe distance, it gazed up at Saroja with be-
seeching eyes. Saroja rushed back into house and returned
with a chipped china saucer holding two idlis, the only
food she could lay her hands on at short notice. The

ravenous way in which the puppy pounced on the food, bland south Indian vegetarian fare, moved Saroja no end.

With the clockwork precision that would have delighted a Swiss or Japanese watchmaker, the pup turned up every day, giving a confident, friendly yelp to announce his presence. Without fail Saroja would open the door and feed him scraps of leftovers, more of the bland south Indian vegetarian fare. But the puppy lapped it up without complaining. Though this ritual was followed for a long time, it remained a kind of arms-length master-pet relationship because Saroja's family thought it unclean to let dogs into the house.

A few months into the semi-official adoption, Saroja gave the latte brown Manikyam a bath, tying him first to the slender trunk of a guava tree growing in their front yard. She directed a ferocious jet from the garden hose at the panic-stricken puppy and then scrubbed him with Lifebuoy, a raspberry-red carbolic soap. When the last of the lather was blown away by the Niagara gushing out of the wire-wrapped black hose, what was left standing was not a coffee coloured animal, but a sodden dusty-white one with a large tan coloured patch on his back, as if somebody had spilled a cup of Hyderabadi chai on him. But for his uniquely shaped tail, epitomising the mystery of the universe, even Saroja, his arms-length mistress, would've been hard put to recognize him.

It was around this time, when he received his baptismal bath, that Manikyam acquired his name. The name had suggested itself to Saroja's mother, a lady whose sole source of entertainment and enlightenment was the cinema and the periodicals devoted to it. At that time a popular

Telugu film called *Mattilo Manikyam* was running in the local cinema halls.

Mattilo Manikyam meant "the jewel in the dirt." He was unquestionably a jewel, as the subsequent events bore out. Despite being under Saroja's care, he lived in the open, growing up foursquare to the elements. Yet, he grew so attached to Saroja that, whenever she stepped out of her house, he left whatever he was doing — rummaging in the garbage or even wooing she-dogs — and followed her to the main road like a bodyguard. He waited patiently, chasing his tail or licking sundry parts of his body, until Saroja got into a bus or an auto rickshaw, and only then did he return. In the same way, whenever Saroja appeared at the top of the lane, he'd race up to her and welcome her with ecstatic barks. He'd escort her home, his interrogative tail wagging with excitement. A true knight in shining armour, even if a four-legged one.

There is a task, however unwelcome, that she can't put off, either yielding to lethargy or lassitude, or whatever label she chooses to give. She has to call the Raos, and make an appointment to visit. The Raos, a stupendously successful immigrant family, always make her feel nervous and inadequate. They're all well settled, have good jobs or are comfortably retired. They eschew Bollywood films, the grandchildren attend expensive private schools, and are into hockey and lacrosse. Some of them ski, or have at least taken lessons, she was told.

When she thinks of the Raos, she pictures them as a

perfect family: Mr. and Mrs. Rao seated in ornate chairs, flanked by a daughter, her husband and two children on each side. The two spaniels are curled at their feet. It's very much like the actual photograph on the Raos' mantelpiece, displayed in the gilt-edged photo-frame bought at the Bombay store. It was a good picture, imbued with traditional family values—all the people in it looked personable and successful. The only shortcoming was that the photographer couldn't quite capture the haloes around their heads.

She calls, but it goes into the voicemail. Calling a bereaved family is always a tricky business, and leaving a message in such circumstances is even more so. She records her message, feeling highly self-conscious:

"... I hope Uncle has not taken it too badly ..."

Why wouldn't he take it badly—he's been married to her for over sixty years, for Chrissake! Ramya is suddenly overcome with a sense of ineptitude; flustered, she aborts the message.

She could be neither kind and deferential like Sudhakar, the elder son-in-law, an import from India, nor urbane and savvy like Jayanti, a product of the Canadian education system. She was a first-generation immigrant, the nowhere woman.

Instead of trying again and leaving a more cogent message, she decides to call later.

⸺◦─────◦⸺

Despite his reservations, Daddy agreed to buy Ramya a pet dog for her 10th birthday. Agreeing was one thing, but actually acquiring a puppy was something else, which Daddy discovered quite early in the process. Buying a dog wasn't as easy as entering a shop, choosing a canine, coughing up the money, coming out with the article perched on the crook of your arm, and with an invoice along with a two-year warranty safely tucked into your pocket.

For starters, he couldn't locate shops actually selling pet animals in Hyderabad. He rang up all his friends who had pet dogs, and naively enquired whether they had any puppies to spare. While some of them promised to give Ramya one when their she-dogs conceived, none of these animals were pregnant at that time. Many dogs Daddy discovered to his disquiet were neutered so they could have no progeny at all. One of his friends advised him to look in the classifieds of Sunday papers where private sellers advertised.

But there was a hitch. Unfortunately, Ramya's birthday fell well before the weekend. So to make up, Daddy ordered a birthday cake in the shape of a cute, cuddly lap dog—never mind that the baker of Golconda Bakery used turquoise blue and strawberry pink icing to decorate the cake.

This was the only birthday when Ramya showed no real interest in the proceedings—all her thoughts were focussed on the upcoming weekend, when she would be presented with a puppy. She cared neither for the party nor for the cake, nor for the various gifts her classmates and friends from the neighbourhood brought her. The only thing she wanted to think about and speak about was the unique if delayed birthday present her Daddy was going to give her.

On the following Sunday, a tense Daddy woke up early in the morning and waited for the paperboy to coast down the lane on his bicycle, jingling the bell. No sooner than the boy yelled, "Paperoo!" with a Telugu accent, that Daddy rushed out to fetch it. Normally it would lie on the front veranda, the sheets all higgledy-piggledy, the way it was tossed by the indifferent paperboy, until retrieved by a servant maid, reassembled, re-folded and placed on a teapoy in the living room.

Daddy riffled the paper, and pulled out the classified section, neglecting the weighty developments in the international scene, news like a natural disaster in Mexico and a political coup in the Middle East. He ran an unpractised eye over the page unsure where in the serried arrays were the 'Puppies for Sale' ads. The only time he'd scanned the classifieds was when he'd been searching for a groom for his sister. But that was aeons ago.

"There it is!" he yelled, like a castaway who has sighted land in the distant horizon, much to Ramya's delight. She'd been seated on the sofa, with bated breath, watching her father clumsily turn the pages of the newspaper. She'd defied Amma's orders to go and brush her teeth, preparatory to having breakfast and a glass of Ovaltine.

Ramya ran up to her father, as he folded back the newspaper. He looked at her and said: "There's a man in Mehdipatnam who sells puppies. Let's pay him a visit right after breakfast."

Ramya was so excited that she could hardly touch her food even though it was her favourite—crisp-roasted dosas stuffed with sautéed potatoes and served with cocoanut chutney. But when Amma threatened her with dire

consequences, saying, "Enough is enough!" Ramya managed to swallow a few shreds of the rice pancakes. Left
untouched, the Ovaltine went cold, and a skin of cream,
as wrinkled as Amma's cheeks, formed on its surface.
Soon Daddy put down his coffee cup, and said: "Let's go!"

The game was afoot. An excited Ramya scrambled
into the passenger seat in the front, wishing the car was
a helicopter. They also took with them the servant boy
Sailoo, who sat at the back, as was his wont, striking a
princely pose, shoulders pressed back, and arms splayed
out in a casual fashion. Amma had given them a wicker
basket, lined with a folded piece of an old worn out bedsheet. Sailoo took custody of the basket and placed it next
to him on the seat, as a king may do with a royal orb.

It took them a good half an hour to reach Mehdipatnam, and an equal amount of time trying to locate the
house. Daddy stopped often to ask passers-by for directions only to discover that many of them were new to the
place and were looking for an address just like him. Such
was Hyderabad! Eventually they reached the house, after
going this way and that, guided and misguided by well-
meaning but ignorant residents of the locality.

There was a high compound wall, with only the roof
of an imposing building and some tree-tops showing
above it. The enormous gates, clad with metal sheets,
were left open, and they drove up the semicircular gravel
drive to the portico. The house, despite its magisterial
size, appeared marooned in the large compound. The
portico looked over a pond with a fountain that threw
up debilitated jets of water, like wobbly silver strings, its
pipes clogged with years of lime deposits.

The owner of the house and Daddy had much to talk about as they had many friends in common, some of whom were Daddy's patients. An old manservant brought tea in rose-patterned china. When Ramya shook her head, he asked: "Would baby like to have a soft drink?"

"No," Ramya said, shaking her head violently as her impatience mounted.

Despite her saying no, the servant brought her a tall glass of iced Rooh Afza, a traditional rose-flavoured summer drink. Ramya wanted to weep; drinking up the tall glassful of sherbet would only delay her mission further.

"Try it, baby. If you don't like it, you can leave it."

Arbitrarily, Ramya decided to dislike it, and after taking a couple of sips set it down on the end table. The glass began to sprout beads of restless sweat, as Daddy and the owner continued to engage in small talk. A peeved Ramya stared at the condensation on the tumbler — as more droplets formed, the smaller ones coalesced with bigger ones, and then suddenly and quickly slid down the side like a tiny rivulet.

Then at long last they all came out of the house and went around to the back where a series of kennels had been constructed against the rear wall. The backyard was shady with ancient trees brooding over it. The kennels were clean, but the smell of animal urine and dog-food fluttered in the air like a banner. Also wafting towards them, like rollers from an ocean, was the strong spicy smell of non-vegetarian cooking from the kitchen of the main house.

There were at least a dozen pups of various ages up for sale, in groups of threes and fours clustered around their mothers, in separate enclosures. When the dogs heard them coming, some of them snarled, as if calling out a warning, and then turned their heads away with indifference. A few puppies ventured out of the kennels, unfearful of strangers, and approached them as if they were old friends. Ramya, being unused to pets, was frightened of animals in general; she would scream when even a kitten brushed past her.

Some of the bigger dogs in the kennels looked fearsome, with their mouths open, and wet tongues lolling out. But the friendly puppies won Ramya over completely with their convivial curiosity. Picking up a small reddish-brown pup which looked so angelic to her eyes, she said: "Can I have this one?"

"Are you sure?" the owner asked.

Ramya nodded her head vigorously. The puppy was already licking Ramya's face with clammy painterly strokes.

Before the man could complete the sentence, Daddy interrupted him: "Let her have it, if she likes it so much."

"It's only a few weeks old ... but it is a Doberman, and it will soon grow up to be a big, strong dog," he said, more as a warning than just providing product information.

While Daddy settled the commercial aspects of the deal, Ramya and Sailoo placed the puppy in the open basket and clambered into the back of the car. The excited puppy got out of the basket and ran over their laps and was in danger of falling into the gap between their knees and the back of the front seats. Soon Daddy returned and got into the car. As he turned on the ignition and pulled at the starter switch, he asked: "Happy?"

"Yes!" Ramya said, as she tried to evade the generously sticky licks from the puppy.

"What are you going to call him?"

Tommy? Rusty? Brownie? Bruno?

"I don't know. I'll have to think of a good name."

Casting a glance at the rufous puppy, Daddy said: "What about Reddy?" And laughed uproariously.

When the car had gone a few miles, the puppy changed its mood all of a sudden, and began to mewl. It grew restless and jumped from one lap to the other, yelping so piteously that Ramya was quite alarmed.

"Daddy, the puppy is missing its mother, I think. Let's go back! He looks so miserable."

Her father slowed down the car, and would've heeded to Ramya's plea, but for an unmoved Sailoo's wise counsel: "Don't worry so much, Ramya-amma. He might miss his mother right now, but if you look after him well, he'll forget all about his family in a few days' time."

When they reached home, Ramya carried the whimpering puppy into the drawing room. No sooner had she set him down on the floor than he passed water. A servant maid was sent to bring a mop and a pail to clean up. By then Amma had brought some warm milk in a bowl, and instructed Ramya to feed the dog. The puppy waddled over, and noisily began to slurp up the milk. After he had his fill, he seemed to be satisfied and didn't look so woebegone.

In the first few weeks, Ramya devoted all her spare time to the care of the puppy. When Ramya left for school every morning, the puppy mewled heartbreakingly. In the afternoons, it would hang around near the open front door, waiting for Ramya to return. The moment she appeared, in fact well before that, when the puppy heard

the metal gate creaking open, it would hurry outside taking fragile mincing steps, its eyes afire with adoration.

Without waiting to get the overloaded canvas school
bag off her back, or kicking her dusty leather shoes away,
Ramya would scoop up the puppy and coddle him, mut-
tering sweet nothings. Thus, she would break the age-old
house rules to change out of her uniform and wash her
hands and feet the first thing after returning from school.

Ramya even neglected to have her afternoon tiffin,
usually a light snack of bondas or samosas or curry-puffs,
something she would've pounced on hungrily the minute
she'd washed her hands. She had to be reminded umpteen
times by Amma, her voice growing sterner by the minute,
to change into civvies and have a bite. Ramya stopped
going out in the evening to play with her friends or take
her small bicycle for a spin. If she went out at all, she took
her puppy with her, cradling it in her arms, much like an
ayah taking her ward for an outing. The children playing
in the street would abandon their games and come up
to her, some of them begging Ramya to let them carry
the puppy.

Ramya stopped doing her homework, and her grades
began to plummet. Only Mummy, in spite of her sacred
aloofness, remarked aloud about Ramya's undue preoccu-
pation with her newfound pet. Amma, though she disap-
proved of Ramya devoting so much time to her pet, was
reluctant to chide her, as she was staying as a mere guest.
Daddy, blissfully oblivious to what was happening, was
content to see Ramya happy.

One afternoon, Ramya's teacher sent home a handwritten note addressed to Daddy about her poor perform-

ance and lack of attention in class. For Daddy it was a bolt from the blue; he was horrified to read the terse missive. Nevertheless, he was stung into action. He instructed Amma to take more control of Ramya's leisure time. Though Amma was well-versed in the art of putting undisciplined children to rights, it took her a few weeks of threats and entreaty to bring back the perennially indulged child into the groove.

The entire household, except for Mummy, had been mesmerized by the antics of the puppy in the first few weeks, and doted on him, not at all put off by the name Barghest that Ramya had bestowed on the hapless animal, after poring over many a formidable book, all gifts from Atom Auntie. The servants never questioned Ramya's choice of name — pet dogs were always given outlandish names, especially English ones, a carryover from the British Raj. To their ears a Norse name sounded as familiar or unfamiliar as Lassie or Goldie.

Only Mummy asked: "Ramya, what kind of a name is Barghest? Has your Atom Auntie got something to do with it?"

The question felt like a rapier thrust. Mummy's sharp tone and uncomplimentary reference to her beloved Atom Auntie made Ramya bawl; she felt both chastised and belittled.

"Why do you talk to a small child like that?" Amma said, bustling into the living room. "Don't cry, Ramya. Your Mummy was only joking."

By and by, Barghest stopped being the beloved cynosure in spite of his beguiling ways. This happened because Amma and the servants noted with increasing alarm his progressively growing appetite. When Barghest was brought home, he was a wee little thing, and they'd somehow assumed that he'd remain his small self, and if he did grow at all, he'd do so in modestly incremental steps.

But a purebred Doberman pinscher was no lap dog. His appetite was enormous, his growth explosive. As weeks passed, Barghest grew and grew, and the intake of food was in step with his size. Within four months he was as big as a full-grown cocker spaniel, with an appetite to match.

The servants resented the extra work of another mouth to feed. When shopping they had to buy and carry more groceries than usual; the cook had to cook more than was customary; and worst of all, Barghest not having been potty-trained properly, dirtied the house indiscriminately, and the servants were constantly being summoned to clean up after him. Daddy appeased the servants to a certain extent by hiking their salaries, but not everything was as easy as that.

Amma likened Barghest's growth spurt to that of the mythical fish in the story of Manu, the first man on earth, after whom mankind was named. One day Manu, the son of Brahma the creator, went early in the morning at a sacred hour to the bank of a holy river to offer prayers. When he was performing his ablutions, a tiny fish swam into the vessel he was using. The chit of a fish spoke to Manu in human tongue, and commanded him to take it home and look after it. If he obeyed the fish, the fish in turn would come to Manu's aid in the near future when a cataclysm would befall the earth.

Manu did as he was enjoined and took the fingerling

home and housed it in a small jar. Like Barghest, the fish grew, but even more exponentially. Every few days, Manu had to exchange the fish's temporary home for another larger container. This went on until the fish, according to Amma, grew the size of a Leyland lorry.

"Amma!" Ramya said, well versed in the subject of mythology thanks to Atom Auntie. "There were no trucks in those days."

"Don't interrupt elders. I know there were no lorries then, but I used it as an example, so that you got an idea of the size of the fish. Anyway, the fish was transferred to a pond."

Soon even the pond proved insufficient. "Because he had grown as big as a ..." Amma faltered.

"A jumbo jet," Ramya suggested.

"Whatever," Amma said. When it was at last released into the ocean, the fish, who was none other than Lord Vishnu in his piscine avatar, told Manu: "Soon there will be a great deluge. Build a large ship so that you can take in as many species of plants and animals as you can." Within a short span of time, the skies curdled over, and incessant rain poured down, day after day, until almost all of the earth was covered with an endless sheet of water.

The fish having grown more gargantuan than ever showed up as promised, and steered Manu to safety, with one end of the celestial serpent Shesha tied to the prow of the ship, and the other to a horn on its head.

"What kind of fish has a horn on its head, Amma?" Ramya asked. But she liked the notion of the ship being towed by the fish to a safe haven. She could picture her beloved Barghest on a leash, leading her out of a Minoan maze, if ever she found herself in such a predicament, and deliver her back into the bosom of her family.

When Ramya celebrated Barghest's first birthday, the pup had grown into a handsome specimen. A shiny coat clothed his muscles, which rippled as he walked. He weighed forty pounds and was as many inches tall. Ramya observed Barghest's birthday with all the traditional pomp and circumstance one associates with an anniversary party for humans: streamers and balloons, caps and whistles, ice cream and coke. The baker of Golconda Bakery was up to his old tricks again, and made a cake in the shape of a bone (a short stubby femur with lime green icing) on a candyfloss-pink plate and "Barghest" written in Mediterranean blue.

Though Ramya made a point of telling her invitees to bring their pet dogs, if they had any, it was a good thing that only two other dogs showed up. Saroja, who gave the beautiful collar with the medallion, brought Manikyam, smelling of Lifebuoy, having been hosed down for the occasion, and a girl of Ramya's age named Maunika brought a snow-white pom called Toughie, a small cowardly beast that snarled ferociously all the while but turned tail if anyone, man or beast, challenged it. Throughout the evening the three dog owners had to hold on to their dogs tightly lest they start a canine affray. Nevertheless, the party was a huge success.

As to Saroja, the mistress of Manikyam, she got married a few months later in an arranged manner to a young man of her caste. Though he was scrawny and bespectacled, his horoscope matched hers to a T. While unprepossessing to behold, he had a steady job in the government and had good prospects — which was what mattered, at least to Saroja's parents. Daddy and Ramya attended the wedding held in a marriage hall on the Lower Tank Bund Road, near the Hussainsagar Lake, giving the young couple an acrylic lemon set as a wedding gift.

After all the festivities were over, and having spent the connubial night on a bed bespattered with rose petals (supplied by good old Arifuddin), it was time for Saroja to move out of her parents' home for good. When the time of the day was most auspicious by the Hindu almanac, the newly-wed couple got into a car that a rich relative had loaned for the occasion. Saroja, along with all her possessions stuffed into three or four suitcases, was going to be borne away to her in-laws' house once and for all. Tearful relatives and friends besieged the car, and the atmosphere was surcharged with heart-breaking emotion. Though Saroja would continue to live in the same city, on the opposite end, on the other side of the gigantic Hussain Sagar Lake, she would now belong to another family, assuming another last name. Even her gotra, an ancient tribal identity, would be changed to her husband's.

Unnoticed by anyone, except Ramya who was peering through the grille-work gate, Manikyam was loitering at the periphery of the throng, looking sad and confused. Just before stepping into the car, Saroja sought out Manikyam, and bent down and patted his head with aching affection. When all the goodbyes were said, the car started to move, the driver honking vigorously to make people step out of the way. The car crawled away, raising a cloud of dust, and the crowd melted away in silence.

After that day, no one saw Manikyam in the neighbourhood again. It was noticed and remarked by some, but nobody paid much heed. He never again turned up at Saroja's parents' house at the appointed time seeking handouts. This puzzled the family a little, but nobody was bothered enough to investigate.

A few weeks later, the people in the neighbourhood were surprised to learn that Manikyam was staying in Saroja's new home. He'd followed the car, nose to the ground, picking up the trail even after losing sight of the vehicle, crossing so many intersections, some with traffic lights, some without, slinking past an unmanned railway gate, running the gauntlet of stray dogs hell-bent on protecting their territorial rights, cantering without pausing for breath, and his thirsty tongue hanging out, along roads brimming with buses, lorries, cars, auto rickshaws, motorcycles, scooters, cycles, cycle-rickshaws, bullock carts and pedestrians, a distance of twelve kilometres, before turning up, exhausted but deliriously happy, in front of Saroja's in-laws' house. A truly incredible journey!

Ramya could picture Manikyam emitting his trademark bark, full of confidence and love.

A disoriented Saroja must have done a double take and burst out the front door, with the thought — could it be … surely not! The curved tail and the tan-coloured patch on the back would've given no room for doubt. After getting her husband's permission and, being a wise young woman, her mother-in-law's too, a jubilant Saroja brought a small bowl of milk and a plate of Parle glucose biscuits for Manikyam. Her husband was so moved by the dog's love and loyalty, he allowed Saroja to keep

Manikyam in the house. He couldn't have given a better wedding present to his new wife.

Saroja's parents had indeed chosen a good match for their daughter.

While Manikyam's devotion to his mistress was acquiring aspects of an urban legend, events in Ramya's house were panning out a little differently. As months passed, Barghest became too unwieldy an animal for Ramya or the maids to handle on their own. So the responsibility fell on the strong and able shoulders of Sailoo. Unable to get the pronunciation exactly right, but being privy to a few English words, he began to call the dog Bar Guess.

"Bar *Guess*—stick!" Or: "Bar *Guess*—ball!" he would shout, emulating but not mimicking Ramya. The dog would race away, chasing the object that was tossed.

Ramya began to notice, with growing disquiet, a change come over Barghest. Subtle and hardly discernible at first, later it became too obvious to ignore. Barghest's adoration, which had once been almost idolatrous in its fervour, was being replaced by an attitude of indulgence, or worse still, condescension. He remained friendly— even gentle, rubbing his velvety neck against her legs, in an affectionate, proprietorial way. But the love-filled gaze of the soulful black-and-brown eyes was completely gone. Barghest eyes lit up only for Sailoo, responding readily to the corrupted name of Bar Guess. Now and then Barghest would even show impatience if there was any delay in taking him out. Anyway, it was Sailoo who was taking him for a run most of the time, Ramya being preoccupied with homework or preparation for exams.

A year later Sailoo left. Daddy got him a good job at

a factory owned by one of his patients. Sailoo needed to earn enough money to marry and start a family. By continuing to work as a servant boy he couldn't have done that.

Once again managing the big heavy dog, whose footfalls might have been those of an approaching baby elephant, fell to the lot of women, women who were either old (Amma), incapacitated (Mummy), puny (most of the servants) or young (Ramya). Most of the time, Barghest was on good behaviour but occasionally he showed signs of bad temper — it always had to do with being taken out. At the appointed time, he'd bark nonstop and pull at the leash in an unholy haste to be let out. But once he was taken out, he'd try to run ahead and drag the maid who was walking him so forcefully that, unable to keep pace, she'd set him free. A delighted Barghest would bound away, to hobnob with the she-dogs sunbathing near the garbage bin at the end of the lane. When it was time to return home, it needed threats and blows with a stick before the lead could be tied around his neck. He had to be forcibly hauled back home.

One day Ramya took Barghest out for a walk. He was now a huge dog and came up to her waist, as he trotted beside her like a well-trained stallion. But when he caught the scent of his female acquaintances, he tried to peel away. Ramya held on to the leash even more firmly, unaware that the maids had made it a habit to unchain him on his walks. Barghest pulled at the lead, and when Ramya didn't let go, he began to tug more violently, and then increased his pace to a gallop. A surprised and frightened Ramya had to sprint after Barghest, her hand clutching the leash and her feet flying over the uneven ground. It began to get more and more difficult to stay in step with Barghest who was hurtling at full tilt, barking with annoyance and impatience.

Then Ramya tripped and fell, and was dragged a few feet by Barghest, until she let go of the leash. When she got up, feeling angry and stupid, Barghest had loped away out of sight. She wanted to follow in his wake, but realized that her dress was torn and smeared with dust. Besides, she felt her hands and legs singe with pain; she had barked her knees and grazed her forearms. Involuntarily, she began to cry, not so much with physical pain, but out of a feeling of abandonment.

A maid had to be sent to recover Barghest. Amma dressed Ramya's wounds as best she could with cotton and strips of plaster cut from a big roll. When Daddy returned home in the night, he gave Ramya a tetanus injection. A chastened Barghest spent the night tied to a tree in the yard.

The next day, the maids had other gory stories to tell about Barghest: how routinely he chased young children, alarmed cyclists into falling off their bicycles, constantly fought with strays over she-dogs, so on and so forth.

Daddy called Sailoo at his workplace and spoke to him. Sailoo turned up that evening to take Barghest away.

"He'll make a good guard dog at the factory," Sailoo said.

When Ramya bent down and ruffled the fur on his head, Barghest looked kindly at her, his eyes full of compassion, and gave her a generous lick. It was almost like old times, but both knew that the time had come.

Sailoo finished his cup of tea, and the bun he was dunking into it. Wiping his hands on the seat of his pants, Sailoo said his goodbyes and took a firm grip on Barghest's collar, saying: "Come, Bar Guess. Let's go."

The silver medallion with Barghest's name on it came loose and fell to the ground. Sailoo and Barghest walked away in perfect amity, as if they were inseparable friends. There was no need for a leash to bind them together. Ramya stood at the gate with moist eyes, tears gathering in them like storm clouds, while Barghest receded into the distance. He didn't so much as give a backward glance as dusk enfolded him.

8

BFF

RAMYA PLUCKS OUT a lipstick from the sandalwood chest. It has a chocolate-brown plastic cap and a golden metallic base which has begun to blacken. A large L with prominent serifs, and ringed with two curved sprigs of laurel, is engraved on the top of the cap. Lakmé was the catchy name the manufacturer chose for a new range of locally developed cosmetics. The company had found a business opportunity when the government cracked down on imports. There was a serious balance-of-payments issue, and the country no longer wanted to splurge its scant stash of U.S. Dollars and Pounds Sterling on bagatelles like rouge and mascara.

Ramya learned much later that the original Lakmé was a star-crossed Indian—Indian as from India—lass in one of Bizet's French operas. Abandonment is a universal theme, spanning cultures and continents.

She tries to unscrew the cap. It resists a little before yielding squeakily to reveal a stick of dark purple. The lipstick looks dry and slightly off-colour. Like a cheap crayon. Ramya has never touched her lips with it, and with good reason; the tumulus shape is almost pristine, save for a light bruise on the top.

She never used purple. To carry off such a colour with her complexion in India you had to be forward, or "fast," as some people would say. Ramya, who would describe herself as dull and demure, preferred more modest shades —a deep maroon or pale pink, something that didn't clash too much with her nutmeg complexion. In those days, wearing lipstick was considered very unorthodox; so much so that when Ramya applied colour to her mouth, her relatives' eyebrows went up. The fact that they themselves applied *kaatika,* an age-old form of mascara to their lashes, and thickened their brows with a black eyebrow pencil was conveniently glossed over. Eye makeup was traditional; lipsticks were modern, even Western, and by implication, decadent.

Maunika, Ramya's so-called best friend, had given the lipstick as a parting gift on the day a loyal Ramya organized a small farewell treat at an ice cream parlour in Abid's, the main drag of Hyderabad. Ramya remembers the day so well. It was the end of April, the annual exams were just over, and though it was spring, the weather was warm as toast.

Picking up the lipstick, Ramya rises from the dining table and shuffles to the mirror above the console table in the hallway. She stands in front of the gilt-framed mirror, holding the desiccated lipstick she received over three decades ago, and wonders: "How would purple look on me now?" Her skin has grown a shade lighter living in the northern latitudes where the sun is an infrequent visitor. Her hand holding the exposed lipstick stays poised like a bird in flight as she is distracted by her reflection in the mirror.

Her hair is unkempt, and here and there, a surge of grey is threatening to rise and overwhelm her shoulder-long tresses. Her complexion is sallow, and her chapped lips pine for the soothing application of a balm rather than lip-colour. When she makes eye contact with herself in the glass, lacklustre irises stare back at her.

In her mind's eye, unbidden, she sees an image of the sadhvi she encountered years ago. She has a serene smile and a youthful look though she is much older than Ramya is now.

Dismissing the recollection, Ramya absently rubs the purple lipstick against her lower lip. The top of the stick crumbles and a few dry bits cling to her mouth like cookie sprinkles. She wipes her lips clean with the Kleenex she keeps handy on the console table.

How untidy her console table is! It has become a safe haven for old receipts, small change, hairpins, loose keys and a comb. How unhappy and uncomfortable must the six-inch-high clay image of Lord Ganesa feel? The elephant-headed god is the remover of obstacles. She placed the idol, gaudily painted with red, blue and yellow, on the console table opposite the front door to usher in good fortune. It is indeed inauspicious to surround him with so much untidiness. She should do something to clear the table so that the god, in turn, can clear the impediments in her life.

Ramya's unwritten "to do" list grows by the day. One

of the items is to write the list itself on a sheet of paper and stick it on the fridge, under the magnetic picture of the CN Tower.

⟡━━━━━⟡

When Ramya was in high school, she had — perversely — chosen Maunika to be her best friend. Maunika was a lanky girl with a dusky complexion who seemed all elbows and knees. She was the youngest of four children, and wore clothes which were obviously hand-me-downs, just a tad faded and fraying at the edges. But they'd been so expertly altered, possibly by Maunika's mother, that they didn't look out of date. In fact, Maunika looked quite chic in them. You'd have to rub the fabric between your thumb and forefinger to discover that it was almost threadbare.

Though Ramya and Maunika lived in the same neighbourhood, they went to different elementary schools. They knew each other by sight, and would run into each other in the nearby park or at a common friend's birthday party. She was the stand-in mistress to the frisky pom at Barghest's birthday party. Ramya hadn't invited her at all; she'd sent an invitation to the dog and his master, a high school boy named Raghu. He and his family were Daddy's patients. But Raghu preferred to take part in a friendly cricket match at the Parade Ground, and sent his pet dog to the party with Maunika, his neighbour, as its chaperone.

Their high school was in the heart of the city, a good distance away. It was big and renowned, with sprawling playgrounds, and drew students from all over the city.

Later, whenever Ramya thought about it, she couldn't fathom what she'd seen in Maunika to make her her very best friend, her thickest pal. That Maunika lived nearby, took the same navy blue school bus, and was in the same class may have influenced her ... And Maunika always knew by instinct on which side her bread was buttered.

Telephones were a luxury in those days, so having a classmate nearby was useful. If Ramya was absent for any reason, she could always find out what had transpired at school by simply walking over to Maunika's house. But there was a flip side: Maunika could do the same. Besides, she had the vexatious habit of not returning in time the textbooks or notebooks she had borrowed. On some occasions, she didn't return them at all. This meant Ramya had to write her exams without sufficient preparation. If asked, Daddy would've bought her a new textbook without giving it another thought. But how could one replace an exercise book in which she'd taken down copious notes?

The same was true of her storybooks. Maunika would borrow her shiny paperback copies of novels by Victoria Holt and Mary Stewart and later return them in a dog-eared condition, if she bothered to return them at all. Novels were meant to be read, but what Maunika did with them challenged one's imagination. Did she give the books to her infant nephews and nieces to cut their teeth on?

Maunika seemed to think her obligation ended by saying: "I'm sorry." If Ramya persisted, Maunika would give a peculiar look and sigh. "I said, I'm sorry, didn't I?" She managed to suggest that Ramya was making too much of a fuss, and her tone implied, come on, it's only a *book*, for pity's sake!

The cost of maintaining Maunika as a best friend was high indeed. Was it a surprise then that Amma didn't like Maunika one bit? Amma wasn't the kind to hide her dislike. "Be careful with her," she'd warn Ramya. "She's not a dependable girl."

"Amma, I'll be careful. But Maunika isn't a bad sort at all," Ramya would say, making an unconvincing, half-hearted defense. Once she had proclaimed Maunika her best friend, Ramya wanted to be loyal and steadfast.

Her father, ingenuous as he was, didn't share Amma's misgivings—the fact that Ramya considered Maunika her dearest friend was enough for him. He made a lot of fuss over Maunika when he saw her, much to Amma's fury.

"Did you give Maunika a slice of the plum cake?" he'd ask. Or: "Why don't you let Maunika ride on your new bicycle?"

It was a miracle Amma didn't explode when Daddy made such naïve utterances. Everyone could hear her grumbling in the kitchen while serving a portion of a sweet for Maunika, taking extra care to cut a thinner slice. But Maunika was too thick-skinned to mind anything; she knew what she wanted, and got it any which way. This quality evoked grudging admiration from Ramya.

When Ramya was in Grade 10, Daddy bought her a proper dressing table, a kind of rites-of-passage event. It sported a bevelled Belgian mirror, and came with a cushioned stool. Ramya populated its Formica faux-wood surface with a modest collection of scents and cosmetics. Deployed like toy soldiers were jars, tins and bottles: Afghan Snow, Charmis cold cream, Tata's hair oil and eau de cologne, Pond's Dreamflower talcum powder, Shringar scented bindi, and a flat round tin of locally made kohl whose brand name she couldn't recall — was it Eyetex?

Ramya wasn't the sort of girl who'd sit brooding in front of a dressing table mirror in throes of pubescent angst, counting her zits. She used cosmetics just enough to look presentable, and smell good.

Ramya had varied interests but reading came first, and her favourite author was Daphne du Maurier. She also liked sports and played shuttle badminton in her front yard with the maids who were utterly hopeless at the game and were apt to giggle uncontrollably whenever they missed hitting the bird. Ramya also learned the traditional dance-art of Kuchipudi, but performed it in lackadaisical fashion.

When Maunika came over, she wasn't interested in playing scrabble or listening to music on the Philips hi-fi Daddy had bought for Ramya, but would make a beeline to the new dressing table. She would settle down on the sumptuously cushioned stool and converse with Ramya's reflection in the mirror. Ramya, reclining on the pillows propped against the headboard of the bed, would address her replies to Maunika's slim back. The drill was the same every time. First, the preliminary small talk, then Maunika would open container after container and sniff at their contents. How often would one want to smell Tata's eau de cologne? The next step was to dig deep into a jar of snow or cold cream (or both), scoop out generous dollops, and pat them on to her face. Then Maunika would apply a large bindi on her forehead, painstakingly filling in the colour with the tiny tip of the applicator stick.

Ramya could only gaze helplessly at her friend's

antics. With liberal daubs of cream on her cheeks, and a large red bindi decorating her forehead, Maunika reminded one of a professional clown. But it was no laughing matter. At least not for Amma. If she chanced upon Maunika with her face slobbered with cream, Ramya got an earful right there in the presence of her friend.

"Have you any idea how much they cost?" Amma would scream. Ramya felt like a whipping boy, and her helplessness only increased. Maunika for her part didn't show a whit of penitence.

Truth to tell, Amma didn't have a clue as to the cost of the cosmetics because she never used them, except for talcum powder. Cosmetics were a luxury beyond the reach of her husband's salary of a lowly government clerk.

In the first year of Junior College, the equivalent to Grade 11, Maunika's father was transferred out of Hyderabad, and her family prepared to leave.

"It's the best news I've heard in a long, long time," Amma said. "This calls for a celebration!"

When Ramya planned a farewell treat for Maunika, Amma said tartly that that wasn't the celebration she had in mind.

Ramya invited another friend by the name of Sujatha to the small get-together she organized. She asked Sujatha to accompany her because young girls from good families didn't sally forth alone, even in broad daylight. Daddy was visiting a very sick patient and couldn't drive them to the restaurant, so they took an auto-rickshaw, the door-less three-wheeled taxi. Known simply as 'auto', it was more expensive than a bus but far cheaper than the yellow-roofed taxi.

Even in those days, Maunika could be described as a
bold thing. (She was too young to be called fast.) She came
on her own, taking a road transport bus, which had cost
her just a quarter of a rupee.

The day was bright and shining like polished brass,
and it presaged a scorching summer. Inside the restaurant
it was cool and dark, the air laced with redolence of the
oil they used for cooking. Ramya was very sensitive to
smells; others didn't seem to mind so much. The three of
them entered a section marked Family, pushing open a
pair of springy glass-paned half-doors. The ceiling fans
overhead whirred frenziedly as if on steroids. There were
other customers in the room, including a legitimate
family, a small noisy group of women unaccompanied by
men, and a young dating couple who whispered timor-
ously to each other, heads bent.

The trio seated themselves in a corner, on bench-like
seats with high backs. Sujatha was an eager, talkative girl
—a charming but intriguing mixture of unworldly naïveté and sharp native intelligence. When Maunika saw
that Ramya had brought Sujatha along, she grimaced.
Sujatha took it in her stride, not making an issue. Ramya
had often heard her remark that it took all kinds to make
the world go round.

The chole-bhathura they ordered came soon, on a
stainless-steel tray perched on the waiter's shoulder. The
chole was in porcelain tubs, and the deliciously puffy
moonlike bhathuras stacked on plates. The chole was excellent and had a taste unique to the restaurant.

"Could it be because they add anardana?" Ramya
hazarded, meaning crushed pomegranate seeds.

Maunika shrugged, busily tucking into the food; she couldn't be bothered with finer culinary points. She took another helping of the peculiar cocktail onions doctored a purple-pink and kept in a cruet on the table.

Sujatha, biting into the luscious long green paprika which came as a side, said: "I wonder if it's that — or is it because of the kala namak, black salt? I don't know much about north Indian cooking, but the chole tastes divine. Even the bhathuras for that matter!"

Sujatha enjoyed the food, making ecstatic comments between morsels. Maunika had a bored expression, as if blasé of the food and the company. Ramya and Sujatha finished every particle of their portions, but Maunika left half a bhathura and a good helping of the chole uneaten.

"Sorry, but I must take care of my figure."

"Really," Sujatha said. "You look like a matchstick as it is."

"Let's order some dessert," Ramya butted in quickly, and looked around for a waiter.

Sujatha chose a modest slice of strawberry ice cream, while Ramya opted for a fruit salad — a handful of anaemic-looking pieces of tinned fruit with a tiny finial of vanilla ice cream. Sujatha rolled her eyes when Maunika went in for the Honeymoon Special — a triple sundae which came in a tall frosted glass with three scoops of ice cream, and a variety of diced fruit, interspersed with jam, jelly, and nuts. The top looked like a Viking's helmet with two triangular wafers stuck on the uppermost scoop. The ice cream cost the earth. It was a good thing Ramya's father always insisted that she take more than enough money with her when she went out.

Sujatha gazed at Maunika with wonderment as the latter ate the ice cream with a detached expression, a sort of urban sophistication. But she managed to polish off every bite — totally unmindful of her figure.

"How was your sundae?" Ramya asked.

"So-so," Maunika replied, with a studied lack of enthusiasm.

Just before the waiter brought the bill, Ramya presented Maunika with a dress — a cream shalwar kameez with an elaborately embroidered yoke, and a tie-dye dupatta to match. In return, Maunika whipped something out of her pocket, and gave it to Ramya. It was brown and gold tube of lipstick. When Ramya unscrewed the top to look inside, the first thing she noticed was that the purple lipstick had been used — the gleaming bullet-shaped stick was scuffed at the top, as if someone's lips had left tread marks on it.

Ramya screwed the top back on hastily, and put the lipstick into her handbag.

⁓————⁓

Standing in front of the mirror, Ramya runs a comb through her wavy hair; it's still manageable, but will become more recalcitrant unless she washes it on the weekend.

Weekend! That word again. What meaning does the word have now? For an out-of-work employee the entire week is one long weekend. It could be one long party, if she started receiving her EI payments. But then she'll have to complete and submit her forms. When will she ever get to doing it?

Still peering into the mirror, she tells herself: "I think it's time I paid a visit to Tressa." Tressa is her hairdresser. Ramya has been her customer for many years now.

"On the other hand, I don't think I should. It will cost me nearly eighty bucks, and I have nowhere to go ..."

Ramya suddenly remembers that she promised her colleague Wilma, when she called her a few days ago, that she'd drop by today. Wilma was laid off at the same time; otherwise who'd be at home on a Thursday morning to receive visitors? They're sisters-in-arms, Wilma and she. But Wilma was a little ahead of Ramya in planning the next stage of the campaign. It would be good to talk things over with her.

Half an hour later, on the way to Wilma's house, Ramya calls her and says she'll be late by a few minutes. It's almost noon. She stops at a Tim Hortons drive-through and buys two double-doubles.

Wilma lives in a nice, quiet neighbourhood with apple trees and manicured lawns. But today, on a grey winter morning, the trees look bare and scorched, and the lawns lie doggo under an eiderdown of snow.

Ramya and Wilma sit at the small dining table in the kitchen, sipping their coffee. It's cold in the kitchen. The furnace is probably set on low to save money. The french windows look on to a backyard covered with snow that looks like a sea of congealed spittle. Ramya nibbles at the Danish which Wilma has picked up cheap at Costco. At 5'8", Wilma is tall for a Filipina. She'd worked on the assembly line before being laid off.

Wilma's husband Jason works a courier-van driver, and still has his job. But courier companies too are feeling the

heat as the economy slowly but surely slips into a reces-
sion. They have three children of school-going age, and a
mortgage for a large house. Coping on one salary isn't
easy, even if their mortgage principal is not huge. They
bought the house when the real estate prices were low,
before all this business of mysterious buyers from China
flooding the market and driving up the prices.

Wilma is trying to cut costs by buying things in bulk
or shopping at discount stores. A few weeks ago, she even
visited Value Village, a shop re-selling the jetsam from
the use-and-throw society. While shopping she'd felt a
wave of shame suddenly wash over her, so she abandoned
her half-full buggy in an aisle, and strode out of the shop
empty-handed.

"It's nearly three weeks since I submitted all the papers," Wilma says. "I don't know why it's taking them so
much time."

Wiping the strawberry filling stuck to her mouth
with a tissue called Truly, an inexpensive substitute for
Kleenex, Ramya says: "Did you speak to Lisa about it?"

Lisa works in the HR department, and, not surprisingly, has managed to hang on to her job. She's a young,
bright, energetic and precise Chinese woman who, when
caught off guard, is prone to call Ramya Lameea. To be
fair, she's friendly and helpful, and continues to be so even
after they were laid off.

"I did. She's says these things take time as it's a government office. They too have laid off their employees,
apparently."

"Downsizing," Ramya says, nodding knowingly. "It's
the in thing with management all over the world. A new

corporate fashion statement, like Kaizen or Quality Circles were once upon a time."

Wilma looks blankly at her. Ramya, who has a management degree from back home, hastily presses on. "I spoke to Jamila the other day. She's heard that our company might hire us back soon. Hope springs eternal in the human breast, I suppose."

"Annie also told me the same thing. The management is planning to reopen one or two lines because demand is picking up in the U.S.A. She thinks there's a good chance that some of us will be re-hired."

"I don't want to get my hopes all up only to be dashed again." Life has taught Ramya that the glass is always half-empty, if not completely so. "I don't mind this break from work, really. But it would have been good if I started getting the EI checks regularly."

"When did you send in the forms?"

Ramya sighs, and shakes her head. "I haven't done it yet."

"Ramya! You should never neglect to do such an important thing. Go home and do it right away. How can you hope to win the lottery if you don't even buy the ticket? In my horoscope today, I read that something good is coming my way."

"It may be the postman with your EI cheque, who knows. When I get back home I'll see what my horoscope in the *Toronto Star* says. There may be something about getting our jobs back."

"We were getting the *Toronto Sun*, but we've put a stop to it. I read my horoscope online now."

"Way to go! Let me know what you discover around

the corner," Ramya says, as she rises from her chair, and picks up her car keys and cellphone.

While returning from Wilma's house, Ramya stops at the Indian grocery shop. It has an unwelcoming aspect: The front door is narrow, and handwritten flyers are stuck on the glass. There are stacks of free south Asian newspapers lying about. At the door, she selects a shopping basket with castors and drags it behind her. Besides groceries and produce, the shop sells everything remotely connected with India: telephone cards, Indian-style brooms, carom boards, mehndi paste, talcum powder, pain balms, and even Eno fruit salts, the white powder that hisses and bubbles in a glass of water, which her grandmother used to take if she thought she was suffering from a bout of acidity.

Of course, she has neglected to bring her shopping list. Jogging her memory, she coasts along each aisle picking up what she thinks she needs, like a street vacuum cleaner that sucks up roadside refuse. She selects Indian vegetables like karela and small round eggplants, and ready-made chapattis. She opts for apples and pears since it isn't the season for mangoes, and picks up yoghurt in the dairy section, not forgetting the homo milk.

She would've preferred to buy fruits and milk products at a mainstream grocer like Food Basics or Freshco because they're cheaper there, but today, she's in no mood to visit yet another shop. To hell with cost-cutting! As it is she feels edgy and impatient as she shuffles about in the dark, smelly, aisles. She wants to get back home as soon as she can. Even this small outing makes her fell exhausted and — she doesn't know why — a little depressed.

When will she learn to start buying cheaper substitutes and save money? Business magazines call it "down-trading," and Wilma does it like a pro, without even knowing the word for it. She should follow in her good friend's footsteps, if she wants to survive. She makes up her mind to buy unbranded bathroom tissue instead of Charmin the next time she visits the supermarket. That'll be a good a start.

———

Even without her best friend by her side, Ramya graduated from junior college with flying colours. It was Amma's unshakeable belief that Ramya's success was entirely due to Maunika's disappearance from her life. Ramya didn't feel Maunika's absence as much as she had feared; there were other friends, like the loyal and faithful Sujatha, who stood in, and even if none of them acquired the standing of a best friend, they weren't so demanding either.

But on the very first day of college, Ramya ran into Maunika. Ramya didn't recognize her at first. Maunika had cultivated a mod look—in her appearance and the way she carried herself. She had a pageboy haircut, and spoke in a fashionably slangy Hinglish, a hybrid of Hindi and English. Moreover, she'd rechristened herself Monica. It was her re-tailored clothes that gave her away.

When last heard of, her erstwhile best friend and her family were roughing it out in Kolkata, a metropolis nearly a thousand miles away. Ramya was more annoyed than surprised to discover that Maunika had returned to the city, and hadn't bothered to let her know. Agreed, she was living in another part of the town—her father had rented a house close to his new place of work, but couldn't she have given Ramya a call? If they didn't have a phone installed in their home (in the days of quotas, God knew how hard it was to get a connection), couldn't she have rung up from a public phone?

"Sorry, *yaar*! I wanted to give you a buzz, but I misplaced my address book when we moved back. *Kya karen?*"

Monica was in the science stream, and claimed airily that she was trying for a seat in a medical college. Ramya knew it was all bull; nonetheless she was amenable to having Monica back as her friend—though she wasn't sure how Amma, peering down from her heavenly vantage point, would perceive it.

Nizam's was a co-ed college, and Ramya felt both shy and diffident there; until then she'd attended girls-only institutions. And she'd heard such dreadful things about the college, mostly about its libertine reputation, from her relatives and friends. It would be nice to have an ally like Monica.

Monica didn't seem displeased at reconnecting with Ramya, but behaved as if befriending a backward girl like Ramya was one of the realities of life. Since their electives were different, Monica and Ramya could meet only during the lunch hour.

Every day it was Monica who would come over to the Arts section of the college to meet up with Ramya for lunch. Monica rarely brought a packed lunch from home. And not having money to buy herself something in the college canteen, she would've had to go without food had not Ramya in her generosity offered to share hers. Ramya made a point to bring extra food every day, just in case. They ate their lunch together, sitting down on a grassy patch under a shady tree — the college was dotted with such agreeable spots. Monica usually sat cross-legged, even if she was wearing a skirt, whereas Ramya, dressed in a salwar-kameez, would sit down with her legs modestly fold back to one side.

When Ramya wanted to eat in the college canteen or go to Mohini, a restaurant nearby, just for a change, she would always invite Monica to accompany her. Monica came along without any qualms, pretending she was doing it just to humour Ramya. Though it was Ramya who bankrolled their lunches, Monica always had the gumption, when the waiter appeared with the salver which had the invoice and a handful of mouth-freshening fennel seeds, to make jokes like: "Now, who'd like to play 'foot-bill'?"

Over lunch, whether it was in the canteen or the restaurant or on the grassy patch, they would share gossip about college and common friends.

"What's that *chokri* — whatshername — Sujatha doing now?" Monica asked.

"She's doing Electrical Engineering in Osmania," Ramya said.

"Quite a brainy girl, *n'est-ce pas?*" Monica sometimes abandoned Hinglish for French which she took as her second language in the college. She was forever casting bits of French about like confetti, for some kind of effect. Ramya had opted for German, partly because her uncle, whom she'd seen only once in her life, lived in Dusseldorf, but mostly because she'd hoped, in her youthful naïveté, that she would be able to read Goethe and Rilke in the original.

Or Monica would say: "Everyone says that you and Prahalad are an item, *sacch hai kya?*" She would add a snigger, like a filler word.

"Nothing of the sort!" Ramya said hotly. There was a senior named Prahalad who was stalking her, and Ramya had confided in Monica. But telling Monica was as good as announcing it over the mic in the Salarjung Hall, the college's assembly room.

Six months into college, Ramya began to detect a change in Monica. At first, she couldn't exactly place a finger on what had altered. It was partly to do with Monica's clothes. Most of the girl-students wore saris, or its shorthand version, the half-sari, or shalwar kameez. A few fashionable girls wore tops with skirts or jeans. But it was always some full-length garment, at least something that fell well below their knees. But Monica's clothes had something bold about them — sleeveless tops with or without plunging neck lines. And, surprise of surprises, her clothes ceased to look like renovated hand-me-downs.

Almost at the same time, there was a change in her behaviour towards Ramya: Sometimes she got unnecessarily impatient or showed irritation with no justifiable cause. It was as if Ramya's very presence grated on her nerves. Then there were occasions when she tried to shake off Ramya's company all together.

Ramya couldn't comprehend Monica's conduct. She felt puzzled at first, and then hurt — it wasn't a nice feeling to realize that you'd been used as a doormat. One fine day Ramya decided enough was enough and stopped seeing Monica. It wasn't such a difficult thing to do: they didn't have any common subjects, and the imposing Arts Building and the modern shapeless Science Block stood far apart, aloof from each other. The students from either stream didn't even have to use the same gates to enter and exit from the spacious grounds of the college.

A few months passed before everything began to fall into place. While Monica's experiments with clothes turned bolder and bolder, it became common knowledge that she was going steady with a fellow-student named Amar.

Ramya remembered seeing him, in the early days of the first term. A light skinned, plumpish young man of medium height, he was doing BSc. He wore clothes that were shiny and seemingly expensive but not necessarily stylish. His hair was always groomed with loads of sweet-scented hair oil and a fine-toothed comb. Dandruff, the size and colour of snowflakes, could be seen trapped in his hair.

Even in those days, it was a well-known fact that he was not only married but had a toddler son (chubby and fair, a carbon copy of his father, but too young to have dandruff). It was also equally well known that he had tons of money. He was one of the few students who came to the college in his own car. He would park his Premier Padmini—an authorized Indian clone of the Italian Fiat—under a shady tree. The snow-white car was pimped up to be a rich man's conveyance: tinted windows, large, shiny hubcaps, and a long radio antenna that arced back like a bow. Amar and his male friends would hang around the car in their free time, chatting and listening to Hindi film songs on the stereo.

The car became a standard fixture under that tree, with all its doors open and music flooding out. But at some point in the month of March, when the final exams were just around the corner, it was no longer seen at its habitual haunt. All the hangers-on too had melted away. On a couple of occasions, Ramya spotted the car sitting sedately in the designated parking area opposite the Salarjung Hall. It gave Ramya cause to wonder, but she put it out of her mind.

In the weeks that followed, whenever she caught sight of the car, it always had Amar at the wheel and Monica in the passenger seat. Just a few days before exams, Monica and Amar stopped coming to the college altogether. Nobody seemed to know the reason. Surely it couldn't be that they were cramming for the final exams?

Soon there was a rumour circulating in the college that Amar had eloped with Monica, deserting his family.

Years later, when Ramya was working as a junior executive in a pharmaceutical firm in Hyderabad, she ran into Monica again. She was seated in the office foyer with a binder on her lap. Clearly, she'd come for an interview. From the way she was dressed — no printed silk sari or a business suit, it was obvious that it was only for a junior position. She wasn't sporting anything unorthodox or daring either, just a sober shalwar kameez that had seen better days. Her dusty feet were stuffed into a scuffed pair of Bata sandals. Instead of eye shadow, she had bags under her eyes. She looked tired and careworn.

Ramya greeted her and started a conversation. Monica's response was polite but unenthusiastic. After Ramya returned to her desk, she decided to call the HR Manager and put in a word for Monica. But she came to know later that, the moment Ramya went back into the office, Monica got up and left the place without saying a word to the receptionist. She didn't attend the interview.

9

The First Kiss

Ramya brings in the mail which had been sitting in her mailbox from God knows when. There are stacks of offers from pizzerias, real estate agents and dentists. And there's an envelope from her ex-employer which fails to ignite any excitement. She has become incurious about the world around her, and she knows the envelope will bear no lifechanging news, though she's heard rumours about rehiring. The letter, when opened, professes concern for her well-being, and outlines the ways laid-off employees can upgrade their skills to cope with a rapidly changing world.

Skills, and rapidly changing world? If she recollects correctly, it was not *her* lack of skills that brought the company to such a pass. It was obvious to any sane onlooker that it was her employer's lack of skills in adapting to a rapidly changing business environment that brought misery upon its own and its employees' heads.

The company wants the out-of-job employees to meet

with consultants who will develop customized individual plans for their rehabilitation.

Back to school, says Ramya to herself. Come on, she's forty-nine going on fifty! Too late to learn or unlearn. Unbidden that mawkish song about a girl who's sixteen and going on seventeen from *The Sound of Music* floats into her head. Ramya was taken to the film by her school, and she'd watched, like the rest of her schoolmates, completely mesmerized.

But right now, Ramya cannot readily recollect any songs that celebrate her circumstance. Surely, there must be a song about a golden girl, even if only a gilded one?

At her age, Ramya doesn't see any need to enrol in a college. If a fifty-year-old needs to learn anything, it must be about retirement and estate planning. But why would Ramya want to know about wills, testaments and death duties? Who does she have to bequeath her fortunes? Besides, what legacy would she be leaving behind?

A wasted life, she sighs.

Later in the evening, Ramya gravitates to her sandal-wood chest. She espies a smuggled made-in-Japan Hero fountain pen. When she was growing up, all the attractive items were the ones which were smuggled into the country. There were places in Chennai like Burma Bazaar and Kasi Chetty Street where shop after shop would stock serried rows of breath-taking foreign stuff. You could buy openly if you had a gift for haggling and didn't mind the extortionate prices. The contraband goods were all so exquisitely packaged while, in comparison, Indian merchandise seemed sloppily produced and came in lack-lustre packaging. Generations grew up in India believing that the grass was always greener abroad.

The pen has a dark green softly contoured body wit
a gold cap that has the name 'Hero' etched on the clip.
Her father had a similar pen, but in ebony and gold, with
which he'd write out prescriptions, on a letter pad that
boasted a large R.

When she was very little she'd thought the R on the
prescription pad stood for Ramya — after all she was the
apple of her Daddy's eye. Later she discovered that the
letter with a cross bar on its right leg stood for the Latin
word *recipe*, and under which doctors wrote, in their il-
legible scrawl, directions on how to take the medication.

While playing doctor-doctor with an unwilling Barghest as the patient, and using all of Daddy's professional paraphernalia, she'd discovered that the plastic portion
of the pen had a magical quality: if you rubbed it vigorously it would turn into a magnet that could pick up
small bits of paper. Yes, at times, a pen is mightier than the
magician's wand, a realization which didn't fail to sink
into Ramya's impressionable mind.

The dark green and gold pen was given to her by a
good-looking young man, following the tradition of gallant males giving gifts to their lady-loves. Though it
wasn't deliberately intended, it was more of a phallic symbol than just a writing utensil. Prahalad, her senior in
Nizam College, was a jock, aware of his good looks, and
not averse to using them to further his designs. A prick if
ever there was one.

When she'd opted to join Nizam's, it was indeed a
bold step for a girl student who'd attended only gender-
segregated institutions until then. She'd lain awake many
a night wondering if it was a wise move. Since Amma had
passed on, she had to do all the worrying for herself.

Though Daddy always presumed that Ramya knew what was best for her, and usually had little or no objection to anything she chose to do, he had some reservations about the college she'd chosen.

"Are you sure about it, dear? People tell me that Women's College too is a very good."

"It's easier to get to Nizam's by bus than to Women's College. I can't expect you to drop me off and pick me up every day. According to Arati, Nizam's is a wonderful place."

"What would Arati know about colleges?"

Arati was a distant relation who'd discontinued her studies to get married to her maternal uncle. That was the local custom — a girl was expected to marry her maternal uncle, and only if a suitable one wasn't readily available, did the parents range out to look for other candidates. Anyways, Arati's marriage was a success in some respects at least: She and her husband/maternal uncle produced three children in as many years.

Many of Daddy's friends and relatives — busybodies masquerading as well wishers — expressed either puzzlement or concern, or downright outrage at Ramya's choice of college.

It scandalized Mr. Parmesan, Daddy's very close friend and a very learned man. (He spent at least ten hours a day reading the Great Books of the World by all sorts of authors, starting with Augustine and ending with Zola. He could afford to do so because his wife was a successful gynaecologist — nothing to sniff at in a country where millions are born every year.)

"Nizam College!" he'd spluttered. "It's... it's like a fleshpot of Egypt!" Noting Daddy hadn't understood a

word of what he was saying, Mr. Parmesan elucidated:
"The students there are very permissive. I wouldn't send
my daughter there."

Since Mr. Parmesan didn't have any children, let alone
a daughter, it was a moot point. Mr. Parmesan was too busy
perusing classics to take time to procreate. It was widely
believed that, had his wife worn a dust jacket instead of
a white coat over her sari, he'd have taken more interest
in his conjugal obligations.

Another friend, Mr. Radhakrishna, a bank manager,
said: "A new college for women has come up in Nehru-
nagar. It's called Kasturba. Maybe Ramya would like it
better there?"

Sharada-auntie, Daddy's colleague and a gastro-
enterologist, said: "Isn't Ramya interested in medicine? If
she wants to do 'arts', why does she have to go to Nizam
College? It's so far away. Why doesn't she join Arts &
Science College in Secunderabad? It's so much nearer and
perhaps just as good?" In her opinion, only a medical college merited a long trek.

There were suggestions aplenty. Though her father
was very suggestible and could easily be swayed, he wasn't
the sort to force his ideas on Ramya.

"I have a patient who teaches in the university, shall
we see what he has to say?"

They drove to the Osmania University campus. How
vast it was! God knows how many tens of square miles!
It had no compound wall, she noticed — it would cost a
fortune just to build one. When she wondered aloud
about the picturesquely situated building on top a hill,
Daddy said: "That's the library."

"What a lovely location for a library!"

Holy places were usually located on summits of hills. In a way a library was a very sacred place, the abode of Saraswati, the goddess of learning.

Daddy parked the car in the shadow of the magnificent Arts block, a jewel of Islamic architecture in India. They went into the cool exquisite building built of pinkish brown granite, climbing the two flights of stairs flanked by stone balustrades. The professor received them in his room which was shabby and smelled faintly of must. Books and papers were everywhere — strewn on the table, stuffed into and even on top of the cupboards. The Professor wore a dark-coloured suit and a pair of thick black-rimmed glasses. His bold yellow silk tie was askew at this throat.

He rang a bell, and an attendant appeared like a genie. The Professor ordered tea, sweeping aside Daddy's protests. The Professor and Daddy indulged in small talk, while Ramya looked around. There were a couple of framed certificates on the wall, and a photograph of a thin worried-looking young man in a mortarboard and a black robe, clutching a rolled-up diploma, as if it was his dearest possession. Perhaps it was. You had to look hard to find any resemblance to the stout middle-aged man with a pleasant smiling face who was seated in front of them and talking affably.

"The college has nothing to do with it," the professor said, dismissing all the negative comments they'd heard about the college with a wave of his hand. "It depends on the nature of the student. If he wants to wile away his time, it's a perfect place. If they're serious about learning, it is just as perfect a place. Just so you know, most of the toppers and successful professionals in the city have come from Nizam's."

Ramya had no doubt that the professor too had studied there. The attendant returned with a tray which bore three small china cups and saucers. The reddish Hyderabadi chai was a bit oversweet but piping hot and incredibly tasty.

"Are you interested in arts, paapa?" the professor asked, putting down his cup and turning to Ramya. "Nizam College has an excellent faculty. Their English and foreign languages departments are unmatched. They have very good lecturers in economics and political science, too. If you're interested in sports, they have many facilities. Though Nizam's is bang in the centre of the city, do you know how big their grounds are? They have both cricket and football fields."

The professor stopped and looked expectantly at Ramya. She felt tongue-tied in the presence of elders, more so stranger-elders. This was considered a comely attribute, and so her Daddy went to bat for her.

"Besides sports, Ramya is interested in quiz and elocution. She has won many prizes in her school."

"Is that so? Very good, they have all sorts of extracurricular activities like debating and dramatics. I'm sure they must have a quiz team too."

When they took leave, the professor said: "Your father is a very good doctor. He keeps me and my family in good health. I'm surprised you didn't want to become a doctor. But as a professor of sociology, I'm glad you chose humanities."

Ramya left for her new college on the opening day
with expectations tinged with nervousness. Instead of
sending her on her own by the Road Transport Cor-
poration bus, Daddy took the morning off to drop her
off at the college.

The college had old imposing buildings in a confused
yet charming mixture of colonial and Indo-Saracenic
styles. The almost rundown structures showed their age
and government's apathetic maintenance. Nonetheless, as
a college it had a casual and informal air, almost festive,
and promised to be a fun place. The students old and
new were wandering around free of any care or responsibility in the world.

As days passed, she learned that the students attended
classes only if they felt like it. At any given time, the college canteen would boast of more students than any classroom. Apart from the canteen, there were many vantage
points where groups of students congregated and talked
shop. When the bells rang to mark the start of classes,
bodies simply gravitated to the lecture halls with a kind
of insouciance.

Ramya quite liked the democratic idea of attending a
class only if it interested you. It was like voting with your
butt. She admired the staff who taught her subjects, especially English literature. They had a ready wit to counter
the rowdy elements. She wouldn't want to miss their class
for anything.

It was all very different from her idea of school; the
unfettered freedom that was thrust on her was dizzying
at first, without the guiderails of rigid rules and the
supervisory, all-seeing, Big-Sisterly eye. All this seem-

ingly convivial mixing of boys and girls was also a bit too much. When she spotted her long-lost friend Maunika during the lunch hour, she was delighted to discover someone she thought was a kindred spirit. Apart from showing an exaggerated amazement at reconnecting Ramya, Maunika, going by the name of Monica now, was cool and composed and looked very much at home in this large co-ed institution.

But, by and by Ramya got used to the place, and began to revel in its friendly, unstressful atmosphere. In her classes, she met many nice girls and young men with whom she wanted to be friends. She was surprised how informed and well read some of her college-mates were, despite playing hooky all the time. A few of them were so passionate about politics that Ramya wondered why any teenager would want to get so entangled in it, but when she came to know them better she had nothing but admiration for the purity of their zeal and commitment.

There were a few bad apples too, students who indulged in what was known as "eve-teasing": making cat-calls behind a girl's back or passing lewd comments within her earshot. While she felt uncomfortable with this at first, it was Ramya's opinion that such students, mostly boys, had personality issues, and she learned to ignore them. Her Daddy used to say: What cannot be cured has to be endured. Thus, spake the good doctor!

In the very first month of the academic year, the senior students hosted a party for the 'freshers', as the first-year students were known. At the party they served light snacks on flimsy paper plates, and tea and coffee in small glass tumblers. The real crowd-pleaser was a mock beauty

contest which seemed to evoke a great deal of merriment.
The awards, meant to poke fun at the freshers, went
mostly to girls: A student with spots on her face got the
Miss Clearasil award; a hirsute one the Missy Hairy Legs;
and a well-built girl, the ultimate title of Mister India.
Ramya had goose-bumps as the program progressed;
when it was finally over, like many other first-year girls,
she sighed with relief, glad that she hadn't been selected
for some belittling title or the other.

After that there was much music and dancing. Only
a handful of the newcomers were bold enough to dance
in full view of the college. Ramya sat with a group of her
classmates, watching. But Monica was on the dance-floor
having a whale of time as she flounced around with a
roly-poly senior Ramya didn't know. From time to time,
Monica looked in Ramya's direction, and bade her to
come on to the floor. A horrified Ramya shook her head
vigorously.

When the pair got tired they came over to Ramya's
group and sat down on the vacant chairs amidst them.
Monica seemed happy as a lark and was very voluble.
Sweat poured down the rotund face of her dance partner.
Soon another young man, ostensibly a senior, joined
them. "Hi Prahalad!" Monica's friend said.

"Hi Amar!" he said, his eyes scanning the group. The
gaze hovered briefly over Monica before moving on. It
paused over another girl before coming back to rest on
Ramya, as if for good. Ramya looked away quickly.

When the DJ — one of the seniors, enjoying the
chance to show off — changed the track to a song with a
fast tempo. Monica squealed: "My favourite number!"

"Let's dance," her friend said, rising from the metal folding-chair, which grunted back into shape.

"Would you care for a dance?" the man named Prahalad asked.

Ramya turned to say no curtly. But no words came out. She hadn't realized how good-looking he was, with clean cut features and light brown eyes, and a day's stubble giving him a rakish appeal. Yet she saw no reason to dance with a stranger just because he was handsome. Luckily for her, Monica tugged at her hand, saying: "Come along." Just to escape Prahalad's attention, Ramya got up and went along with Monica to the dance floor.

Once on the dance floor, Monica whirled away with her partner, cutting Ramya adrift. She stood alone in the middle of the floor like a gnomon of a sundial, not knowing what to do amid wildly gyrating bodies careening all around. Then out of nowhere Prahalad appeared, and taking her by hand, began to dance. Willy-nilly Ramya followed along, though she'd never danced to disco numbers in public before. Having been a student of one of India's classical dance traditions, she was able to imitate the steps of her college-mates, keeping perfect time to the number.

"Wow! You dance so well," Prahalad said. He had a gravelly voice, a little irritating to the ear, like a voice on the radio which is not tuned-in fully to the station.

"Thank you."

"Do you attend a lot of parties?"

"No. Why do you ask that?"

"Because of your dancing. You must have had a lot of practice."

"This is the first time I've stepped on to a dance floor."

"Really? You must be a natural then."

Ramya didn't want to tell him that she was trained in Kuchipudi. It could be off-putting to a student of a hip college! But here she was, not even one month since the college opened and openly dancing with a young man she'd only met minutes ago. She recalled Daddy's friend's remark about the fleshpots of Egypt. Inwardly, she shook her head and sighed—she didn't want her college life to be marred by an inane and abortive romance.

All through the dance, Prahalad kept plying her with questions: "Which high school did you go to? What's your favourite band? Who's your favourite author?" Even though Ramya was giving noncommittal, monosyllabic answers, he was persistent, like a policeman giving third degree treatment. When the song stopped, Ramya said, "Thank you," and left the dance floor. She had danced to one number only, but how long it had seemed!

Mercifully, Ramya didn't see Prahalad in the next few days. Later she ran into him a few times at different spots of the college. He tried to strike up a conversation, but Ramya discouraged him. They ended up merely acknowledging each other's presence with a nod. Afterwards, not even that. They reverted to being strangers—thankfully.

⁂

With the consultant's appointment looming, Ramya thinks that a modest makeover is in order. She drives to Short Cuts, her usual hairdresser located in a strip mall less than a kilometre from her home. It is run by a South

Korean woman who calls herself Tressa. The name is a little too apt; Ramya doesn't know if the hairdresser got the name by accident or design. Perhaps it started off as Theresa and got clipped to its present rendering by an association of ideas.

There are no customers waiting; the plastic chairs ranged along the walls are empty—no butts on seats, no bucks in the till. But it's not all that bad; Tressa's assistant Lolita is busy with another client seated on a swivel chair. No nymphet, Lolita is tall and heavy, more like a masseuse. Her scissors go clipitty-clip, her mouth yaketty-yak. The customer's eyes are closed, in Zen-like tranquillity, as if she has switched herself off from the concerns of the world. She has switched off from Lolita, that's for sure.

"Good Morning! How have you been?" Tressa asks. Lolita stops her juggernaut rush of chatter and gives Ramya a welcome smile. Ramya gets a warm reception wherever she goes—unlike many immigrants, she's not miserly when it comes to tipping.

"I need major renovations," Ramya says with a sigh, mussing her hair.

"It's a long time since you came here, eh?" Tressa says. Without further ado, she leads Ramya to a chair and, forcing her into it, trusses her up. She runs a comb through Ramya's knotty hair. Then she applies the dye—a natural black, no browns or blond highlights for Ramya—in generous swathes. Tressa, who could be as inveterate a talker as her colleague, speaks to Ramya guardedly, as if walking over a minefield. She knows Ramya has recently lost her job.

"Have you read any good books lately?" Hairdressers

rarely talk about books. They like to enquire about family and vacations. But from past conversations, Tressa has learned that Ramya likes to read. Even a penniless person can borrow a book gratis from a public library.

"Nothing interesting, really," Ramya says, remembering the stack of unread books she needs to return to the library. As for Tressa, once upon a time she used to read a tacky local newspaper in Korean which one could pick up for free outside Korean restaurants. As decades have passed since her arrival in Canada, she's lost interest in the humdrum events happening in the Orient. Nowadays the only reading she does is of junk mail advertising liquidation sales.

"Did you take your usual vacation in December?" Ramya asks. Tressa has acquired a taste for the Caribbean in the winter, like many Canadians. Mexico, Cuba, Dominican Republic. She's seen them all, courtesy cheap chartered flights.

"We didn't go anywhere last year. We spent a quiet Christmas with family," Tressa says. "You could call it a staycation." Despite her name, Ramya would have expected Tressa to be a Buddhist, but many immigrants to Canada from the Far East have taken to Roman Catholicism. "We couldn't afford to travel last year. Business has been bad. People now only want the cheapest haircuts. I guess it's the economy."

Tressa becomes suddenly quiet, as if she's bitten her tongue. Put her foot in her mouth, more likely. Lolita too falls silent, maybe in sympathy.

In a deathly hush that reminds Ramya of Remembrance Day, Tressa plucks out excess facial hair from

around Ramya's eyebrows, while waiting for the hair dye
to sink in. She then massages Ramya's face, and says,
breaking the silent spell: "It'll bring out some colour in
your cheeks." After what seems like ages to Ramya, whose
patience and fortitude have taken a serious beating of
late, her tresses are trimmed, faithfully in a fashion stipu-
lated by her years ago.

When at last it is done, Tressa says, marvelling at her
own handiwork: "You look gorgeous!"

"You got to be kidding," Ramya says, glancing first
at herself in the mirror in the front and then her back in
the mirror Tressa was holding, like a beaming lottery-
winner holding an enlarged cheque to the press. Ramya
makes a moue. Her hair looks stiff, as if it has been painted over. And while there's a smidgeon of sheen on her
face, it looks — yes — *old*. But she concedes, grudgingly:
"I don't look half as bad as I did when I walked in. Thank
you, Tressa."

She may not have won a lottery, at least she won't
look a loser to the consultant.

In the middle of September, the drama club in the college
put up a poster announcing the production of a play. It
was a call for auditions. They were staging *A Streetcar
Named Desire*, with the director, a final year student of
English Literature, bowdlerizing the script to suit the prud-
ish expectations of an educational institution in India.

Ramya attended the audition, and to her utter surprise was selected for the role of Blanche. It was a coup

of sorts as she was a rank newcomer, and it set a lot of
tongues wagging. There were to be two months of rehearsals before the performance on the last day of college in
advance of Christmas and New Year holidays.

Rajnish, the director, was a gangling, energetic man
with a pronounced Adam's apple, but his eyes shone with
a fiery passion. The entire cast met for practice every evening after classes. They'd rehearse in the Salarjung Hall or
the open-air stage behind the Languages building. Soon,
much to Ramya's discomfort, Prahalad also began to drop
by. Though he hadn't got a part (something to do with
the gruffness of his voice perhaps), he was allowed to come
to the rehearsal apparently as an understudy, but actually
as a dogsbody to run errands for the cast. The latter role
he did so effectively that it made him quite popular. Soon
he was as much a permanent fixture as the rest of the
props for the play. Ramya quite forgot that he'd been trying to hit on her. She even stopped noticing that Prahalad
was never too far away from her.

During the rehearsals they'd order tea and coffee from
the canteen. A boy came with a large aluminum kettle and
a stack of glasses. But every now and then after the day's
practice, they headed to a nearby restaurant for a bite.
They'd go on scooters or motorcycles, or occasionally
squeeze into a car. One day she found herself going with
Prahalad, sitting on the pillion of his Vespa. Prahalad was
on his best behaviour, to Ramya's relief. She'd half-expected him to try his hanky-panky stuff on her. After that
she relaxed and lowered her guard.

A week later, Prahalad approached her during a break
in the rehearsal. She was seated on a wickerwork chair

drinking the oversweet tea. She was alone, as her co-actors had gone to the loo or to have a quick puff outside.

"Would you like to come to a film with me tomorrow?"

It was most unexpected. Ramya didn't want to seem primitive; after joining the college drama troupe, in her own estimation she'd gone up a notch or two on the scale of sophistication. What the hell, she was an actress now! It would be churlish to decline ...

∽────────∾

Ramya gets into her car to drive down to the consultant's office downtown. How generous of the company to pay for such rehabilitative services. Personally, Ramya would've preferred if the company had shown its generosity by not throwing them under the bus.

The drive is bad, atrociously so. It snowed in the wee hours of the morning, and the traffic is exasperatingly slow. A snowplough has haphazardly cleared the road, leaving trails of snow on the surface and mounds of dirty snow either side. A salter has scattered granules of salt on the road, over which the car tires roll, sounding as if they're gnashing their teeth.

The building where the consultants have their office looks as if it's made entirely of bottle-green glass. The office is on the 14th floor. Actually, the 13th but re-designated to appease the superstitious. She's been asked to bring two copies of her résumé.

She along with fourteen other laid-off co-workers, some of whom she didn't know, are shepherded into a small conference room. A director of the company gives an introductory talk about the current economic situation, the job market and the need for upgrading one's skills.

For the next two weeks, they're required to come three days a week. During those times, first they'd review their résumés, and provide tips to improve them. Right from the day Ramya landed in Canada years and years ago, she's been writing and rewriting her résumé. If she'd directed all that effort and energy towards creative writing, she may well have written a book or two by now. Become a bestseller to boot, and would be in no bind to look for a measly job again. Ramya sighs — talk about wishful thinking! From what she's heard, you could count on your fingers the number of authors in Canada who earn a living exclusively from writing.

In the third week, the laid-off employees will be taught the powers of cold calling — the greatest strategy invented by man, the failsafe jimmy which would unlock all the doors of the hidden job market.

To Ramya it all sounds like hogwash. Unbelievable really, like spiels for weight loss pills on TV shopping channels she finds herself watching involuntarily.

At first Ramya wanted to tell her father about the date with Prahalad. It was nothing serious, just a harmless outing, so she thought better of it. But she didn't like the unsavoury feeling she had of not taking her Daddy into confidence.

On the day of their date, Ramya and Prahalad skipped their respective afternoon classes, and went to Kamat's in

Basheerbagh for a quick bite. Ramya ordered a masala
dosa, a folded pancake stuffed with sautéed potatoes,
while Prahalad asked for a thali, a platter which came with
a full spread of a traditional south Indian meal. Ramya
toyed with the food as a host of butterflies swarmed in her
stomach.

"Aren't you liking the dosa?" Prahalad asked.

"No, it's good." Ramya forced herself to peck at the dosa.

In the middle of the lunch, Prahalad whisked out the
Hero pen and gave it to Ramya. She didn't understand
why he'd do that. Did he want her autograph? The play
was a good two weeks away from being staged. What guarantee was there that it would be a success and that she'd
become a star overnight?

But no typical autograph book, small and velour-
bound, emerged. Seeing the look of incomprehension on her
face, Prahalad said: "It's for you. A gift from me." His voice
sounded extremely gravelly, like two jostling boulders.

"Oh," Ramya said. Not that she was ungrateful, it was
just at that instant that the gift of the used purple lipstick
came to her mind. That exchange too had taken place in
a restaurant.

"You don't look too happy."

"Oh, no! I'm quite pleased. It's only that my stomach
feels a bit queasy."

"Is the date making you nervous?"

Before she could think of a reply, the waiter brought
the bill on a small stainless-steel salver. Ramya began to
fossick in her handbag for her wallet, when Prahalad
said: "This is my treat."

He paid the bill, and tipped the waiter generously. He

popped a handful of sugar-coated multicoloured fennel seeds, which came on the salver along with the receipt, into his mouth. Outside, he was able to start his Vespa only after six unsuccessful attempts, and not before tilting his scooter first this way and then that way to get the petrol flowing. They drove to Skyline cinema not too far from the restaurant. Prahalad bought tickets for the balcony, the most expensive but least crowded section of the cinema hall.

When they entered, the hall was in darkness, with a series of advertisement slides being projected on the screen. An usher popped up like a spectre, with a torch in his hand. He peered at the seat numbers on the tickets and then led them to their row. Standing in the aisle like a lighthouse, he trained the beam of his torch on their allotted chairs. Prahalad and Ramya wended their way, rubbing their shins against the knees of the people already seated.

After the slides came the commercials for detergent and cold remedies, their trademark jingles loudly bouncing off the theatre walls. This was followed by a mandatory government newsreel, a black and white short about a dam being constructed in some remote part of India. A sepulchral voice-over, sounding like a prophet of doom, described the notable and proud achievement. A good twenty minutes later the actual feature film started. Ramya, who can't recall the title of the film, remembers that it featured the superstar Amitabh Bachchan, looking very angry all through.

Ramya was watching the film with concentration when Prahalad suddenly took her hand. She was reminded of bangle sellers for some reason—they were the only men who routinely take a woman's hand, and did so only to slide the fragile glass bangles over their knuckles. Ramya felt icky all over and tried to wriggle her hand out of Prahalad's grip, even as she was steadfastly focusing her eyes on the screen. But he pulled at her hand roughly and put it on his crotch. She gave a gasp, and turned her head towards him. Somebody in the row behind them said: "Ssh!"

Prahalad leaned forward and tried to plant a firm kiss on her lips—because of the darkness, he missed his mark slightly, and his lips fell heavily on the corner of her mouth, almost bruising her. Ramya felt as if she'd been boxed on her jaw.

Prahalad's breath smelled of cigarettes, spicy food, and the recently ingested fennel seeds. To add to it all in the background there was a strong whiff of halitosis. (Ramya was a doctor's daughter and knew her diseases: A for Angina, B for Beriberi, C for Coryza …)

Her hand, firmly in Prahalad's grip, felt something like a tube of toothpaste on one side of his lap. Full-bodied, but still soft.

As Prahalad leaned towards her she could feel his warm foetid breath on her cheeks. He whispered into her ear in Urdu: "*Mereko garam hone ke liye zara time lagta.* It takes time for me to get excited."

Ramya's stomach retched and vomit rose to her mouth and then shot out. Prahalad recoiled as if stung. He got up and scrambled out of the hall, wiping his face with his palm. Ramya sat alone for some time unable to decide what to do. She rooted in her handbag for her handkerchief, and after wiping her mouth, she too got up and left the hall. She had to go to the ladies to wash her mouth. The washroom was smelly and the washbasin none too clean.

Prahalad was waiting for her in the foyer. They walked out of the theatre without saying a word to each other. It took an age for the grumbling parking attendant to extricate Prahalad's scooter from the tightly jammed row of two wheelers.

"Where should I drop you?" Prahalad asked, when they were on the road.

"At the bus-stop."

Arriving at her house seated behind a male classmate on a two-wheeler was an image neither of them could visualize.

"What about the drama practice?" Prahalad said.

"I'll give it a miss today. Please tell Rajnish that I'm not feeling well."

That was the last time they spoke to each other. Though they ran into each other during drama practice, they kept a frigid distance.

❧────────❧

A meeting with someone described as a Job Developer has been scheduled by the consultants. Ramya is given a folder to review. It lists all the relevant courses which the jobless could take to make themselves competitive in the job market. She and the Job Developer are to go into a huddle to decide on what courses to apply for.

On the night before the meeting, Ramya opens the file, and her eyes skim over the contents. A tsunami of ennui overcomes her. "I've no appetite for homework at my age," she tells herself and tosses away the file. A single glance was enough for her to realize that it's all poppy-cock — just another ruse for the consultants and the course providers to extract money out of the plight of people like her.

Having nothing better to do, she takes the topmost from a pile of unread books. She may as well read some-thing which she might enjoy rather than the folder on retraining. It's a book she bought for a dollar in the local library from a stack of unread, discarded or donated books which the library hopes to sell to raise money. The book was written by a slew of eminent British detective story-writers of the Golden Age, each one writing a chapter. She'd read and enjoyed the works of many of these writers like Agatha Christie and Dorothy Sayers when she was a teenager. She'd bought their books at AA Hussain on Abid's, or borrowed them from the British Library on the Secretariat Road.

The book promised to be most fascinating but all the fuss about time-tables and tide-tables left her a bit con-founded. She turns to the page where she inserted the bookmark — an old Walmart receipt — and begins to read, and immediately starts to feel better. Reading these writers is like meeting old friends again, tide-tables or time-tables notwithstanding ...

Ramya's amatory troubles did not end with Prahalad.

It wasn't just Rajnish's eyes which had fiery passion. Apparently, his loins too had it in good measure. The director of the play couldn't keep his paws off Ramya. She came to know later that he did so with all the leading ladies, or any female actor for that matter.

"Turn your face to the left, let the footlights shine on you. You're so beautiful, why hide your beauty?" he'd say, taking her by the shoulder and turning her. Then his hand would slide down her back, and rest briefly over her backside.

Luckily, he had a steady named Alka. She was the previous year's leading lady, playing the courtesan Vasantasena in the English adaptation of the ancient Sanskrit play called *Mricchakatika, The Toy Clay Cart*. Alka would often show up at the rehearsals for *Streetcar* though she'd graduated the previous year. Extremely jealous and very temperamental, she was apt to create scenes at the drop of a hat. She regarded Ramya as competition, and was cold and unfriendly towards her. Ramya didn't care; as long as Alka was around, Rajnish was on good behaviour and kept his restless hands to himself.

By the time the play was finally staged, Ramya was fed up. Though the play lacked the professional touch, the audience uninured to good theatre enjoyed it. Her acting was much appreciated, but it meant nothing to Ramya. She was glad to put her only foray into showbiz behind her, once and for all.

～·────·～

She's waiting in a long queue to take a left turn. Though the line-up is getting shorter, it's only at snail's pace. A smoky haze hangs over the city. The traffic lights look like jewels stuck in the gossamer fabric of the fog: rubies, emeralds and amber.

There's a silver Jaguar, just ahead. It's crouched low, waiting for the cue to lunge forward. When she was young, Ramya had wondered what it would be like to own a Jaguar. One of Daddy's close friends who lived in the Banjara Hills in Hyderabad owned a chocolate-brown one, the small figurine of the leaping animal on its hood.

"It's best if I give up such ambitions," Ramya tells herself. "Jaguar's not for the jobless."

Despite the best efforts of the consultant, Ramya is convinced that she won't land a job anytime soon. Would all the training and retraining in the world make a potential employer hire her? She had nothing going for her — her age, her credentials, her skin colour, and her accent are all wrong.

"Shit! I don't want to be mired in negativity," Ramya tells herself aloud. It's bad enough that the day itself is so depressing in its overarching greyness. She doesn't want to worsen her mood by dwelling on an uncertain future.

Ramya makes a conscious attempt to think of something nice, something pleasant ...

If her favourite detective storywriters could be described in terms of car brands what would they be? There was absolutely no doubt about the Jaguar — it was Dame Ngaio Marsh, classy and stylish. Dorothy Sayers would be a Daimler, undeniably. Sir Arthur Conan Doyle, a Rolls Royce Silver Shadow. Dame Agatha Christie, for sheer numbers, the bestselling Beetle, albeit a gold-plated one. Christiana Brand would be the nifty Mini Cooper. Margery Allingham — this was difficult, she couldn't think of a suitable brand right now, something on the lines of an Aston Martin or an Alfa Romeo. Josephine Tey, the striking but short-lived gull-winged De Lorean, a car like no other. Gladys Mitchel, naturally (or supernaturally) a Triumph Spitfire. Georges Simenon, a Citroën for sure, classic and yet pathbreaking. As for the American writers of hardboiled fiction ... Hammett a Thunderbird, painted black all over, and gem encrusted. Raymond Chandler a Dodge Charger, revving down his mean streets. Ross Macdonald? A zebra-striped hearse, most definitely, thinks Ramya, laughing at her own joke.

It's with a more positive frame of mind that she goes to the appointment. The cool and unbusy receptionist who is surreptitiously biting into her delayed breakfast asks Ramya to take a seat, and immediately picks up the telephone and mumbles into it. After setting down the receiver she tells Ramya, gulping down the remnants in her mouth: "Jack will be here in a moment."

Ramya finds herself involuntarily taking stock of the room — the heavy table lamp on an end table, the clutch of leather chairs, and the coffee table with a folded newspaper, and company brochures.

A couple of minutes later, Jack strides into the reception with a smile and an extended hand. He is in his forties and has the bluest of blue eyes she's ever seen. He looks — what was the word? — ripped, and doesn't have a pot belly like most North American men. He gives Ramya's limp hand an extra squeeze before releasing it. He leads Ramya to his box of a room, and once she enters it, shuts the door.

"Keeping yourself busy?"

An opening gambit to make her feel comfortable; but

it only reminds Ramya of the idle hours ticking away unprofitably. He keeps taking sneaking glances at her file even as he's talking to her.

"What does your typical day look like?"

Ramya paints a verbal picture of her daily activities in the days following her lay off: buying groceries, going for walks, visiting the library ... but it peters away like a fading melody, seeing Jack's apparent noninterest.

"Go on, I'm listening," he says looking up.

"I like to read."

"That's good ...what kind of books do you read?"

"Fiction, mostly. I wish I had an appetite for self-improving books."

"They're not for everybody. Any particular book you liked?"

"I'm reading a book called *The Floating Admiral*. I find it very interesting."

"Is it about naval warfare? My grandfather was in the Royal Navy ... He saw action in the Scapa Flow ..."

"How interesting!" But Ramya sighs inwardly. For a wannabe writer her vocabulary seems extremely limited. She could've at least said: "Amazing!" Or even: "Awesome!"

"... I see you are a graduate with a post-graduate degree in management ... oh, but that was in ... Hide, hide ..."

"Hyderabad in India."

"And in Canada you'd been working for eight years as a clerk in procurement."

"Yes."

"That's a very specialized field. While the job opportunities aren't many, as you know the manufacturing industry has been on the decline in Ontario ... What are your thoughts on relocating? There may be openings in Alberta."

"Certainly not!" Alberta, of all places! He may as well have asked her to return to Prakash!

"That's the most passionate refusal I've ever heard. I hope I've not touched a raw nerve."

"It's too much of a hassle, selling my house and transplanting myself in a strange place. Not at my age."

"Come on, you're not old at all, and there's no mandatory retirement age in most of the provinces. However, I understand moving may not be an option for everyone ... It's my considered opinion that it would be useful if you could upgrade your computer skills."

"I've learned all there's to learn in MS Word, Excel, Access ... you name it."

"A refresher course will enhance your résumé, and make it attractive to your potential employers."

"I doubt it. Honestly, I don't want to waste my time and my company's ... I mean my ex-company's resources." Too many exes in my life, Ramya says to herself.

"I'm afraid we have very few options. But do you have anything in mind?"

"In fact, I do. How about something like the creative writing program at Humber School for Writers?"

Jack gives a small chuckle which sounds like a car's starter on a cold day. "That's quite out of the question. At best we could consider a technical writing course or a re-port-writing course in a community college. But then we'll have to assess the suitability to your particular situation —whether it would lead to better employability or not."

"Please do. My heart is set on a writing course."

"The one Humber offers must cost a packet."

"Only workers are cheap, everything else in Canada is expensive. Like the useless computer courses you want me to take ..."

"Well, I'll look into your request, but no guarantees. I hope you don't mind if I'm frank with you."

"Not in the least. If I may speak in the same vein—please don't put me through some boring and useless personal development course. I'd rather stay unemployed."

"Being unemployed has its own charm, I guess," he says.

When the interview is over, he stands up and extends his hand.

Ramya artfully avoids taking it by picking up her belongings—a pen and a black leather folder—from the table. But Jack is persistent; he still has his hand poised in mid-air. Like a servant's hand in India seeking baksheesh.

She takes his hand reluctantly. He gives it a squeeze, a telling squeeze, and says: "Let's keep in touch." He seems to have liked his baksheesh.

"Aren't we doing it right now?" Ramya almost says it aloud.

When Ramya's car glides up the ramp from the underground parking, it's already dark. It's beginning to snow, the flakes falling gently like jasmine petals.

⚮━━━━⚮

There were jasmine trailers strung around the cot, Ramya's and Prakash's connubial bed, and rose petals strewn on the lily-white sheets. The petals looked like big drops of virginal blood.

The first night, how nervous she was. Her first kiss had been a disaster. And for the remaining years in college she'd carefully kept herself out of any romantic entanglements.

She'd lost faith in the chivalry of men. They all wanted to have a good time—with no encumbrances, no responsibilities. They wanted a boundless world where there were no asterisks directing you to the rules and conditions in fine print.

She felt shy, not having any practical knowledge of sex, other than hearsay or what she read in books. Prakash was also shy—just shy of being completely drunk. He'd loaded himself with smuggled Scotch, a gift from his colleagues. Maybe he too was nervous, though he must've had more practical knowledge of sex. Men always do—in matters of car repairs and sex, if not anything else. She hadn't known then that he was married.

Prakash offered her a drink. There was a wine bottle and a couple of glasses on the bedside table. She shook her head. He suddenly switched off the light and was all over her—for a moment she thought he was wrestling with her. In violent jerks, he removed his clothes, and proceeded to disrobe her. Pulling out a sari, and the petticoat guarding her chastity, is a cumbersome job for the impatient. So he pushed her back on the pillow, rolled up her sari and petticoat, which were all askew by then, and spread her legs apart. He tried to dive-bomb into her. When he failed to hit the target, he made her take his member in her hand to insert it. It felt much harder than a tube of toothpaste. More like a fresh field cucumber.

Prakash's mouth clamped on hers; it was wet and slobbering, and smelled of whisky and cigarettes. When the expected moment of searing pain came, she wanted to scream, but Prakash bit her lips.

10

Maid of Dishonour

Ramya takes out a potentially hazardous item from her casket, a small bottle with the alpha numerals 'Tik 20' printed on the label. The printing looks coarse and the yellowing label has turned stiff and has begun to peel. Tik 20 is a commonly used pesticide for bed bugs in India. Though Ramya can recall the events associated with the bottle, she's unable to fathom why she bothered to secrete it in her box. Did seeing so many people trying to grab the vial make it covetable?

Newspapers and news channels in Toronto have been agog with stories about bed bug infestations in condos and hotels. Ramya finds it difficult to believe that bed bugs should be a problem in an OECD country like Canada. But Canada being a nation of immigrants, the pest must've entered as a stowaway, hiding in personal baggage. Undeclared by passengers, unseen by border officials. Like immigrants' dreams and aspirations.

Ramya picks up the bottle again. It's full to the brim.

Could its contents be effective after all these years? It's a pity that the only token she has of the many maids and cooks who worked in her father's household is a small bottle of insecticide.

There's no gainsaying the important role played by servants in their household. A rich and successful professional like Daddy in those days needed a retinue of servitors to keep the homestead going — a cook, a night watchman, gardeners, and sundry maids. And what with Mummy being so eccentric, the cook and the maids had to step in to take care of Ramya, each in her own way, however crude, ignorant and illiterate. Surrogate mothers they were to Ramya, though different from the kind of surrogacy talked about now. Their love was alloyed with a trace of pity, but it was unstintingly showered upon Ramya, a poor waif of a child. Poor, only metaphorically. Poor in terms of maternal love and care. Ramya felt in her heart that she was forever in debt to the servants. A debt she'd never be able to repay.

In an age before machines usurped the work of maids, her father needed the proverbial seven to keep the house in order, often requiring more than just mops. Brooms, rakes, and pope's head, being other likely implements.

Ramya looks around her room. It's far from ship-shape: There are newspapers and mugs scattered about. The sofa cushions are all out of kilter. Ramya sighs; she's neglected to care for her home. Never house proud, hitherto she had at least gone through the motions of trying to keep her immediate surroundings tidy and clean. But in recent months her housekeeping has gone downhill. Of late she has little enthusiasm for anything in life. A feeling of languor envelopes her like a shroud.

Ramya's very much aware that cleaning has a therapeutic effect on the mind. The entire house needs a good once-over with a Hoover, and her laundry basket is so full that there's a danger she'll run out of clean clothes to wear.

Spring cleaning. That could be the ticket to her well-being. Ramya resolves to dive into a marathon session of cleaning and washing. She hopes to emerge with healthy mind and healthy body into the salubrious surroundings worthy of a doctor's daughter. After all, when she was a young and impressionable student in a convent school, she was taught that cleanliness was next to godliness.

She separates her unwashed clothes into white and coloured heaps, as if she's an uncompromising segregationist. She loads the washing machine with white clothes and tosses in a Tide pod, like throwing a coin into a sacred river. She calls the enormous twin washer and drier Rajaiah and Ramuloo — the father and son duo who laundered unwieldy stuff like bed sheets, quilts and curtains. They'd turn up on a Sunday morning, on their bicycles, with a stack of freshly laundered linen, and take back a huge bundle of soiled stuff. First, was the elaborate ritual of counting the cleaned linen, which would be checked off in a notebook with the word Laundry written on its cover. This job was done by Amma or the cook (a self-appointed caretaker, as Mummy was absolutely useless in such matters). If there was any discrepancy, a war would break out. Accusations and counter accusations would fly like mortar shells. Once peace was established again, the number of dirty clothes would then be entered in the notebook under each heading — cotton saris, bed sheets, pillowcases, curtains ...

When the washing machine starts to fill with water (sounding much like Rajaiah's disgruntled mumblings), Ramya brings out her red Dirt Devil upright, which she affectionately calls her Sanna Lakshmi. She starts the machine and drags it over the area rug in the living room. After going over the rug, she resets the head height before taking on the hardwood floor. As the weeks' accumulation of dust vanishes into the vacuum, the floors begin to lose their blurred look, like a scene brought back into sharp focus in a camera's viewfinder ...

⌒───────⌒

Ramya grew up in an age when Time sauntered by at a leisurely pace. It was common for people of Hyderabad in those days to live in villas which would have a lawn (even if bedraggled) in front, and a fountain (often malfunctioning) in the middle of the lawn. It was understandable that such establishments required a lot of extra help. This was before mini apartment buildings mushroomed everywhere, like a blight on the landscape of the city. People started living in what are called flats, and because of the reduced size of homes and families only part-time maids and cooks were needed.

In days gone by, it was a tradition for maids to assume the professional name Lakshmi (a *nom de broom*, to coin a phrase), whatever their given name. Lakshmi was the Hindu goddess of wealth, and by calling themselves after her, they implied that they brought good fortune to the homes where they were employed.

Ramya believes the English word "luck" is probably

derived from a version of the goddess's name — Lakmi or just plain Lakki. (The French turned it into Lakmé — talk about chic!) Perhaps the wandering gypsies, the most persistent migrants ever on the earth, had imported the word from India centuries ago.

Since there were many Lakshmis around, it was common to give them a prefix to differentiate between them: Sanna Lakshmi meant thin Lakshmi, Potti Lakshmi meant short Lakshmi, Dobba Lakshmi meant plump Lakshmi and so on.

There was such a large turnover of servants that even Ramya couldn't recall the names and faces of some of them. The maids had the habit of leaving just like that, without giving any notice. They left because they'd found a better job, or got married, or somebody gave birth, or somebody died. Sometimes they went back to their villages because of good rains, or sometimes if there were no rains at all. It was as if the servants lived on another planet where different rules applied. They didn't live in constant terror of losing their jobs, and gave more importance to life events.

Ramya wishes she had their insouciant attitude. But no, she has an Indian middle-class mindset, where the importance of employment and paycheques — such cherished objects! — is indelibly ingrained. No work, no money ... So everything leads to the elephant in the room: *The EI forms are yet to be completed.*

Must she drop everything and start filling in the forms that very instant? Perish the thought!

While it's true that when Ramya looks back she has nothing but affection for their maids, not all of them

were likeable souls. There were bad ones too — the out-
liers. And liars.

But the most remarkable of them all, whether good
or bad, was Devamma. She was a sincere and hardworking young woman. Tall and well built, she could do a lot
of heavy work too, the kind of tasks that would usually
fall on Sailoo's shoulders. One day, one of Daddy's patients came to the house. He was a film producer. When
he was offered the customary chai, Devamma brought it
in gold-rimmed china, laden on a german silver tray. The
guest scrutinized Devamma from head to toe, as one
might inspect a cow at a cattle fair. Daddy was puzzled,
even disconcerted.

Later the producer rang up Daddy, and through him
offered Devamma a minor role in his upcoming film.
There was confusion, consternation, elation and jealousy
— in different quarters. Devamma was dark complex-
ioned, and in a colour conscious society, her looks went
unnoticed and much less admired. One needed the eyes
of a film producer to recognize her photogenic beauty.

Devamma changed her name to Devayani, and started shooting. Unfortunately, it wasn't her lot to have a
Cinderella moment. She appeared in only a couple of
scenes, the bulk of her shots was left behind on the cutting desk. The movie was a flop, so not many noticed the
new actress Devayani. The film producer too went bust.

Except for Daddy and Ramya, the world seemed
overjoyed at Devamma's debacle. It would've been too
much if a duckling of maid had become a swan of a star.
While she didn't become an overnight sensation, a few
odd roles did come her way. Daddy and Ramya made a

point to see each and every one of her films. But even
these stray roles petered away when films switched to
Eastman colour. Indian audiences, especially south Indian, wanted their heroines to have skin the colour of a
jasmine petal.

One day, years later, the newspapers broke the news
that Devayani had committed suicide, and in a bizarre
way. It was reported that she'd swallowed the diamonds
from her ring. The ring had been given to her by her
live-in partner, but he'd never acted on his promise to
divorce his wife and marry her.

"Amma, are diamonds poisonous?" Ramya asked.

"What a funny question! I don't know."

"Would you die if you ate diamonds?"

"What an expensive way to kill yourself! I've only
seen it happen in cinema—but why do you ask?"

Ramya showed her the paper which carried the news
of Devamma's death. Amma looked at the newspaper,
focusing on the picture of the beautiful woman, with a
sad, wistful expression. Amma couldn't read English,
though she could make out a few words, and sometimes
she deciphered the headlines all by herself. Often, she'd
enlist Ramya's help if the newspaper contained a human-
interest story (the return of a long-lost child or the outing
of a prolific polygamist).

"She's very good-looking. Who is she?" she asked.

"She's Devamma. She used to work in our house."

"Oh! I've heard about her."

"She took her own life."

"Poor soul. But Ramya you're much too young to
read about these things. Put the paper away. These papers

are always full of such stuff—murders, accidents and war. I don't know why they can't print good religious things."

"Amma, I'm fifteen! I was told that at my age you were already married!" She folded the newspaper and put it away. She neglected to add that in her opinion, young and callow as she was, more violence was caused in the name of religion than anything else. Ramya was used to writing scathing editorials about social issues in her school magazine, but her convent school had drawn the line at religion.

Once they had a cook named Ramulamma, and she was one who was definitely not up to par. While she was an expert at cooking party dishes, she was tardy and care-less—forgetting to add salt, or allowing some dishes to char on the stove. It also turned out that Ramulamma was a dipsomaniac. Every now and then she stole out of the kitchen for a chota of country liquor which she'd kept hidden in the cabinet under the wash basin in the back verandah. When she returned indoors after taking a large draught, she'd pop a pod of clove into her mouth to mask her breath. One day before she could pop anything into her mouth, Amma walked into the kitchen. Amma didn't have to wear a deerstalker on her head to realize what was going on. Ramulamma was sacked forthwith.

The worst of the worst was most decidedly Kant-hamma. She joined service at short notice when Potti Lakshmi suddenly left to return to her village to care for her house and her siblings following the death of her mother from pneumonia. Kanthamma showed attitude right from day one, driving Amma mad. The funny thing was that workwise Kanthamma was brisk and efficient. Once she finished her work, instead of resting in the verandah or going home, she'd loiter about the house. Amma always had to order her to leave.

There was a practical reason for her behaviour. Apparently, she was scoping the house. There was nothing she didn't think was worth stealing. Food, clothes, curios, money — not even Ramya's story books were spared — anything she could tuck into the fold of her sari, or toss over the back wall. Later, when it was time to leave, she'd make a great show of opening her carry-bag in front of Amma to prove she wasn't taking anything that didn't belong to her. Once outside, she'd slink around the house to recover her spoils. This went on for many months with no one the wiser, for Kanthamma was very shrewd — she'd pilfer nothing that would be missed immediately.

It was no wonder that Amma was in a bad mood all the time — she never seemed to find anything in its rightful place. She often rooted about for some object thinking it was mislaid, not realizing that Kanthamma had already snagged it. Instead of turning the house upside-down, Amma should've paid a visit to Kanthamma's house, where most of the stolen property was stashed.

But on one occasion, greed got the better of Kanthamma, and that was her undoing.

It happened when Ramya was eight. She insisted that she wear an expensive necklace she'd received as a birthday present. It was a hideous affair — a string of pearls with a peacock-shaped pendant studded with emeralds. Mummy was as usual uninterested, but Amma, who was visiting at the time, forbade Ramya from wearing it. Ramya

went crying to her Daddy, her court of last resort. He told
Amma that it was no big deal if Ramya wore the necklace
for a while. Amma pursed her lips but let Ramya have
her way.

When Daddy was out of earshot, she said sternly to
Ramya: "Don't blame me if you get robbed or kidnapped.
I've warned you!"

Ramya ignored her grandmother's dire utterance, and
joyously pranced around the house, the emerald pendant
bobbing on her chest. The matter was forgotten until late
in the evening.

At six o'clock, when it was time to switch on the
lights in the house and light wick-lamps for the gods in
the alcove, Amma said: "Ramya it's time you returned
the necklace."

Ramya's hand flew to her throat, but the necklace
wasn't there.

"Ammamma, I don't have it!"

"Did you remove it and leave it somewhere?"

"No."

Though Amma didn't exclaim, "I told you so!" the air
was thick with the unspoken comment, and Ramya
began to cry. Amma made everyone in the house hunt
for the necklace, but it couldn't be found. Amma threatened the servants that she'd call the police if the necklace
didn't turn up in the next half hour. True to her word,
when the necklace didn't show up, she called the nearby
police station, making Ramya look up the number in the
telephone directory.

Daddy was at the clinic then, but the local police
knew him. The inspector came with two constables and

interrogated the servants. At that time of day, only the cook and Kanthamma were present. The cook began to weep, but Kanthamma was cool as a cucumber — at first. But when the police decided to take her to the police station to do a body search, she was terrified. It was getting dark. She began to make a scene. She fell at Amma's feet and said a hundred times that she was not a thief, and not to send her to the police station.

"They will beat me!" she said. "They will rape me!"

She began to sniffle. There was such naked terror in her eyes, the earlier supercilious indifference having all but vanished. She ran into the back verandah, to the stinky cabinet under the wash basin where supplies like phenyl, bug spray and Tik 20 were kept. The same cabinet where Ramulamma used to hide her hooch. Kanthamma flung open the cabinet door, and reached for the bottle of Tik 20. As she attempted to drink the poison, Amma tried to wrest it out of Kanthamma's grip, spilling some of the liquid on the ground. Then the police inspector, who'd followed them, strode up to Kanthamma and prised the bottle out of her hand.

"If nothing else, we'll book you for attempted suicide," the inspector said. It was an empty threat because he left the evidence, the bottle of Tik 20, on the kitchen counter.

The constables were dragging a protesting and struggling Kanthamma into their jeep, when Daddy arrived in his car. He stepped out and spoke to the inspector. From where she stood in the verandah Ramya couldn't hear anything that was being said. While Daddy and the inspector were having a man-to-man talk, the constables held on to Kanthamma as if she were a dangerous criminal. Kanthamma was twisting and squirming wanting to break free. Then the inspector barked out something, and the constables released Kanthamma. The police got into their jeep, and left. Kanthamma too left, wiping her eyes with the pallo of her sari.

After that, they never saw Kanthamma again.

The next morning a maid sweeping the front yard found the emerald necklace. It was lying on the ground in the exact spot where Kanthamma stood, struggling to get out of the clutches of the two burly constables. The necklace must have got dislodged from Kanthamma's blouse or sari or wherever it was tucked away.

"… in the darkness nobody noticed it," finished Amma, pronouncing the final judgement on the matter. But Ramya wasn't so sure — the necklace could have fallen off while she was running about in the front yard earlier in the evening.

11

Midnight's Child

THERE'S A COPY of *Midnight's Children* in the sandalwood chest. Ramya picks up the book and riffles the pages. The flyleaf boasts Salman Rushdie's signature, a bold scrawl, as if the signatory was aware of his impending greatness even in his salad days. The signature looks like a silhouette of a boat with sturdy masts braving the tempestuous winds.

The book, an inexpensive trade edition, was a gift. It's one of the items she placed in the box long after she moved to Canada. Nikki Lodha, who gave her the book, wrote a brief message on a notepaper, saying she hopes Ramya too will become a writer someday, realizing her juvenile dream.

Ramya sighs. Her desire to be a writer was meant to be a secret, like an unwanted pregnancy. But somehow, her childhood friends, being keen as a knife, knew of her secret desire.

Isn't it time she did something about her dream? In

the past weeks, she's done nothing about anything, post-poning even urgent matters. She must change! She must do something! *Kuch karo*, do something, was the customary advice for youth in India.

Rise and shine, sleepy Ramya, she tells herself, para-phrasing a song which students sang in her convent school during the music period. But it's easier said than done.

What should she do? Where should she start?

⌇————⌇

In August 1983, there was an announcement in the *Deccan Chronicle* that Salman Rushdie would be visiting Hyderabad to give a talk at the Women's College. The college was housed in a stately and beautiful building, once the home of the British Resident in Hyderabad, the largest of the independent states in India, a country where most of the territory was ruled directly by Britain. The ruler of Hyderabad was Mir Osman Ali, HEH the Nizam, the richest man in the world until his dominion was mail-fisted into becoming part of the Republic of India in 1948.

Salman Rushdie was a rising star, and had recently won the Booker Prize. Even though the Indian political establishment had turned up its nose on him, he was welcomed everywhere, even in the so-called second-tier cities like Hyderabad. It wasn't a surprise; with one flour-ish of his magical quill he thrust Indian writing, which was suffering from a stubborn colonial hangover, onto the centre-stage of world literature. Until then, Indian literature in English was, for the most part, obsessed with poverty, partition, and hill-station preoccupations. Going to see such a man was as good as a pilgrimage for any wannabe writer.

For long Ramya had harboured an ambition, like an undisclosed fetish, to become an author when she grew up. Her trifling verse and stray, short articles published in her school magazine doubtless gave fillip to her aspirations.

And why did she keep her desire a secret? Whenever Daddy proudly told his friends that Ramya wrote poetry, they'd turn around ask her:

"So, you want to be the next Kamala Das, is it?"

Kamala Das, a beautiful person and a sensitive poet, was famous for all the wrong reasons. People were more acquainted with her opinions on sex than her poetry.

Besides, the realities of socialistic India, with few openings in any field, let alone in writing, put paid to her ambition. She yielded to social pressure to take up a college course that would lead to a vocation. Artistic pursuits were to be indulged only in childhood; as you grew up, you were required to drop them, much like a space rocket discarding its spent fuel tanks, as you progressed in the trajectory of your lifecycle. Taking up fine arts for study or as a profession was violently frowned upon.

Rushdie's visit was well advertised. It was uncommon for any eminent writer to visit Hyderabad — while a historic and fascinating city, it was not perceived as a happening place. Or perhaps other writers' visits didn't get such wide publicity. Whatever the case, Ramya never had the opportunity to see an author in the flesh, not even

the hacks who wrote for the local papers. If an internationally famous author did visit, he went usually to
cities like Delhi, Mumbai, Kolkata or Chennai, as if they
were the four cardinal points of the socio-cultural map
of India. Hyderabad wasn't even considered a minor point
on the compass.

When she called the number on the press release to
wangle an invitation, she thought that she would be
staved off with objections. That was the climate of social-
ist India — there was never enough of anything, other
than people. But an old man with a quavering voice answered, and when he learned she was a young student of
English Literature, invited her to the meeting in incredibly precise English, and without making any fuss whatsoever — to her utter surprise and delight.

When Salman Rushdie had started making news, for
political rather than literary reasons, she'd borrowed the
book from a library out of curiosity. She found the going
tough despite the bedazzling quality of the prose. (Who
wouldn't be impressed with the use of a phrase like "the
clock-hands joined their palms in respectful greeting" just
to denote midnight?) Nevertheless, she recognized that
the book had all the hallmarks of a masterpiece. She
slogged away at the book, though it took her a long time
to finish, and when she returned it she had to pay a hefty
fine. She may as well have bought the book, so punitive
was the fine she had to cough up.

The evening before Rushdie's talk, Ramya made her
father drive her from pillar to post, or rather from bookshop to bookshop, to find a copy of the book. They drew
a blank at India Book House on RP Road and at JC Pinto

on MG Road. Night was falling thick and fast, and any time soon, the bookshops across the twin cities Hyderabad and Secunderabad would be pulling down their shutters, and no amount of joining her palms in prayer could avert that. It was pointless to go all the way to Abid's on the other side of the Tank Bund where A.A. Hussain was located. She was about to shed tears of disappointment, when Daddy had a brainwave. He thought of Kadambi, a small roadside bookshop on a busy thoroughfare near the Secunderabad Clock Tower. He doubled back, driving as fast as he could while steering the car through the evening rush of bicycles, buffaloes, and buses. Kadambi was still open, even though it was well past closing time. The owner, a gentle soul, was having a friendly chat with a customer, though the latter was merely browsing, having no intention of buying anything. It was here in this small hole-in-the-wall bookshop that they hit pay dirt. It was the last copy on the shelf, a more expensive edition, and Ramya grabbed it with unseemly but triumphal haste. She wanted to hug and kiss her Daddy then and there, so ecstatic she felt. But of course she didn't; one couldn't be so demonstrative of affection in public.

After returning home with her catch, Ramya called Sujatha, who'd previously shown interest in attending the talk.

"Let's meet at the entrance to the Durbar Hall ten minutes before the start of the programme," Ramya said.

"Sure. I'm so happy you could find a copy of the novel. I know it means a lot to you to see Rushdie in person and take his autograph. Like having a *darshan* of a god."

Ramya was embarrassed. She didn't know she was so transparent.

"See you tomorrow," Ramya said. "Your idea about the newspaper is a good one, by the way."

Sujatha's parents, being parsimonious, hadn't agreed to buy her a copy of *Midnight's Children* just for the pleasure of getting Rushdie to sign on it. The only books they bought were textbooks for their four children. Moreover, they weren't inclined to shell out money for a book by a new writer who had the gall to mix literature with politics. In Sujatha's family, only R.K. Narayan, of all Indian authors writing in English, was worthy of esteem or expense. (In all fairness to Sujatha's family, her father did try Raja Rao's *The Serpent and the Rope* after reading a glowing article about the eminent writer in the *Illustrated Weekly of India*, and learning that he hailed from Hyderabad, but the poor man couldn't make head nor tail of the voluminous novel.)

Sujatha wasn't disappointed, being by nature an understanding person. But she was resourceful, and planned to take the newspaper which carried an article about Rushdie, and have the author autograph it.

The next morning Ramya woke early, unable to contain her excitement. She was going to skip college, and Daddy too took the day off to drive her to the venue. Durbar Hall was once the glittering audience chamber in the rambling mansion of the Resident of Hyderabad. It was said that when Colonel James Kirkpatrick, the British Resident at the court of Hyderabad, showed the architectural drawing to the then Nizam, the building looked so immense and magnificent that the latter refused to approve it, fearing that the mansion would out-shine his many palaces. The crafty Resident simply had the sheet showing the plan of the building, and not the building itself, drastically reduced in size and hood-winked the great Nizam into giving his nod.

The Nizams were no ordinary vassals of the British Crown. Being fabulously wealthy, one of the Nizams, it was said, had loaned a substantial sum to Queen Victoria in her empire-building efforts. In return, the Empress bestowed on him the exclusive E, squeezed between the two run-of-the-mill H's. It stood for His Exalted High-ness, separating him from the rabble of over five hundred princelings in India.

But just as Daddy picked up the car keys from a brass bowl on the hallway table, the telephone in the living room rang. To Ramya's ears, the tone of the telephone conversation didn't bode well. She knew, as a doctor's daughter, that their plans were beginning to unravel.

"Ramya darling, one of my patients' condition has become very serious. I'll have to rush to his house. I'll come back and take you to the event."

"It'll be too late, Daddy," Ramya said. Tears of dis-appointment welled in her eyes.

"Would you like to go in an auto rickshaw? You take one of the servants with you ... Or why don't you come with me? If the visit gets over quickly, we can proceed from there."

So, Ramya accompanied her Daddy to the patient's house. The day was bright, the sky the colour of faded denim, with a few thin lazy puffs of clouds drifting across. When they drove over the bund of the Hussainsagar

Lake, she got a glimpse of sailboats scudding on the vast expanse of blue water. But Ramya's heart had already sunk into her boots.

The visit to the patient wasn't going to get over quickly as his condition had become worse. Since they didn't have the time to wait for a taxi, and ambulance services being practically nonexistent, Daddy had to drive the patient, who sat groaning with fever in the back seat, to the hospital.

So that was that—Ramya never got to see the Great Master and take his blessings. In a way, it portended her insubstantial literary achievement. Her expensive copy of *Midnight's Children* remained virgin, without the author's Hancock decorating the flyleaf.

A few days later she met Sujatha. "Do you know how long I waited for you outside the Durbar hall?" Sujatha said. "When I went in, all the introductions were over, and Salman Rushdie was walking up to the podium to give his talk."

"How was the talk?"

"It was good, but it wasn't what I expected. He kept reading from a prepared speech, raising his head now and then to look at the audience."

"Did you get his autograph?"

"Yes. But I got the impression he wasn't too pleased that I hadn't bought a copy of the book."

"Don't worry about that. After all, I did buy one but couldn't have it signed by him. It kind of makes up, I guess."

"He had such piercing eyes, so full of intelligence though. He was so fair, almost milk-white, like marble."

"Yes," Ramya thought to herself, "a literary idol, in

every way—but I didn't get the chance to genuflect before him. Just my luck."

"Do you know who else I saw at the venue?" Sujatha asked.

"Who?"

"Make a guess."

Ramya shook her head.

"Monica. She came along with her beau. What's his name?"

"Amar. I never knew they were the literary types." Ramya added with a sigh: "Some people have all the luck in the world."

———

When she enters the drawing room, she sees that there's a message on the telephone. Her first impulse is to ignore it. She changes her mind and picks up the receiver.

The disembodied voice informs her that there are four new messages.

The first one is from Jack: *Hi Ramya, just thought I'd touch base with you. I've got a couple of ideas for your professional development strategy. Give me a ring when you have time.*

The second one is from Renata: *Good Morning, Ramya. It's unfortunate that we haven't been able to connect …*

The third is from Wilma: *Hey Ramya! You know what? My horoscope prediction has come true! Give me a call, and don't forget to check your letterbox. (I know you don't do it that often!)*

She hopes the last voice-mail is from her employer,

but it is from Sandeep, her stepson: *Mom, please call me back. We're leaving for India tonight.*

Ignoring the first three messages, Ramya calls Sandeep. "Hello, Mom!"

"Are you all packed and ready to go? When do leave for the airport?"

"In another half hour or so. Vidya's still doing last minute packing."

"Vidya's a good girl! Hang on to her."

Sandeep chuckles, and says: "I will ... Mom, I spoke to Dad a while ago."

At the mention of Prakash, Ramya stiffens and lapses into silence, a silence she hopes more audible than speech. Sandeep should know by now — Prakash was a closed chapter to her.

"He enquired about you," Sandeep says.

"Is he in need of a maid?" Ramya says, annoyed into finding her tongue. "Or a financier, perhaps? Or both rolled into one? By the way, does he know I'm out of work?"

"Mom, you sure do have a sharp tongue. Yes, he knows you've lost your job. I think he's just lonely and getting old. He wasn't his usual cheerful self."

"Why? Has he stopped drinking? Maybe he doesn't get enough opportunities to say 'cheers!' before downing a bottle of scotch."

"Mom, he stopped drinking ages ago."

"Good for him. In some ways Prakash drunk was more companionable than Prakash sober. Anyway, when you reach India, give my regards to your grandfather and your mother."

"I will. Mom, forgive me for saying so. I think you

and Dad must patch up. After all, it's not that you're legally divorced."

"Truth to tell, we're not technically married either."

"What do you mean, Mom?"

"Thereby hangs a tale. I don't want to go into it now. About our patching up, it's out of the question, Sandeep."

Sandeep has steeled himself to persist with the conversation. Ramya can almost feel him grit his teeth as he speaks.

"Mom, you must let bygones be bygones. There are many divorced couples who've remarried. Marriage and divorces are everyday stuff in the West."

"Really? You seemed to have learned a lot about the West from your six-month stint in the USA." Coldness creeps into Ramya's tone.

"All I'm asking you to do is give Dad a second chance."

"*Second* chance? I must've given him a dozen already."

"OK. Please give him another chance."

"I'm too old now to learn to play Happy Families, Sandeep. Besides, I don't believe it'll work at all. It's so pointless." Ramya shudders at the thought of sleeping next to Prakash on the bed. His loud snores, his farts, and the way he shakes the bed when he turns over—you'd think he was an elephant.

"In your old age, both of you will need companionship."

"I'm not old!" Ramya says.

"I know. Young in spirit and all that. Even you could do with some companionship."

"Sorry, Sandeep. Life with Prakash is not in the retirement plans I have for myself. I wish you a happy journey!"

"Dad was right. You are just a poor little rich girl. You

were born with a silver spoon in your mouth. So you've no need for anybody or anything."

Ramya slams down the phone.

were born with a silver spoon in your mouth. So you've no need for anybody or anything."

Ramya slams down the phone.

Ramya's literary career had progressed in fits and starts. While in school, she wrote sporadically, at the behest of her English teachers. In the final year of high school, she even became the editor of the school magazine which had the sabre-rattling name *Excelsior*—after all, the pen was considered mightier than the sword. Ramya wrote trenchantly, revelling in writing editorials with headings such as "Whither India?"

But writing was something you couldn't take too seriously. There were few avenues for getting published. Just a handful of magazines published poetry and short fiction in English. The English language publishing in India then was in a nascent stage—mostly a textbook and reprint market. Any Indian author worth his salt was initially published abroad—Raja Rao, Kamala Markandaya, Anita Desai to name a few. Even R.K. Narayan, the quintessential Indo-Anglian novelist, had his first book published in England, though he was to publish many of his later works in India under his own imprint of *Indian Thought*, with the cover and content of the novels matching Indian sensibilities.

So, who would publish her in India? She put her ambitions on the backburner (however much she would've liked to see her name on a best-seller list) and prepared to get married off like a nice Indian girl.

When they immigrated to Canada, Ramya had a

faint hope that she could rekindle her guttering desire to become a writer. But the thing she found herself writing and rewriting innumerable times was her CV, and of course Prakash's, which went without saying. Prakash had brought home a *Résumés for Dummies* kind of a book from the local library.

"What we call a biodata, or a CV, is called a résumé here. It's also a bit different. They don't need all the biographical details of marital status and hobbies. We should recast our CVs to make them more meaningful for Canadian employers."

"We" meant Ramya, in Prakash's vocabulary, especially when the chore promised to be a thankless grind. She took the fat book from him, and spent an hour or two trying to decode it. Later, they looked around their neighbourhood for a resource centre—a place that provided word processors and reference books for newcomers. Such spaces were often sponsored by organizations like the YMCA, or some enterprising group which saw profit in a completely not-for-profit activity. Once they found such a place, they had to visit it many days in succession as they were allotted only one hour of computer time. The résumés took a long time to finish. While Ramya worked hard at it, Prakash would wile away his time reading the *Times of India* or the *Deccan Chronicle* online. (Later he would feed her with tidbits of news from India, like a know-it-all.)

They applied for jobs everywhere: responding to help-wanted ads in newspapers; visiting employment agencies, at their offices or kiosks at job fairs; dropping off un-solicited résumés with receptionists of various companies; handing them over to acquaintances (friends were really hard to come by in Canada). All this amounted to playing what she called Canadian roulette: scattering their résumés in the wind, hoping one will be picked up by a serious employer.

Nothing worked. Maybe, Canada is no match for Russia, its Arctic neighbour. Their famous roulette worked on occasion. But one day, they were on their way to an IT firm to drop off yet another unsolicited résumé — what else? While waiting for an elusive bus, Prakash felt thirsty. There was a filling station at the street corner nearby with a convenience store attached to it. Prakash nipped across, leaving Ramya behind in the bus shelter. As usual she was on tenterhooks, until at last he returned. Empty-handed, without even the envelope containing his résumé.

"What took you so long? Didn't they have bottled water or pop?"

"What they had was a job opening, love. I gave them my résumé, and they offered me the job then and there. I start from tomorrow. Sorry, I all but forgot about the water."

"Never mind, I'm not feeling that thirsty. You mean they just handed you a job on a platter, without asking you any questions?"

"They did ask a couple of questions. But the most important one was: Are you willing to work in the night?" Prakash chuckled. Prakash had that quality — he inspired confidence, however misplaced, the very first time you saw him.

They went back home, feeling pleased. A job was a job, even if a person who was a high-placed executive in India had to work as a cashier in a petrol bunk on the graveyard shift. The job did not assure them of a cushy life, but at least it staunched their seemingly unmanageable expenses.

Once they were home, they slaked their thirst, raising a toast to their good fortune with tap water.

Within a few weeks, Ramya too was offered a job as a nighttime security guard in a condominium building in the Lawrence-Finch area. The neighbourhood was a hot-bed of crime, and it took more than two hours to get there, so Ramya turned it down. All the jobs available for im-migrants were hard or unsafe and required them to work at night.

New immigrants were truly the children of the night …

If looking for a job was hard, getting published was even more so. The first few months Ramya was too pre-occupied with the challenges of settling down in Canada—job search, housework, grocery shopping—to even think about writing, let alone actually sitting down to write. She kept a small notebook she bought in a dollar shop, naming it "Cauldron of Ideas," where she would jot down themes for poems, or the germ of a notion for a short story. None of those hastily scrawled entries came to fruition. Now and then she'd try to fan the small spark of an inspiration for a poem, but after the first couple of stanzas, it invari-ably ran out of steam.

It was only after she started working full-time, when she really felt she had a toehold in the new country, that she applied herself seriously. While she managed to flog her poems — which had been left for dead for so long — into rising unsteadily and trotting with halting steps, the going was tough.

How amazingly busy the literary scene was in Canada! She'd heard of many internationally famous Canadian writers even before she came to Canada—Margaret Atwood,

Alice Munro, Mavis Gallant, Michael Ondaatje, not to mention authors of Indian origin like Rohinton Mistry and M.G. Vassanji. They were all churning out books and stories, busier than the proverbial beaver. There were so many places offering creative writing courses, so many publishers, so many awards, so many grants, and so many avenues to get published—mainstream magazines, literary magazines, community newspapers, online sites, e-zines, blogs and what have you. Yet, for a new writer to see his or her work in print, let alone be suitably remunerated for the effort, seemed next to impossible.

One day Ramya decided to flesh out the jottings in her notebook into a full-fledged poem. Calling it "Karma's Daughter," she sent it out to the many literary magazines whose names and addresses she'd gathered from the local library. The poem, she thought, had an ethnic appeal, something which might be appreciated in a country boasting multiculturalism:

> *With hope in my heart, and a prayer on my lips*
> *Like a grain of sand I lie on the rocky bed of Karma*
> *Giant waves of trials and travail*
> *Lash as I buffet against them to no avail*
> *Predator sharks of ego and greed*
> *Widen their menacing jaws to feed*
> *As hope dwindles and prayers go waste*
> *Wild winds soften breakers abate*
> *The Orange-robed Boatman, in a divine state*
> *Arrives, and a new hope kindles in the heart*
> *Alas, he only passes by, while I wait*
> *I know now, it will be eons before I can earn His grace.*

Not one of the periodicals found her worthy of publication. While she wasn't sure about the quality of her own writing, she did become aware that the concerns and preoccupations of the editors weren't the same as her own. An immigrant deemed a "visible minority," and the "establishment," which was predominantly white, couldn't see eye to eye. When will the twain ever meet?

Rather than indiscriminately accuse people of racism, Ramya never lost sight of the need to refashion and improve her sensibilities to suit her new country of choice.

So she rewrote her piece "Karma's Daughter," giving it not just a thorough makeover but a new title:

Karma's Child

I lie belly up on the sands of Time,
beside the Ocean, whose incessant waves
tirelessly murmur, *Aum, Aum, Aum*

Beyond the knife-thin horizon,
where the sea meets the sky,
in a lover's embrace,
there circles a school of sharks,
baring their sword-sharp teeth
as if smiling ...

No laughing matter,
when I've to step into the water —
a fleshy tidbit I'll be,
for those gigantic, masticating *Jaws*

O, Sun! Helios, Ra, Savitr, or whatever,
forgive me my many transgressions.
But the day of judgement's near —
Is there room for plea bargains?

In my declining years, adrift and bereft,
my stash of good deeds has come to nought.
A thousand prayers die on my lips.
For the throat is parched, sore for a dose
of something spiritual, of something sublime.

A tall, icy glass of coke and rum!
No! A modicum of *amritam* —
the heavenly nectar of immortality.
Shame! So degenerate has become
My tongue, so steeped in banality.

Shadows lengthen, as the day darkens
as if blinds are being drawn along the horizon.
Plangent notes emanate — like incense smoke,
Suffusing the world with sadness —
Music of the spheres! No, it's a dirge,
the strains of *Nirvana*.

And then I hear — Knock! Knock!!
"Who's there?"
It's Yama with his noose.
No minion, no Myrmidon,
The Lord of Death himself.

Let me stay a while longer
On this Earth — this dome of pleasure.
But Yama says,
Whirling his lariat in the air:
"No, I'm your master —
for now and Hereafter"

Only one year more! I implore.
How about a week? I entreat
A day? An hour? A minute?

"Not a moment more will you get.
Pack your bag and say your *adieus*."

When it's time to board the caboose,
nothing in the world matters:
No piety, no supplication
No tears, no medical intervention
No *revoirs,* no till-we-meet-agains.

Hey! Where have all my playmates and partners gone?
There's no one to hobnob with on this road.

It's a journey I'll have to undertake alone.

She sent out her piece, expanding the list of addresses to
include even minor periodicals. To her intense delight it was
accepted by the editor of a small privately produced magazine of poetry. But when the only payment she received
was two copies of the magazine, she was scandalized.
How could poets subsist on this kind of remuneration?

It looked as if society was making monkeys out of writers by paying them peanuts.

Even so, from then on Ramya was always on the look-out for themes that would resonate with the editors and readers who lived in this cold, sparsely populated country north of the 49th parallel, unlike the tropical, riotously passionate country she came from.

On a chilly Sunday morning in early May, when Prakash and Ramya went for a stroll in a nearby park, they came across a tree which Prakash said was cherry. It had shed all its short-lived blooms, making a carpet, verily of floral design, on the ground. Ramya pulled out her pocket-book and pen, and made a couple of entries — an idea for a poem inspired by the fallen pink petals.

Curious, Prakash asked: "What are you doing?"

"Nothing," Ramya replied.

That very night, when Prakash had gone to bed, his snores rising like rumbles of a geyser priming to erupt, Ramya was busy at her computer, writing, and revising profusely, a poem called "Pink Snow."

That year, winter lingered
well into May —
Like an uncherished guest
Who has overstayed his welcome.

Slivers of ice were entrenched
In the crevices of the roofs.
Dirty snow, like frozen surf,
took refuge in shady nooks

The sky was rumpled and grey
like an unwashed hoodie.
The park was cold and unsmiling,
where birds refused to sing.
The leafless trees huddled together,
trembling in the wind.

And as I walked, the ground
Was soft and alive beneath my feet —
a reminder of last night's
needle-sharp rain.

When the trail turned —
all of a sudden,
blindsiding me,
was the mystical vision:

Drifts upon drifts of pink snow!

Two cherry blossom trees
Standing gauntly on a rise
Have shed their flowers,
making an eiderdown of petals,
to comfort the shivering earth.

She sent it out, hoping time and again that it would catch
the attention of at least one editor, but it wasn't to be —
the publishing world had clammed up. There was no
response whatsoever. Not even peanuts were cast in her
direction.

Karma's Child must have been just flash in the pan. A fluke. A false dawn. Ramya bitterly assumed that she wasn't cut out to be a writer, at least not in Canada. At least not for now.

On a whim, having nothing better to do, Ramya decides to attend a meeting of a writing group which she learned operates at The Beaches. Purposeless living is grating on her nerves. She needs to do something, something to put meaning back in her life.

She's beginning to shake off her lotus-eater's life, taking baby steps ... she made a sortie to the grocery shop, visited her hairdresser, did the laundry, and even attended meetings with the consultant.

Yet, she recoils from the prospect of completing the long overdue EI forms. More daunting than filling in the form online is the need to cook up an excuse for her tardiness. She realises that the more she delays, the more difficult it'll get. She has unwisely allowed the situation to snowball ... Ramya peremptorily dismisses the pointless train of thoughts, a train with no destination.

She doesn't want to dwell on unpleasant things. Attending the writing group meeting, by comparison, seems a more pleasurable alternative. Like a picnic. Though this'll be her n^{th} attempt to resuscitate her aspirations to be a writer, she sees writing as a lifeline that could lead her out of the morass her world has become. Hope springs eternal ... even in Ramya's breast.

The trick is to cling on to the lifesaver long enough

to be rescued. Will she have the perseverance? The stamina? Or will she let her habitual lethargy, something that has grown to monstrous proportions of late, take over?

She found the writing group by surfing the internet. When she emailed a tentative enquiry, she received an enthusiastic reply. But that was long ago, just after her layoff, when she was still smarting from the insult, and she still had spirit left. She wanted to hit back at her company for treating her like dirt. She would write, get published, become a bestseller and show them! Like that mystery writer who wrote novels about the detective Aurelio Zen. The author had lost his tenure at a university, so he decided to write a book to cock a snook at his previous employer. In the event, he cocked more than a snook—he snagged the Crime Dagger award for his debut novel.

Was writing an antidote for sagging self-esteem? Was it something with which to bolster your *amour prop*? Was wanting to become an author one big ego trip?

No wonder there was such a demand for self-publishing!

The writing group meets in a tavern at 6:30 pm the first Wednesday of every month. The tap house is called Denny's or Benny's, she can't remember clearly now. She'll have to look it up again, and send an email to the group, alerting them of her impending visit. Authors don't like surprises; they reserve them for their readers.

In the evening she leaves for the meeting. Though cold, there's light, as the days have begun to grow longer, if ever so slightly. The rush hour traffic is petering down.

Why is she going to this damn fool meeting? Wouldn't she be better off completing the EI forms? She was supposed to submit them within a fortnight of being laid off, now it's more than a month. How many more days does she need to complete it? Why has she developed this incorrigible habit of putting things off? Could anything be more urgent than submitting forms which will guarantee a sizeable income for eight months or so? Though not comparable to what she'd been earning, it wasn't chicken-feed either.

She enters the restaurant. She divests herself of the heavy winter jacket, an indecisive cream with darkish faux fur around the neck. She hangs it on a tree-like structure with stumpy branches. There aren't many coats hanging there. Neither is there anyone to greet and conduct her to a table.

Ramya scans the place. Most of the customers are legitimate diners, in ones and twos. In the far end, there's a group of four people, the biggest congregation in the thinly populated restaurant. They're in a huddle; she can hear their chittering faintly from where she's standing. Ramya was told the group was eight-member strong.

As Ramya walks up to them, four disparate faces look up — two brown, one white, one yellow. They offer uncertain smiles of varying warmth, from sub-zero to a toasty thirty degrees Celsius.

"You must be Ramya," one of the women says, beckoning her to the empty chair they'd kept for her.

"I was expecting a larger group," Ramya says, planting her backside gingerly on the chair.

"Not everyone can make it every time," the only man in the group says. "Especially on a day like this. I'm John." He's wearing a shabby jacket and has brindled hair and moustache. And three days of stubble. Maybe he finds time to shave only once a week. Must be a busy writer.

They make introductions. Apart from John, they are Jeannette, Brenda and Chantal. They're all on the older side, in their late fifties or early sixties. Ramya isn't yet fifty, but she'll soon be. The ladies have tried to conceal their age with the aid of hair colour, but when she stood over them she noticed the telltale roots showing on a couple of heads.

"Why don't we begin?" Jeannette, who Ramya learns is Chinese, says.

The one who calls herself Brenda, (her given name Ramya discovers in due course is Vrinda) reads from a story set in an office on Bay Street, in Toronto's financial district. She's got all the particulars of an office setting correct, right down to the reception counter, the cubicles, the photocopier, and the coffee machine. The story opens with a scene in the lunchroom, the employees sitting in clusters with their friends, opening their lunch boxes. The contents are different depending on the nationality of the employee. The piece is two thousand words long and takes nearly thirty minutes for Brenda to read.

"Brenda, the atmosphere is so authentic. It's amazing," Jeannette says.

"The introduction is really good. But it would be nice if you could bring in some action and more dialogue early on," John says.

Brenda jots down this input from her fellow members assiduously.

"It's a nice beginning for a novel," Ramya says.

"It's actually a short story," Brenda says.

"Brenda, Ramya's reaction is proof that the introduction is taking up too many pages," John says. "If you can introduce plot details, rather than beating about the bush, you'll be able to sink your hooks into the reader. Otherwise you'll lose him."

"Or her," Jeannette says.

"What's the story about, if I may ask?" Ramya says.

"It's about a group of friends in an office who collectively buy lottery tickets every month. The time they get lucky, one of the members hadn't bought in because she's on mat leave. This leads to bad blood, litigation and so forth."

"It's a lot of stuff for a short story," Chantal says.

"It's meant to be about five thousand words long," Brenda says.

"The way it's shaping up, even fifteen thousand won't be enough," John says. "You should expand it into a novella."

"You must learn to work faster too, Brenda," Jeannette says. "In the past six months, you've not progressed beyond the opening scene. I'm aware that you faithfully incorporate all the suggestions we make into your story, and it no doubt takes up your time."

"I often suffer from writer's block," Brenda says, with pain in her voice. "But I'll see what I can do."

The other south Asian lady, named Chantal, is writing a memoir of her early life in India, growing up amidst dozens of relatives and relations. Her husband was a high-flying businessman, and they made frequent trips exotic places in the world — Paris, Zurich, Madrid, London, and even Rio de Janeiro. But at long last, they decided, quite perversely, to settle in Canada, a country which is in deep freeze for the better part of the year. Her memoir is all about herself, and how privileged her life was. Everything else, whether people or places, are merely props.

A surly waiter appears, putting a brake on Chantal's longwinded narrative. He stands patiently, without enthusiasm, with his pad and pencil at ready. It's obvious that he knows from experience that these struggling writers place small orders and tip poorly as well.

The ladies, especially Brenda and Chantal, make a great show of going through the wine list. Eventually Brenda asks for water with a wedge of lime, and Chantal, the self-confessed jet-setter, orders a glass of the plonk known as the house wine. Ramya asks for a cup of coffee, and Jeannette for herbal tea. John orders butternut squash soup. Having to cope with a quartet of women at the table requires nourishment.

Once the waiter leaves, Chantal resumes, like an unstoppable juggernaut, until the waiter returns a good twenty minutes later with their order. She's eager to continue after the waiter retires, but Jeannette intervenes. Chantal for one doesn't suffer from writer's block.

Jeannette asks Ramya: "Do you have a short story or something you want to read from?"

Ramya delves into her handbag and pulls out a sheet of paper. She puts on her glasses, and reads from her poem, "Pink Snow."

"You write well," Jeannette says when Ramya finishes reading. "But Ramya, I hope you don't mind my saying so, the tree in your poem is most probably a crab-apple tree. Cherry blossoms are white, but crab-apple blossoms are pink."

"Thank you," Ramya says. "As an immigrant one is always learning. But substituting crab-apple for cherry blossom sounds so unpoetical!"

"I'm not a poet, but do poems always have to be about flowers, trees and birds?" John asks. "I've very little patience with all this nature stuff."

"This isn't just a nature poem," Ramya says. "It's about sacrifice."

"Maybe you should call it Red Snow?" Brenda says. "Red is the colour of sacrifice."

"As you can see, we aren't in the least bit qualified to critique poems," John says.

"We once had a poet in our group," Jeannette says. "She moved to BC last summer."

"She had a chapbook published by a small independent press in Toronto," John says.

"Each one of us had to buy a copy," Brenda says, as if still unable to get over the grudge.

"She sold fifty-two copies of her chapbook in all," Chantal says. "Quite an achievement, when you think about it."

"If you had something in prose, perhaps we could help you," John says. He'd been looking at her with unwavering gaze all through. When Ramya looks up, his eyes are boring into her.

"As a matter of fact, I do," Ramya says, averting her eyes and fishing out a sheaf of papers from her miraculous handbag.

"Wow, quite a magician, eh?" John says. "I wish we could bring out stories like that. Out of a hat, at the drop of one."

Looking at her wrist watch, Jeannette says: "We have fifteen minutes. Would you like to read?"

Ramya reads from a short story called "Down Under" that she wrote when she first realized that she couldn't sell her poems. The story, which needed much polishing, was about a young family from south India living in a basement. The man's mother visits them to help with the young children. One day she decides to cook a delicacy, which her son liked, made from smelly sundried fish she'd brought from India, tightly wrapped in a polythene bag. The heady but foetid aroma fills their underground flat and then wafts up to the first floor where the owner lives. The suspicious owner, unable to decipher the strange smell correctly, calls 911, thinking there's a marijuana grow-op thriving in his basement. The irate police and firemen who've arrived on the scene aren't inclined, as her son might've been, to appreciate the old lady's culinary skills.

"I've an issue with the title," Chantal, the well-travelled one, says. "'Down Under' refers to Australia. This story is set entirely in Canada, even though in a basement flat. It will confuse the reader. If I were you, I'd change the title."

"I'll think of another title," Ramya says.

Brenda, who had already evinced a keen passion for details, suggests: "Why don't you include the recipe for the fish curry? It'll add to the authenticity of the story."

Though Ramya is at a loss to know who'd be interested in making the offensive dish, she's in no mood to argue, and so she says: "That's a good idea."

"The scene and conversation with the police doesn't ring true," John says. "I don't think policemen in Canada speak like that."

Ramya sighs. Being a prissy, law-abiding soul, she couldn't even begin to guess how Toronto police would behave and speak. While she's seen them zipping up and down the streets in their cruisers, she hasn't so much as received a traffic ticket in her life.

"The story is very interesting," Jeannette says. "If you have a bunch of such stuff maybe you could get them published as a collection."

"But collections are very difficult to sell to publishers, Jeannette," John says. "And to have individual stories published, literary magazines take months to decide. Even if the story is published, very rarely do you receive any payment."

"Max two copies of the periodical," Chantal says. "Sometimes I wonder why I want to be a writer at all."

"Vanity," Brenda says with a sigh, "like the rest of us."

"If you're serious about being published, I suggest you write a novel," John says.

Then they all leave, collecting their coats from the stand. Outside on the sidewalk, John says: "Hope to see you next month." The tip of his tongue sneaks out and wetly caresses his lower lip. The restaurant was overheated and dry. "Maybe, the next time you'll pull out a novel out of your handbag."

"Your vanity case," Brenda says.

"So that's that," Ramya says to herself as she's driving back home.

Her spirits have plummeted to their nadir. The literary outing, far from accomplishing the goal of showing her how to proceed with her literary ambitions, has only revealed more pitfalls. All she learned was that she didn't have the required talent to write saleable poetry—and there was no ready market for her short fiction.

The evening was such a waste of time and effort. Whatever John said about her talents in his mock-serious way, unfortunately, legerdemain wasn't one of them. There was no way she could materialize a novel out of thin air!

Maybe she was better off filling in those EI forms. She must use her creativity to come up with some credible excuse for the delay. Something the labour department functionary will fall for. Pogey seems more lucrative than poetry.

She returns home exhausted and depressed. She switches on the lights one by one in her dark unwelcoming home, hoping they'll ward off her depression. But the dolefully quiet rooms with all their redundant furniture only deepen her loneliness.

In the evening the following day Ramya drives to Mrs. Rao's house to pay her condolences in person. She was careful to call earlier in the day and make an appointment. The Raos have little patience with the typical Indian way of doing things; they think it's too slapdash.

The evening is gloomy and cold. There's a mild fog stroking the city with its wet fingers. As she nears the Rao residence, the fog seems to grow thicker, maybe because of all the tall old trees in the posh area. The Raos had moved to an upscale neighbourhood, rubbing shoulders with well-heeled neighbours consisting of doctors, business tycoons, drug dealers, and illicit pot growers.

The house has a slate grey façade with black doors and windows, and turret-like projections on the roof. It looks back at her with a baleful gaze, and on that wintry evening, with a low grey sky and the dark denuded trees, the fashionably built house might be mistaken for a vampire's lair.

A female relative, whom Ramya doesn't recognize, opens the door. She gives an uncertain smile, and conducts Ramya wordlessly to the living room. The house is uncomfortably cold and unnaturally quiet — as though everything in the house, people, furniture and appliances, are observing silence in honour of the late Mrs. Rao.

Mr. Rao is seated on a winged chair. He's idly holding a walking stick which ends in four prongs at its base. He's staring at the floor, as if he's trying to find meaning in the pattern on the hardwood. His face has become a tissue of wrinkles; there are wayward strands of hair protruding from his ears and nostrils.

"I'm sorry to hear about Subbu-Auntie," Ramya says like a parakeet with limited vocabulary.

Mr. Rao's answer sounds something like 'mmmff'. He continues to stare at the ground.

"I hope she didn't suffer before she passed away."

"What suffering? She had a nice life right till the last few days. Anyway, she died in her sleep."

"That's comforting to hear."

"How's Prakash these days? Don't hear from him at all."

"He's moved to Alberta."

"Why haven't you gone with him?"

"We're separated." To her, her words sound as if she's

talking about a pair of Siamese twins who've been surgically parted.

"So are Subbu and I now." Mr. Rao had another take on separation.

"In a different way, I guess."

The old man looks up and says: "You're damn well right."

Why do most men turn uncaring and crotchety when they grow old? Even her father was no exception. It was only in his later years that he revealed an acerbic side of his tongue, bidding goodbye to his reputation as a modern-day Buddha.

Interacting with the Indian community always makes Ramya feel depressed. It's been so ever since they first arrived over a decade before. She detected an undercurrent of envy, and jealousy, or even contempt sometimes, when one would've expected sympathy and kindliness towards new immigrants. With one or two exceptions, the only real help she's received was from people of other races.

After she separated from Prakash, things became more acute. Men try to take advantage, and women are needlessly judgemental. The pettiness of character, which may have gone unnoticed in her native land, when transplanted to Canada, seems all the more magnified.

Ramya's feeling of isolation is complete.

12

The Stain on the Mattress

THE MANAGALSUTRAM, a special wedding necklace made of twenty-two carat gold, is the most expensive object in her box. Also, perhaps, the least valuable. A thin rope-like chain with a disc-like pendant. Traditionally, it's a symbol of wifehood; the chain that a groom places around the bride's neck to proclaim his ownership.

The chain reminds her of her failed marriage, the wasted years. Nearly two decades of living together, and nothing to show at the end of it. Even while it lasted there were few shared delights, few shared triumphs. There was neither companionship nor commonality of interest. Over the years they became complete strangers living under the same roof, sharing the same mattress. Just roomies — and not very cordial ones at that.

It's not only Ramya who's paid a heavy price for the misadventure. Daddy had parted with a big sum as dowry and picked up the enormous bill for all the wedding expenses, as was the custom. In the bargain, he'd bought himself a lemon of a son-in-law. Mercifully, he never came to know of that, at least not from Ramya. It's possible he'd suspected that all wasn't hunky-dory between his daughter and son-in-law; word has a way of getting around.

<hr>

Like many fathers in India, Daddy searched high and low for a perfect match for his daughter, the apple of his eye. He was very well off, so he was in the position to call the shots.

As for Ramya, she was a prize catch in the marriage market — born into a rich family, educated, and even talented. It meant Daddy had to be vigilant, and filter out unsuitable suitors, separate grain from chaff. Unfortunately, he wasn't a very canny person. A trusting soul, he habitually accepted things at face value.

In those days any male who entered an arranged marriage preferred a full-time homemaker for a spouse. Housewifery was a demanding job. The country being beset with shortages of every kind offered a great opportunity to show off one's talent for economy and efficiency. If a wife could moonlight, and earn some money as a teacher or an office assistant, so much the better. A welcome bonus, no doubt, but not a dealmaker. The jobs earmarked for women were humble dead-end jobs, but yielding a small steady income to supplement the family earnings. This was considered a good thing as it wouldn't eclipse the husband's status and salary. A man liked to be the primary breadwinner and the maker of all decisions. The unquestioned king of his castle.

Ramya never let on that she hoped to be an author,

and prayed that Daddy would do the same. Writing was considered a rather kinky pursuit — suitors would probably be more in awe than be enamoured of it. Hobbies like embroidery, tailoring, and fabric painting however were understandable, and there was a practical money-saving side to those.

Sometimes, during a conversation with a prospective groom, Daddy would let slip that Ramya wrote poems and articles in the local newspaper.

"Really? Has she been published in *Eenadu* or *Andhra Bhoomi*?" the suitor, or his father or his uncle, would ask — suddenly wary.

"No. Her work has appeared in the *Deccan Chronicle* and the *Hindu*."

"Oh. So she writes in English?" There would be puzzlement and sometimes suspicion in the tone. Was Ramya too good a match for them?

That's how even Daddy, a trusting, guileless man, learned to soft-pedal on Ramya's writing abilities.

The proposal for Prakash had come from a marriage broker. "The boy" seemed to have everything: education, an excellent job, well settled siblings, and parents who were of independent means. He seemed a bit on the older side, but nowadays didn't men tend to marry late?

Daddy was both delighted and relieved to settle the obviously suitable match, and did it with alacrity.

With too much alacrity, perhaps. He should've delved deeper into Prakash's antecedents. People did a more thorough job of checking the background of a candidate when hiring for an entry-level position. The shadow of failure in Atom Auntie's case must have hung over Daddy.

His daughter was growing up to be more and more like his sister. He didn't want Ramya to remain single—with nothing but books as companions.

The wedding was conducted with great fanfare. There were lots of lights, noise and smoke to mark the occasion. After returning from Srinagar in Kashmir where they spent their honeymoon, Ramya and Prakash left for Bengaluru. Prakash had a good job with a Swedish engineering company and lived in a posh well-appointed flat. That he had a drinking problem and was prone to violence came out in bits and pieces, and by then they were already a year and a half into their marriage. Ramya blamed it on fate and continued with her life. She would do anything to spare her father pain and disappointment in the evening of his life.

In all the years she spent with Prakash, she had to call the police only once. The police came a couple of hours later and heard her out with patient resignation, while Prakash sat penitently silent on a sofa. The police counselled her, despite her bruised face, to learn to live with her husband in amity. They gave a kid-gloved warning to Prakash before they left. In the eyes of the police, wife-beating was a normal pastime for a man. Like betting on racehorses or throwing darts in a pub.

A few months down the road Ramya and Prakash met a marriage counsellor at a cocktail party—some of these counsellors were real high-flyers. Her name was Payal Singh, a wellspring of unbounded optimism, and with her help they tried to reconstruct their life. The first thing that struck one, upon beholding Payal, was her self-confidence. Being a glib talker, she gave the impression that she was extremely knowledgeable.

"Nothing is impossible," Payal said. "If you set your mind to it, you can achieve anything."

Payal lived in Delhi, but flew around the country as she had well-heeled clients in all the major cities. After a few consultations, she recommended Prakash join a substance abuse therapy group, and advised Ramya to take fertility treatment.

"In some parts of the world, people may think my methods old-fashioned. But in India things are different. There's nothing like children to hold a marriage together."

Prakash decided to give abuse therapy a try, and Ramya encouraged him. Prakash said: "I doubt it'll help." Then added, with a chuckle: "But what the heck!"

After a couple of trial sessions, he signed up and stuck it out — to Ramya's utter amazement.

"That Payal," Ramya thought, "she can really work wonders." For once, husband and wife were united in their admiration of something, or rather someone. Payal succeeded in bringing the mutually antagonistic Ramya and Prakash together on the same plank, even if fleetingly.

Ramya underwent fertility treatment with a local doctor who had a miraculous reputation in the field. Every time Ramya visited the clinic, she couldn't help wondering how many issueless couples there were in a country with nearly a billion people. Pinned on one of the walls of the clinic were scores of snaps of proud, beaming parents holding their firstborn. Despite many expensive cycles, Ramya couldn't conceive.

"Just my luck," she thought.

It was in the aftermath of the unsuccessful rounds of treatment that Prakash told Ramya about his first marriage and his son. Ramya felt neither jealous nor angry about his first marriage. She merely shook her head in mild wonderment — and, if it were possible, Prakash sank further in her esteem. But when she heard the whole story, she experienced nothing but compassion for Sandeep and his mother. Prakash's first wife had contracted leprosy, and it wasn't diagnosed as such when the first discolouring patches appeared. While there was a cure for leprosy in this modern age, a severe stigma was still attached to it — hence the separation.

But Payal's therapy for Prakash was apparently a success. He was declared clean. Later Ramya learned that Prakash and Payal had had an affair.

No, it wasn't Payal's blood-red lipstick stain on Prakash's collar. A couple of Ramya's friends tipped her off that they'd seen Prakash with a fashionably dressed woman. On one occasion, through the car window Ramya glimpsed two people who looked like Prakash and Payal, at least from their backs, walking arm in arm on MG Road.

When questioned, Prakash said: "Today? No, I didn't meet Payal. But I've taken her shopping a few times to Commercial Street."

Prakash would've made a good chess player. But she knew Prakash. He always had his eyes on the main chance. For that matter she knew Payal too — a fling with Prakash would only be a minor distraction for her, something to occupy her leisure hours on her trips to Bengaluru.

Not surprisingly, Payal and Prakash fell out quickly. After he was dumped, Prakash was moody and irritable for a few weeks, and he seemed to get fewer phone calls and text messages on his mobile. Ramya could never understand what Payal, an intelligent and sexy woman, saw in Prakash—a coarse-grained hunk. Maybe it was a strategy Payal employed to secure success. It explained how Prakash, a person totally lacking in perseverance, persisted with the program. That he didn't take to the bottle again immediately after the break-up was testimony to the fact that it wasn't an intense affair. It must've been just casual recreation for them—not that Ramya really cared.

Soon afterwards they applied to migrate to Canada.

Ramya telephones Wilma.

"So, what's the good news? Did you receive your first cheque?" Ramya asks.

"It's much better than that. True North is restarting one of their lines. I received a letter from them asking me to return to work. Lisa also called me. I was hoping you too would've received the letter."

"No, I haven't received any such letter."

"Did you check your letterbox? How long has it been since you last checked?"

"A week," Ramya says.

"Ramya! You're too much! When will you change? How many times can I tell you, you won't win the lottery unless you buy a ticket!"

"I receive mostly junk mail. Anyway, I'll check the

next time I go out." Ramya's letterbox is at the end of her
not so long driveway. It's an effort to pick up mail, especially in cold weather. As far as Ramya's concerned, the
cast iron letterbox is just an ornament decorating her
smallish lot.

"No, do it now. As soon as I disconnect."

"Ok, ok."

Ramya puts down the receiver. The news hasn't stirred
any excitement in her. If she did get the job back, it
would mean returning to her old life. She's not sure if
that's what she wants. But then she's not sure exactly
what she does want in life.

<hr />

When Prakash was preparing to leave for Alberta, one of
his businessman friends threw a farewell party. Prakash
had found a respectable job in the field of engineering,
thanks to his excellent networking skills.

"No more survival jobs for me," Prakash said. "Boy,
am I sick and tired of lifting crates in a warehouse!"

It was loosely decided that Ramya, who had a reason-
ably good job, would follow Prakash once he settled
down and got to know the lay of the land. They didn't
want to the run the risk, as they had when they first came
to Canada, of both having to start life anew, right from
scratch.

The party which Raj Mehta hosted for Prakash was
lavish in every way. So different from the slapdash pot-
lucks immigrants usually held. It was coincidentally the
weekend of Deepavali, or Diwali as it's known in north

India, so there were twinkling coloured lights strung along the eaves of the house. The party was held in the open, beside the private swimming pool. That year Diwali came early, and fall was late, so there was only a rumour of a chill. Guests sat around the open-air stoves, women wearing shawls and men pullovers. All the guests were Indian, and most of the conversation was about India. Many had returned from their annual holiday there, and had lots to say about its growing prosperity in the wake of privatization and liberalization — words which just meant the government had given Nehruvian socialism the unceremonious boot.

The evening had an enchanted feel to it. There was outside catering and the best of wines and liquor. Waiters circulated with delicious hors d'oeuvres made of roasted vegetables and meats on small skewers, and cheese and seafood on crackers. All the meats at the party were either chicken, fish, prawn, or goat. No beef or pork — the first a taboo for Hindus, and the latter for Muslims.

Prakash who was on and off the wagon depending on his whim decided to go in for the kill. He started with beer and then moved on to hard liquor. Now and then he'd glance sheepishly at Ramya. His looks seemed to say: "It's only for today. Let me enjoy myself."

He was ignorant of the fact that Ramya, so inured to Prakash's impetuous decisions, didn't let anything about him bother her. Anyway, Ramya didn't know what got into her on that night; she too decided to let her hair down. Perhaps it was the gorgeousness of the party, the likes of which she'd never attended, at least in Canada. Wan evening stars in the darkening sky, the coloured lights reflected in the pool, the conviviality of the guests, the aroma of fabulous food — what exactly it was, she never could quite tell, that gave the evening an enchanted feel. But she felt a little sad too and missed India, and longed for the loved and cherished feeling she had when she was growing up. But not for a moment did she feel unhappy that Prakash would be gone in a couple of days.

She had some of the champagne and liked it immensely. She lost count of how many glasses she had, as no sooner she finished one than somebody would replenish it. She was pleasantly high, but not drunk. She was sure of it because she felt slightly embarrassed when Prakash, tight as a fiddle, made a maudlin speech. When he was done, there was much cheering from the guests, especially the male ones. Then one of them, with a reedy off-key voice began to sing "For He's a Jolly Good Fellow." Mercifully others were quick to join in, and the song turned into a boisterous performance.

After the elaborate dinner which had many Punjabi dishes, tastier than what she'd had ever eaten in restaurants whether in India or Canada or anywhere for that matter, they left. Indian parties end when dinner is over, as if a curfew is declared, and the guests leave *en masse*. Neither Ramya nor Prakash was really fit enough to drive. Prakash took charge of the wheel anyway, though he was more sloshed than she was. It was just their good fortune that nothing untoward happened.

That night, after she switched off the bedroom light, and prepared to go to bed, Prakash pulled her violently towards him and kissed her, smothering her with his butter chicken laced bad breath barely concealed behind the flavour of minty Colgate. If Ramya had been in complete control of her senses, she would've shouted, "Rape!" and threatened to call 911. But that night the champagne she'd guzzled took over her soul. She responded to Prakash's overture, and they made love in a way they'd never done before. Ramya's entire body was on fire, painful, pleasurable. Prakash dug into her like a maniac. Both grunted as they thrust their hips at each other. Ramya stopped only when she was in the throes of an orgasm. She screamed as her pubis turned into a river, flooding their limbs and soaking though the sheets.

Next day when they woke up they were both embarrassed. Prakash pretended nothing had happened while Ramya felt shy and ashamed. Their marriage was too far-gone to be saved by a night of torrid sex.

The following day Prakash took a plane for Calgary from Terminal 3 at Pearson airport. When she turned her back on him in the foyer, after saying her goodbyes, Ramya decided that she wasn't going to follow Prakash to Alberta. She was turning her back on her past. Their marriage was over.

The stain on the mattress, which Prakash left for Ramya to clean up, was the only thing to show for over two decades of marriage.

A few months later she visited India because Daddy wasn't keeping well. He was over eighty and wasn't so much ill as simply growing old: His tired overworked organs were slowly giving up on him.

Most of the day he'd sit in the drawing room with eyes closed meditatively; Ramya never knew whether he was dozing or merely resting. On one occasion he opened his eyes and demanded: "Why hasn't Prakash come?"

"He has a new job, and it isn't easy to get leave,"

Ramya said, surprised how fluently she could dissemble. Cohabiting with Prakash for over two decades must've made her adept at giving evasive answers. Prakash always played fast and loose with the truth, calling his mistruths white lies.

"Your mother and I were always together," Daddy said. "Never was there an occasion when I sent her out alone."

"I know."

"Only when death parted us," Daddy said, and fell silent, closing his eyes, as if he'd fallen asleep.

Ramya idly picked up the *Deccan Chronicle*, and glanced at the sensationalist news on the front page. Looking at the papers in India, anyone would think the end of the world was close at hand.

Daddy suddenly opened his eyes and started to speak, spooking Ramya. "Do you know how your mother died?"

"It was jaundice or something like that, wasn't it?"

"Something like that, but not quite. Imagine! All the top doctors of Hyderabad were consulted but what was the use? We were treating her for jaundice when she had another disease all together."

"I didn't know about that. Were you not able to detect it?"

"It's a bacterial disease that's common only in some parts of coastal India like Tamil Nadu. Leptospirosis. That's the name of the undiagnosed disease. The symptoms are very similar to those of hepatitis. Your mother contracted it when we visited Chennai for Ramu-uncle's son's wedding. I came to know of it much later. I've never been able to forgive myself."

"How is Ramu-uncle?"

"Dead as a dodo. How else could he be? He always had a weak heart. Told him many times to go slow on smoking and drinking. All my old friends and classmates have predeceased me."

Ramya was silent. There was an inkling of glee in his voice when he spoke about his acquaintances.

But his tone changed. "I should've been the first to go —hanged for murder. I killed your mother with my ignorance."

Ramya sighed. It wasn't just the Indian press that was sensationalist.

———

After copying Sandeep's number in India from the voice-mail recording to her old phonebook, which was almost in tatters, she dialled it.

"How are you, Sandeep? How is Vidya?"

"I'm fine, so is Vidya. We have some good news for you. I was meaning to call you. But before that I want to apologise—I spoke too much last time. I got carried away. I'm sorry."

"Never mind. I know Prakash is your father, but for me anything to do with him will always leave a bad taste —and I'm sorry for saying so. But what's the good news?"

"Vidya is … expecting," he said.

"It's good news indeed! So I'm going to be a grandmother soon. You made me an old woman with this one bit of news. But I don't mind it. I feel nice that there's a grandchild on the way. When is the baby due?"

"In mid-August."

"A Leo or a Virgo. Your mother must be so happy!" Ramya said. Ramya had lately begun to read the horoscope section in the newspaper. Even there she hadn't found a shred of hope, though it mentioned an unannounced arrival of a relative—but the astrologer meant it differently.

There was a pause. "I've not told my mother yet. I wanted you to be the first person to know, Mom."

It was Ramya's turn to be silent. She was touched. In a way it was understandable. He met Prakash and Ramya often, dropping by for vacation when they were still in India. He saw his mother maybe once a year.

"You should tell her as soon as possible. If it is difficult to call her, you must go to the ashram."

"We're planning to meet her this weekend," Sandeep said.

While leprosy began to be called by the euphemistic name of Hansen's disease, and modern medicine could contain the infection, the social stigma associated with it still prevailed. Prakash had already planned to leave his wife because cohabiting with someone with the disease was a serious health risk. He was young, in his late twenties, and didn't want to jeopardize his future.

Sandeep's mother voluntarily took herself out of the picture by moving to an ashram. Hers was a different kind of separation. And Sandeep, only two then, went to live with his maternal grandparents.

13

To Dust Returnest

It's the day of Subbu-Auntie's funeral. Ramya wakes early, takes a bath, and has a quick and light breakfast of coffee, jam and toast. Anything she cooks now, if she does any cooking at all, is quick and easy. Gone are the days of making a south Indian breakfast like dosa or idli or vada, where grinding, steaming or frying were involved. Being made of lentils and rice, they're nutritious, loaded with proteins, but come with a lot of prep work.

The hastily slapped together sandwich tastes like nothing and she has trouble ingesting it. Maybe she's too frugal with jam and butter, wanting to consume less sugar and fat, the two tasty killers. Or, perhaps, it's the mild stress she feels at the thought of going to a funeral. It's not just the funeral *per se* that troubles her, though god knows how unsettling that can be, being in the presence of Death, and all that. The real reason for the stress is that she feels ill at ease hobnobbing with Indians in large numbers. It has always been so, even when she was with

Prakash, and now that she's separated the discomfiture is more acute. The preoccupations of her countrymen (their children and their activities, and/or their homes and the ever-rising real-estate values) and Ramya's outlook of life, to live and let live, don't seem to find common ground.

But go she must. Not just to "show her face" as they'd say in India, but because she really wants to say goodbye to Subbu-Auntie. She was one of the few Indians Ramya had met in Canada who was genuinely willing to help others.

Ramya steels herself and enters the garage by the side door. Ms. Peggy is waiting for her with her habitually dour expression. Possibly, she too doesn't like the prospect of going to a funeral in this weather.

❧────────❧

When Prakash and Ramya left for Canada, her father was already old, nearing seventy. He continued to live alone in their house in Hyderabad. Of course, there were a couple of servants and a watchman — but that provided only Dutch comfort to Ramya. The local newspapers were full of stories of servants murdering and robbing their elderly employers. But Savitramma the old cook and Anjali the young maid were not the stuff assassins were made of, Ramya was sure. Though Das the watchman was reliable as to character, he took his guard duties lightly. Since he had a day job too, he was a heavier sleeper than Daddy himself. But there was always the chance that Das's loud snores, more akin to a hungry tiger's growl, could keep a not so determined cat burglar away from the premises.

Though Daddy was in good health and was comfortably off, Ramya still worried after him. Her father told her firmly that she was better employed in making a success of their decision to immigrate than worrying about him. He'd heard from his friends that immigrating to Canada was no cakewalk. He assured her that their neighbours, who'd been known to him for decades, were more than willing to give him a helping hand even before being asked. Aside from being innately kind and helpful, they felt obliged to Daddy as he'd given them free medical advice when they fell ill. They called on him regularly, and helped him with things like shopping, and paying property taxes and utility bills.

Daddy died fourteen years after they left for Canada. The call came at 3 am. In that wee hour, the ring sounded loud and shrill, like a heavy-duty drill boring into the mantle of the night. Roused violently from her sleep, Ramya jumped out of bed to answer the phone, having not yet acquired the habit of letting calls slip indifferently into the voicemail. A late-night call always spelled bad news. A young man calling himself Kumar announced her father's death. He turned out to be her childhood friend Raghu's son. They'd lived down the street in a villa-like house which hid behind a veil of creepers and climbers. The house was later converted into a block of apartments with nary an inch of open space anywhere for a skinny shrub or even a tussock of grass to grow.

It wasn't the peak season for air travel, so Ramya managed to get a ticket for the same day. But she had to fork out a large sum — the airline management know that people who buy their tickets at the last moment don't have the luxury to blanch at the price on the sticker.

The journey was gruelling—twenty-eight hours with two tiresome stopovers. When she arrived in Hyderabad at the crack of dawn, surprisingly she felt neither tired nor jet-lagged. Bereavement can be numbing.

It was a new and different airport she landed in. All swanky and shining, with high vaulted ceilings, god knows why. So unlike the cramped old airport in Begumpet, which though small, was conveniently located, just off one of the busiest thoroughfares in the city.

The passengers filed out into a glass-walled corridor, and started to shuffle forward. But after a couple of hundred yards, they discovered their way was barred by a locked door. Most of the passengers, though tired and sleepy, were reduced to waiting in silence. But some, more irate or less patient than others, began to shout randomly for the airport officials. It was all quite useless. The place beyond the glass door was as deserted as a cemetery, and there was nobody around to take notice. Not even ghosts. From where she stood imprisoned, she could see posters hanging from the ceiling trumpeting the fact that the new Hyderabad airport was voted the best in the world in its class.

Nearly fifteen minutes later, a sleepy janitor arrived and set them free. The planeload of temporary captives erupted into rapturous applause. Despite her circumstances, a spectre of a smile formed on Ramya's chapped, travel-weary lips. It must've been the first flight of the day, and the janitor probably dozed off. This was Hyderabad, and some things never change. It was still in some ways a sleepy, medieval city with domes and minarets defining its skyline, a city of a thousand and one nights.

It had a reputation for its courtly and leisurely ways, where Father Time too would stop by to dally over Irani chai and mini-samosas. But now the city was being goaded into the digital age by politicians and businessmen, where software development centres of Microsoft, Oracle, Apple, Google, to say nothing of scores of lesser-known firms, kept cropping up like the proverbial mushrooms.

The new airport was miles away from the city, and she had no Indian currency on her, leaving her to wonder how to get to her house. But there were kiosks where you could change your money, and there were also touts moving like spooks among the passengers whispering about the great exchange rates for American dollars they could offer.

"I only have Canadian dollars," Ramya thought with a sigh. Before she could think of what to do next, she spotted Raghu in the crowd outside holding a placard with her name on it. But when she approached him she realised he was too young to be Raghu, and her small smile of recognition faded away like a food-stain under Resolve. She got confused and thought to back away when the young man gave a coy smile and said: "I'm Raghunath's son."

"You were just a baby when I saw you last," Ramya said, as she allowed him to take charge of her one suitcase, and be led to the parking lot. The drive was long but quick. The traffic was light as it was still dark, and the sun hadn't yet risen. A brand-new flyover miles and miles long conveyed them directly to the heart of the city.

When she entered the house, which seemed to be wide awake with lights on and people milling about, she saw Daddy laid out in a glass-topped contraption, like something you see in a grocery shop in Canada. It was a refrigerated coffin. Cotton wool was stuffed into Daddy's nostrils, and a white band had been tied from his chin to his head to prevent the lower jaw from falling open.

The room smelled of air-freshener rather than flowers or incense, though she could see that both were put to abundant use in the room. She dropped her suitcase, and stood bending over her Daddy's body, gazing into the coffin, when Raghu stepped up, and opened the lid. Ramya bent down to touch Daddy's wizened cheek, tears streaming down her face. Daddy's face felt cold and rock hard. It was the same cheek that as a little girl she would kiss each morning before Daddy left for work.

Within a few hours of her arrival the body was carried out on a bier to an ambulance-like white van parked under the porch. The vehicle, which had the words "Last Journey Van" painted on its sides, would convey Daddy's body to the burning ghat.

Times were a-changing. Though she was a woman she could go to the cremation grounds now. She got into the van rather than the taxi that was ordered for her. The van trundled over the city roads on its way to the crematorium. The suspension of the van was so bad and the roads so pot-holed that she found herself bouncing like a *lailappa*, the yo-yo-like toy that was a small water-filled balloon which Daddy would buy for her at local fairs when she was a child. Daddy's cadaver too bounced on the trestle. He was having a bumpy ride to heaven.

It was Raghu's son who performed the last rites. Times hadn't changed all that much—a male relative had to do them, and it turned out, rather conveniently, that Kumar was a distant relation, with fourth or fifth degree of separation, on Daddy's side.

The next day, after another orgy of pujas, they took the earthenware pot containing Daddy's powdery remains to the sacred temple town of Mantralayam in their small car, a South Korean brand, though made in India. Making in India was always a big thing; it meant independence and self-reliance, a throwback to an age before colonial rule. Few people would know about this better than Indians; after all they made millions of babies in India (and outside the country too) every year.

They cast Daddy's ashes into the holy river of Tunga-bhadra, now little more than a trickle — thanks to scanty rains, and indiscriminate construction of dams upstream in the name of development. The Tungabhadra, on whose banks mighty empires once flourished, would carry Daddy's ashes until it merged into the Krishna, which in turn traversed the Indian peninsula before draining into the Bay of Bengal. Like Daddy said many years ago, all streams and rivers eventually find their way to the ocean. Daddy returned to the place where life on earth is said to have first originated — the bed of the ocean.

On the thirteenth day after Daddy's passing away, an elaborate ceremony was performed to ensure his entry into heaven. At the end of it there was to be a sumptuous repast, but they couldn't start until a crow or an eagle first partook of the meal. Ramya waited on the flat roof of their house for the carrion birds to espy the plate of goodies and come after it, while the guests waited in the house with mounting hunger, the aroma of the dainty dishes teasing their palate. Ramya could see a few birds circling in the sky high above, but they seemed in no hurry to make a beeline to the spread arranged for them. Perhaps, the vegetarian fare wasn't worthy victual in the estimation of carnivorous birds. However, a few minutes later, a lone crow flew out of nowhere, and landed on the parapet wall. Ramya watched breathlessly as it swivelled its head one way and then the other before taking a few tentative hops towards the plate. It dipped its beak and bit off a morsel of food and flew away just as quickly. When the good news filtered down to the restive guests in the living room, a wave of silent delight spread among them. Now the feast could begin!

She had to stay back in India for two months after her father's death as there were many official things to take care of like wills, bank accounts, and property taxes. Not everybody in India was as obliging as that small venturesome crow. To get legal and financial matters sorted out took weeks — not a surprise in a bureaucracy tied up in age-old red-tape. It took pleading, coaxing and a good bit of payola to get things moving. It was a frustrating and boring wait.

One evening Ramya stopped by a new bookshop. The ones she frequented as a child seemed to have disappeared, as if they'd fallen off the bandwagon of progress, and nobody so much as noticing. The new book stores were no longer outlets merely for books. This particular shop, which had a very catchy name (Crossroads? Crosswords?) offered a variety of merchandise like music CDs, toys, dolls, greeting cards and what have you. Fortunately, they also stocked books by the thousands. Bewildering arrays of works by new writers stared back at her from the racks. While some of the old favourites like R.K. Narayan were still visible, she looked in vain for Kamala Markandaya's *The Nowhere Man*. She'd bought a copy long ago, but even before she could read it, Monica had borrowed and mislaid it. Living in Canada for a good number of years made Ramya want to read this classic, well nigh the bible of diaspora literature.

She asked the sales girl, who was hovering around like an undercover agent, for help. The young woman gave a watery smile and set off obligingly on a hunt, peering into the shelves, probing every display table, and even peeking under it. But in the end, she came back empty-handed, with the same smile pasted on her kind mouth. So Ramya picked up a couple of books by new Indian sensations (Chetan Bhagat and Amish) and went up to the counter. The manager got talking, and he was very knowledgeable about books.

"There are so many new writers in English now. And many of them are earning crores of Rupees!"

"That's awesome," Ramya said.

"I believe India will soon be the biggest market for English language books, after the U.S. and the U.K. ... where are you from, ma'am, if I may ask? America?"

Ramya was amazed at the Indian shopkeepers' habitual ability to spot a 'foreign-returned' person, though outwardly she looked no different from other Indians. She could never figure out how they did it.

"Well, almost. I'm from Canada."

"Margaret Atwood! Rohinton Mistry! They sell well here," the manager said, totting up her purchase on the cash register.

"Good to hear," Ramya said, paying with Indian Rupees she drew from the bank after Daddy's savings account was unfrozen.

"I hope you enjoy the books," the manager said, handing over the carry bag.

"What do you think of these new writers?" Ramya asked.

"Well, for one thing they don't have the colonial hang-up the older authors had. These youngsters write boldly and confidently about issues that matter to them and their Indian readers, rather than addressing their work to a Western audience."

"That sounds good."

A few days before she went back to Canada, she thought of visiting the Chilukuru temple. She'd reckoned that a visit to a temple, especially one so far removed from the rough and tumble of the city, would bring some peace of mind. She wanted a break too from the unending flow of visitors who came to condole with her. While they were profuse and genuine in their sympathy, they were far from providing comfort, and only kept Daddy's demise fresh in her mind, reopening the wound every time they spoke of him. But a visitor like her old friend Sujatha was a different matter — one could snatch a few moments of joy even in one's bereavement.

When Ramya told Sujatha about the situation between Prakash and her, Sujatha said: "Divorce is a way of life in the West, isn't it?"

"Perhaps. It's a little different there. Women are on the same footing as men — in terms of rights, status, everything. They don't play second fiddle to them."

Sujatha was silent for a while. Then she said: "You may be right."

"What is it, Sujatha?"

"Two years ago, I was asked by my boss if I would like to head the Singapore office of my company. I had to decline the offer because Srinivas didn't want to leave his job. But if it was the other way around, he would've expected me to dump my job and go with him."

"As Monica would have said, *c'est la vie,*" Ramya said.

But the visitor who made Ramya's day was Sailoo. Ramya was horrified to notice how old he looked. His head was all grey, and his face as wrinkled as a washerwoman's hands. But, as usual, his eyes shone brightly with wisdom. He came with a wiry rust-brown mongrel in tow. The dog directed a gaze of unblinking curiosity at Ramya as though trying to place her.

"What do you call him?" Ramya asked.

"It's a her. She's Bar Guess's granddaughter. Her name is Pennyloopy."

"What kind of a name is that?"

"I asked Sujatha-amma to suggest a name that you may like. She looked into big fat books and came up with the name."

Penelope! The personification of unwavering loyalty. It was a quality Ramya most admired in people. It was both amazing and disconcerting to learn, once again, how well her childhood friends knew her. But she wasn't very adept at weaving, and certainly she'd never wait for anyone to return.

The early morning drive to Chilukuru was beautiful. It was cool and there were drifts of mists where stands of trees grew. Just before approaching the temple grounds, they had to stop to make a small payment at a tollgate. This was a new development; she didn't remember doing it on her previous visit when she accompanied Prakash. But that was more than a decade ago. After the driver parked the car, she stepped out, leaving her shoes in the car—one didn't enter temples wearing footwear. Unaccustomed to walking barefoot, her soles hurt as she trod over the unpaved ground sprinkled with flint. The road to God is always a painful one.

But when she rounded a corner, the tableau which presented itself made her gasp in horror. It was so completely different from the pastoral vision that was etched in her memory. Gone was the bucolic setting! Gone was the numinous stillness! Gone was the unimpeded view of the lovely lake!

Instead, rows of makeshift shops selling puja requirements and cheap souvenirs had cropped up. Scattered among them were dubious-looking restaurants and small fruit vendors' stands. One had to make an effort to spot the lake. In a gap between buildings, and barred by a wire fence, one could see a sliver of water.

Inside, the look and feel was entirely different. While no major renovations were done to the small temple, the courtyard was choked with a circumambulating mass of devotees. It was as if humanity was being continuously churned, but there was no clue as to what was being creamed off. Going by the fact that many of the devotees had some form of counting arrangement in their hands, one could guess that their wishes were fulfilled by the bountiful deity, Venkateshwara of Chilukuru.

Ramya joined a slow-moving queue that wound

round the temple proper twice. It took almost an hour to get into the inner chamber and have the darshan of the deity. The priests bade the devotees to move on as hundreds more were waiting in the line-up. When she at last came out of the temple, which was abuzz with frenetic activity, her heart was heavy. India was changing, there was no doubt of it. It was sloughing off the slumberous covering of decades-old socialism, but Ramya wasn't sure what was emerging, and if the capitalism the country was embracing was of the right kind.

Something was lost at Chilukuru — irrevocably. Maybe, it was India's ancient sense of spirituality. What had taken its place was the stranglehold of superstition dedicated to material well-being. But who was she to grumble? Judging from the sheer number of devotees who were blessed by the gods, the new India was receiving divine sanction.

For her, Chilukuru had changed forever. Maybe, that's how it was with everything in life. Change was the only constant factor. (Who said that?) And sometimes there was no going back.

On the final day of her stay in India, she returned in the evening after a strenuous round of last minute shopping — buying pickles, spices, condiments, spares for her pressure cooker and a hardy mixer-grinder designed to deal with the demands of south Indian cooking.

The cook Savitramma handed over a package saying a woman had dropped by when Ramya was out. Ramya tore open the package. Inside there was an autographed book and a note written on a small loose sheet of paper, inserted into the book like an improvised bookmark:

Dear Ramya,

Just thought that you might like to have this book more than me. Books are not my thing, they never were and never will be.

Have you written anything lately? I hope you become an author and realize your dream. I will definitely buy and treasure the books you may write!

Sorry to have missed seeing you
Your friend
Nikki Lodha

Who could Nikki Lodha be? It reminded her of Nicki Lauda, one of the car racing idols of Prakash. But this had nothing to do with Prakash or his macho interests. The handwriting was vaguely familiar. Surely it was not … Ramya called the number scribbled at the bottom of the notepaper.

"Hi! Nikki speaking." It was the unmistakable voice of Monica, nee Maunika, aka Nikki.

"Monica!" Ramya said. "How are you! It's ages since I've seen or spoken to you."

"Good. Good," Monica said. Her voice had the easy confidence of the well-to-do. "I'm sorry about your father. Sujatha told me you were in town."

"Thank you for Rushdie's book. Is Lodha Amar's last name? I didn't recognize it."

"Certainly not. Amar's business lost a lot of money. We divorced, and I remarried," Monica said, and laughed. Her laughter sounded like the tinkling of rapturous bells. When her husband couldn't provide for Monica, she had the gumption to dump him and move on. Monica always knew which side her bread was buttered. Or which side of the bed was better.

～━━━━━～

The snow is falling thick and fast. According to the forecast it's going to get progressively worse, and may even turn to icy rain. The weatherman is expecting an accumulation of ten centimetres, and has warned drivers to be careful. Though it's ten in the morning, the day looks so grey and sodden that it could be mistaken for dusk.

Ramya starts the engine, and lets it idle for some time to warm up the car. She doesn't have to do it for long, as she always parks her car in the garage. Ms. Peggy abhors cold weather like her mistress.

Prakash always left the car sitting overnight on the driveway. He was that kind of a man — too lazy to put the car away in the garage. The next morning, already late for work, and not dressed properly for the cold, he would shiver and dance around the car, trying to brush off the snow.

But of late, it isn't cold that's bothering Ramya. Even in the middle of the night she wakes feeling hot. Is it only the furnace thermostat that's acting up? Or is it the dreaded M word? The unspeakable word. She doesn't want it coming now, on top of everything else.

Subbu-Auntie's funeral is set at 11 am. Ramya gives herself an hour, though the journey to the funeral home shouldn't take more than forty-five minutes in the worst of weather. She moves the lever to drive, and eases the car out of the garage.

She stops at a Rabba outlet to pick up some flowers before she takes the highway. The traffic isn't very heavy, so she has lots of time to spare. The bad weather has kept many indoors. She heads to a Tim Hortons drive through where she buys herself a double-double and a lightly buttered and toasted poppy-seed bagel. She needs to fortify herself, the stress is making her ravenous. What a contradiction! Hardly an hour ago, she was blaming stress for her poor appetite. She sits in the parking lot, with the heater on, sipping coffee and munching on the bagel. The shop food tastes so much better than what she'd made for herself. She's become an indifferent cook, adding another item to the list of changes which have occurred to her personality of late.

With five minutes to spare, she starts for the funeral home. The building has a red brick façade like a warehouse, but is not unwelcoming. It has some shrubbery and a thin strip of a lawn in front which are well kept. There are acres of paved parking space around the building. More people come to see the dead than when they were alive.

There are solemn-faced attendants just inside the front door. They take possession of Ramya's coat and direct her to the room where the service is being held.

Subbu-Auntie's family is present in full strength. They occupy the first three rows, a solid presence. Subbu-Auntie's going to get a rousing send off. Mr. Rao sits on a chair, erect and immobile, with his palm resting on the grip of his walking stick. He looks like King Canute preparing to order back, if not the tide, at least Time.

Ramya nods to him in a grave manner, and then pro-

ceeds to the coffin. The casket is laid out at the far wall.
Masses of cabernet-red roses have been placed in and
around the half-open coffin. Only Subbu-Auntie's face
and throat are exposed; the rest of her body is submerged
in floral tributes. Ramya places a bouquet of half a dozen
white roses on the torso. She bought white because that's
colour of death in India. Now she wonders if she's done
the right thing. Internally, she shakes her head. She's
always had a knack for sticking out like a sore thumb.

Subbu-Auntie, in the sleep of death, looks pitiably haggard, as if the pain and suffering she underwent in the
last days of her life couldn't be masked by the mortician's
makeup artist. Pain and suffering is the lot of women.
Mr. Rao, though a successful man, had been a demanding and insensitive husband. Subbu-Auntie seems to have
shrunk substantially too. She looks like a rag doll one
could pick up with one hand. It's unimaginable that when
alive she was such a prepossessing figure, so full of life and
good humour.

A couple of Hindu priests in silk kurta-pajamas materialize. They've brought puja utensils which they set up
on the carpeted floor. They also have a portable fireproof
device to conduct *homa*—the ancient Aryan method of
worship. Pre-recorded tapes play the age-old Vedic hymns
over the speakers, while the priests perform the last rites
in an efficient and fuss-free manner—so unlike what tran-
spires in India. When the ceremony is over, the young
male members of the family lift the casket on to their
shoulders and make their way to a black hearse, while the
loudspeakers blare out devotional songs in Hindi which
have been set to sprightly Bollywood tunes.

Ramya collects her coat, and tips the attendants liberally. They're no longer wearing the solemn expression on their faces; it's as if they had removed it with a face-cleaning pad—like it was so much stale make-up. After pocketing the tips, they give her big smile and wish her a good day. One can tell that tips were not something they expected from immigrant mourners.

Once all the mourners are in their cars, the cortege proceeds to the crematorium. Ramya follows at the tail end of the procession. The incurable laggard. By the time she finds a vacant parking spot and goes inside, the service is coming to an end. It must've been short and brisk. Maybe, the priests have other deaths to attend to: "Next body, please!" The coffin-bearers move the casket to a conveyor which leads into the maw of the furnace, red and hungry. The last, but brief, leg of Subbu-Auntie's earthly sojourn has begun.

When the coffin disappears from view, there's a lot of wailing and weeping, the lamentation rising like a crescendo. There's nothing more for Ramya to do. Not born of a maudlin mould, tears don't come easily to Ramya. She leaves.

The drive back from the funeral is slow. The snow has begun to fall harder. Visibility has reduced, it's like driving through masses of white curtains billowing in the wind ...

Ramya remembers the night Amma died. She was seventeen then.

The drapes of the bedroom windows were fluttering wildly. It was a windy night, a precursor to the first monsoon rain. Letting go of Amma's hand, which she'd been holding, Ramya walked over to the window to shut it.

Amma was lying on the cot. She was asleep, but it was a kind of troubled, discontinuous sleep. Whenever Amma seemed to stir, Ramya fed her with a teaspoonful of water, as the servants had instructed her to do.

It was well past midnight, and the night had an unreal feel. Earlier in the day, she'd tried to feed Amma with very soft rice mixed with plain yoghurt. Despite her pleading and coaxing, Amma wouldn't eat even a spoonful.

"Now, I'm giving it back to you," Amma had said, with a weak smile. Her voice had become soft and croaky, and the words came out with a quavering slowness. "When you were young you wouldn't want to eat; whenever I tried to force feed you, you were always turning your face away. Only your Atom Auntie could make you eat."

Ramya eyes fill with tears at the mention of Atom Auntie. Ramya always avoided thinking about her — even the merest mention would bring a lump to her throat. The last glimpse she had of her beloved aunt, frail and vulnerable under the uncertain light of the street lamp, was a picture she would like to banish forever from her memory.

After shutting the window, Ramya returned to the cot, and took Amma's hand — it felt dry like parchment. She knew from Amma's s shallow, stertorous breathing that her end was near.

"Amma, are you OK?"

Amma half-opened her eyes, which seemed oddly sightless, and without a word she shut them.

Ramya called out to her Daddy. Though his bedroom was on the upper floor, he was awake, as if waiting for his cue. She heard his footfalls, the rubber flipflops slapping on the polished-stone treads, as he came down the staircase.

In the sickly light of the zero-watt bulb, Ramya saw Amma trying to take a deep, long breath. Ramya stared absently at Amma's diamond nose-stud, waiting and waiting for her to exhale. Before Daddy who'd entered the room just then could put on the ceiling light, Amma had breathed her last.

***

The line-up of cars begins to move, the trail of red lights ahead inching forward. The cars stop and start again, their progress regulated by the capricious traffic lights. She needs to concentrate on her driving, lest she get involved in a fender-bender, but her wayward mind drifts into the past.

Everyone she loved or cared for or befriended has either passed on or passed by. Her ineffectual Mummy, kind but a bit addled Daddy, her beloved Atom Auntie, Amma, the archetypal mother hen, to say nothing of the dog Barghest, fickle as he was. Even Monica and Sujatha—they're just a couple of fading snaps in a photo-album. Sandeep and Vidya have returned to India, most probably for good. As to Prakash—she'd let him proceed without her. It was the easiest of separations, no words, no emotions. One went ahead, the other stayed behind. It was as simple as that — as clinically precise a separation as was possible. No mess, no bloodletting. Divorce-lite.

Now Prakash is engineering a comeback. Is it fear of old age? He must be well past sixty now, an age when people in India are already retired. Loneliness? Or wanting someone to take care of him in his dotage?

How about her? Is she OK with his returning? Is her life too nearing the end of its course? Does she need companionship? A comrade-in-arms to combat old age and death?

No! There's no question of old age or death. Come next month, she'll be fifty, just half a century old. No, the latter sounds rather bad ... just five decades old. A golden girl! She has one third of her life span, or more, left to live. And live, meaningfully. Live, with some purpose. She's not going to fade away into the sunset, just like that ...

Really?

Is she kidding herself? Easier said than done. What does she have to look forward to? She has no job, she's not particularly rich, no husband by her side, no children to fuss over, and not many friends either ... Maybe, a few colleagues but whose lot was worse than hers.

In India, it's said that everyone should have at least four friends in the world. That's because it requires four shoulders to carry you on a bier once you're dead. Never mind that in Canada you need more than four strong shoulders to carry a heavy wooden coffin made of maple. (Or is it oak?)

As for Ramya, she has none — no friends, no relatives, and *ipso facto* no pallbearers. No one to extend a helping hand on her last journey on earth ...

When she gets on the highway, the traffic starts to move faster. The snow rising from the road surface looks like scudding clouds of gossamer. The day is grey and dreary, with wet snow falling relentlessly. The wipers move incessantly, scratching at the windscreen with a monotonous rhythm, clearing away the bird-shit-like spatters.

As the car nears her cul-de-sac, rain has miraculously taken the place of snow. It's as if all the lamentation for Subbu-Auntie has reduced the heavens to tears.

When she enters the house, Ramya feels low and lonely, and the gathering darkness outside doesn't seem to help much. She doesn't feel like picking up her mail —all she receives are invoices and flyers anyway. The lure of finding a re-appointment letter from True North is simply not enough. She only wants to collapse into a couch and switch on the TV—her only voluble companion. Not that she wants to see anything in particular —the mindless but excited natter of the anchormen, delivering every inconsequential bit of information with gusto, has a comforting ring to it.

What's Death like? The cessation of all sensations, she could guess with her limited knowledge. What Ramya has gleaned about Death has come from scriptures, general reading, and also, in her case, the conversation of maids.

According to Hinduism, Death isn't the final end all. Souls are merely recycled—like empty plastic bottles or aluminum cans. They're reborn in another form. Birth and Death, they're just the two faces of Life, obverse and reverse. Then why does one fear Death so much? Even the terminally ill and those in considerable pain don't often welcome it. The centuries-old conceptions of Heaven and Hell peddled by the religious establishment the world over must surely have a hand in it, feeding on people's insecurity.

Ramya wants to steer clear of the morbid thoughts which are randomly invading her mind, but the shows on TV are unhelpful — not one of them is riveting enough. Death must be a horrendous thing, if one goes by the reaction of the living who are left behind — the grief, the despair, the sense of abandonment. Doubtless there are some who experience joy and profit from someone's death, and surely, there are others who do the despatching themselves. But, on the whole, humanity would prefer Death not to visit their household.

But the dead, to whom one would suspect Death had mattered most, are past caring. Perhaps to some it was a happy release — an escape from the countless demands of Life.

How different and uncomplicated from all this was their servants' take.

"When I die," Sanna Lakshmi said, "I will go to heaven. There I believe I can eat whatever I want, and as much as I want."

"What would you want to eat?" the nine-year-old Ramya asked.

"Mutton biryani, and chicken korma. Every day, morning, afternoon, and night," Lakshmi said. Ramulamma the cook left whatever she was cooking to its fate and came into the room to join them in the serious discussion of thanatology.

On seeing Ramulamma, Lakshmi added: "Anything, but what Ramulamma cooks."

Ramulamma bridled, but before she could snap back, Ramya said: "Ramulamma is such a good cook. With her cooking she makes life on earth a heaven."

"How well you've put it, my little angel!" Ramulamma exclaimed.

"What would you like to eat when you go to heaven, Ramulamma?" Ramya asked.

"Though I'm a cook myself, nothing special comes to mind right now," Ramulamma said, shaking her head, her brow creased with concentration.

"What about drinks?" Lakshmi said, and giggled. "*Gudamba*, perhaps?" Gudamba was a cheap but potent locally-brewed intoxicant made from jaggery.

"You'd know better. I hear your husband drinks and lazes all day long, and sends you to work to bring home money," Ramulamma said.

To them Life, and Afterlife, it appeared, was all about food and drink.

⁓————⁓

Ramya remembers her sandalwood box, which holds only one remaining object. The bottle of Tik 20. The last one standing. The contents of which the thieving Kanthamma had threatened to swallow. In Kanthamma's case, it was all for show, and she hadn't meant to carry out her threat. But Devamma? Though she was a showgirl herself, she'd had the guts to take that terrifying step.

The liquid in the bottle was something that could

fell an elephant, though it was meant to eradicate bed bugs and other creepy-crawlies. Did it still retain its potency after all these years? Ramya is sure that it's still effective. But isn't the proof of the pudding in the eating?

Ramya fetches the bottle, and sits down on the couch, and leans back. The room is in semidarkness. The TV is on, and cheerless light filters in through the windows, painting the interior of her home in so many shades of grey.

Ramya unscrews the cap, places the bottle to her lips and swallows the contents in one quick gulp. Bottoms up! Here's to Death.

14

Groundhog Day

THE SUN IS STREAMING into the drawing room. Its brightness, uncharacteristic for a winter day, could lull you into believing the temperature outside is mild. Nothing could be farther from the truth. The snow-covered landscape is desolate and bitterly cold. Nonetheless, the sunshine dispels the dark shadows that haunted the room the previous evening. Dust motes jive in sunlight. They're the only animated things in room.

Despite being suffused with cheery light, the room is deathly still. The furniture, immobile in their appointed places, crouch restively. The air is still too, the thermostat having turned off the heat on its own. The knick-knacks, mostly bronze and wooden figurines brought from India, look lifeless under their shroud of dust, as though the frigid weather has sucked out their tropical souls. Ramya lies supine and motionless on the couch, like a puppet dropped by a clumsy puppeteer.

The TV, however, is on, accentuating rather than

contradicting the surrounding stillness. It looks tired and
jaded, having stayed awake all night. A news anchor gabs
about the groundhog's shadow which was spotted earlier
in the day in a small Ontario town.

Every year the country goes through the ridiculous
motions of trying to extract a prediction from groundhogs about the onset of spring. There's a clutch of sup-
posedly clairvoyant rodents that the TV channels consult
for meteorological insights. These groundhogs with lame
and lamentable names have a celebrity status. Every year
they bask in their fifteen minutes of national fame. Now
that the groundhog's shadow has been spotted, a short
winter is prophesied.

Whether you're a believer or not, it's heartening news.
The dark and dismal reign of winter being cut short is a
welcome happenstance. Spring! A rebirth of life, when
nature awakens from a slumber akin to Death. Spring! A
time for new beginnings, when the past is sloughed off
like outworn clothes.

It's no surprise that Telugu New Year comes in early
spring. Punjabi, Tamil, Marathi, Kannadiga, and Parsi
New Years too come when winter has bid au revoir, or
whatever. It does make sense that spring should mark the
beginning of the New Year. From what Ramya has read,
even in Europe, the New Year was observed in spring until
the Gregorian calendar arbitrarily fixed on January 1st.

On Telugu New Year, known as Ugadi, a special relish is prepared. It's a concoction made of neem leaves
(bitter-tasting in the extreme) and jaggery (a traditional
substitute for sugar), among other ingredients. As a child
Ramya refused to even sample it, stubbornly turning her

face away. But if Atom Auntie was around, she'd coax her. "Just try a spoonful, dear. You eat *Ugadi Pachchadi* to remind yourself that Life is sometimes sweet, sometimes bitter."

Ramya stirs and lifts herself to a sitting position on the couch. She's been lying there for god knows how many hours. She feels weak and groggy. She remembers waking up in the middle of the night and stumbling to the bathroom where she threw up into the toilet bowl.

Outside the sun is beating down with deceptive brightness. Ramya tries to get up, wanting to wash her face and brush her teeth. But the effort required to stand up seems quite beyond her. She sinks back into the couch. Reflexively, her hand reaches for the remote. She shuts off the TV and with it the hogwash about the early coming of spring.

After lying on the couch for twenty minutes or so, Ramya musters enough strength to rise slowly, and then walk haltingly to the kitchen to make herself a strong cup of Bru, the instant south Indian coffee — the true elixir of life.

She's still alive, sighs Ramya. She doesn't know what got into her last night to make her swallow the contents of the Tik 20 bottle in one gulp. But she's not overly thankful that she's survived: She's still foggy about her life ahead. She always knew the poison wouldn't work. Wouldn't the bug killer, lying in her precious sandalwood box for over thirty years, have lost its lethal edge? No, Amma must have had something to do with it. She may have found the bottle secreted by Ramya, and poured out its deadly contents only to replace it with tap water. No wonder it was full to the brim. Yes, that must be it ... the bottle had been half empty when Kanthamma grabbed it in a dramatic show of bravado.

Ramya pours the coffee from one mug into another repeatedly until the top turns to foam—the way south Indian coffee must be drunk. On her way back to the living room she notices that she has voicemails on her phone. At first, she wants to ignore them and let things drift, but she changes her mind and picks up the cordless.

The first message is from Jack:

"Hi Ramya, you never returned my call. If you're free tonight why don't we go to the *Ten* in Port Credit? We can discuss your future over dinner and a nice bottle of wine."

Ramya presses the delete key.

The second message is from Lisa, good old Lisa, loyal and caring:

"Lameea! Have you checked your mailbox? If you haven't, please do so immediately. You have a surprise waiting you." She hurriedly added: "A *nice* surprise. You'll like it."

Ramya presses 'delete'.

The third message is from Prakash:

"Ramya, I'll be in Toronto for a week to attend a training program. I'd like to meet you."

Ramya presses 'delete'.

She tosses the phone away. Her eye catches the sandalwood box on the dining table. It's empty—totally, comprehensively empty. All her memories lie scattered around it, orphaned and neglected.

She stares ahead wondering about life. Her life. Is a woman always an adjunct—somebody's daughter, somebody's sister, somebody's wife, somebody's girlfriend, somebody's keep, somebody's mother, or even somebody's godmother? Can she not have an independent existence?

She gets up and hobbles to the dining table. She picks up all the mementoes, except for the empty bottle of Tik 20 which has already found its way to the garbage, and stuffs them back into the sandalwood casket. She shuts the lid with an authoritative bang.

The landscape as seen from the dining room window is pristine. The ground is covered by lily-white snow, and a beneficent sun is shining. The day has a newly laundered look, like the clothes in the "after" panel of a detergent ad.

The cup of south Indian coffee has done her good. She's already beginning to get a grip on what she'd like to do with her life. It's just a germ of an idea. A tenuous notion — but will she have the stamina to go ahead and stick it out?

Taking Sanna Lakshmi, her vacuum cleaner, by hand, she goes down to the basement. She gives the place a thorough cleaning, something she hasn't done for a long time. She can see the dust of ages swirling ferociously under the clear acrylic hood of the Hoover.

Ramya wipes all the furniture clean. She removes the last vestiges of Prakash from the small bar. Bottles with some dregs — gold, brown and colourless — at the bottom, as though saved for the day the prodigal returns. Glasses of various sizes and shapes. Ramya can never quite understand why tumblers must come in such a variety of forms. Could the shape of the drinking vessel have an impact on the quality of the contents? On its enjoyment, perhaps? Even though she'd been a barmaid manqué, she finds

drinks, and drunks for that matter, difficult to comprehend. But it doesn't matter now.

After exorcising the spirits from the basement, Ramya
goes upstairs to fetch her old Dell laptop. It weighs a ton.
And looks a bit superannuated, like its owner. She brings
it downstairs, and setting it up on the office table, hooks
it to an electrical outlet.

Ramya sits down on the swivel chair, and lifts the lid
of the laptop. When she jiggles a few buttons, the screen
springs to life. It works — never mind that it has seen
better days. Again, much like its owner. No! This is all
going to change, Ramya tells herself fiercely. Her best
days are yet to come. She opens a new Word document,
and enters the words:

THE TREASURE OF COMMON MEMORIES
By Ramya Prakash

Then she presses the backspace button repeatedly until
the letters h-s-a-k-a-r-P are summarily erased.

She goes to the next page to compose the dedication.
She writes:

This book is lovingly dedicated to ...

Before she can complete the sentence, unexpected tears
film her eyes. There's no debate at all in her mind as to
whom she will dedicate her book.

Blinking the nascent tears away, she begins to type ...
A new chapter in her life.

Acknowledgements

I would like to thank my editor Julie Roorda for all her helpful suggestions. If the book still has shortcomings the fault is all mine. I like to thank Diaspora Dialogues for the support they give immigrant writers. I would like to thank Connie McParland and Michael Mirolla of Guernica Editions for their belief in my story-telling ability.

About the Author

Pratap Reddy came to Canada from India in 2002. When he started writing fiction, he chose as his subjects new immigrants much like himself. His short fiction has been published in Canada, the USA and India. His first book *Weather Permitting & Other Stories* was published by Guernica Editions in 2016. *Ramya's Treasure* is his first novel. He is working on a second collection and also a novel which is about contemporary India as seen through the eyes of a voluntary exile. He lives in Mississauga with his wife and son.